D0976122

THE LODGER

A SPIDER LATHAM MYSTERY

THE
LODGER

LIZ ADAIR

DESERET
BOOK

SALT LAKE CITY, UTAH

Library of Congress Cataloging-in-Publication Data

Adair, Liz.
   The lodger : a Spider Latham mystery / Liz Adair.
     p.   cm.
   ISBN 1-57008-950-7 (pbk.)
    1. Lincoln County (Nev.)—Fiction.   2. Sheriffs—Fiction.   I. Title.

PS3601.D35L63 2003
813'.6—dc21   2003002043

Printed in the United States of America   54459-7069
Malloy Lithographing Incorporated, Ann Arbor, MI

10 9   8   7   6   5   4   3   2   1

To my husband, Derrill, my co-plotter, my constructive critic, and my cheerleader. Without him, this book never would have been written.

A C K N O W L E D G M E N T S

THE TOWN OF PANACA, NEVADA, really exists. It is my husband's hometown, but bears only the slightest resemblance to the town portrayed in the Spider Latham books. I'm afraid I have overlaid my memories of Panaca with memories of Fredonia, Arizona, where I spent my last two years of high school, and Truth or Consequences, New Mexico, where I spent part of my childhood. They are all small towns, all desert communities, all peopled with resourceful, down-to-earth, and sometimes eccentric citizens. And all appear in bits and pieces under the guise of Panaca and Lincoln County in the Spider Latham books.

Thanks go to those rare friends who were willing to read and critique an unpublished manuscript: John Jones, Maretta Taylor, Shirley White, my son Clay and my son-in-law Rich Lavine. Thanks, too, to my brother, Ron Shook, for helping me in that last mad rush to get *The Lodger* off to Deseret Book to be published online. Thanks to those people who read *The Lodger* on *Mormon Life*, and especially those who posted encouraging messages afterwards. And to Elsha Ulberg, Timothy Robinson, and Emily Watts at Deseret Book, thank you for your faith in me.

All the characters in this and other Spider Latham books come from my imagination. However, as my friend Owen Walker gave me permission to use his story on grace in *The Lodger,* I couldn't resist giving the fictional Ethan Walters an Owenesque feature or two, again with his permission. Thank you, Owen, for that sweet story.

To Sara Stamey, your help and suggestions were invaluable in this project, but your belief in me was beyond price. Thank you.

THE HARVEST MOON SANK behind a jagged black horizon, and small night creatures began to venture out into the safety of 2:00 A.M. shadows. On a hill east of Panaca, a mother civet cat, teaching her adolescent kits to hunt, just missed supper as a mouse darted into a pile of rocks. Growling in her throat and pawing furiously at a crevice, she jumped aside when two of the stones dislodged and rolled down the slope. Before she could return to the hunt, the fanning of wings and a swooping black form warned that the great horned owl was about to make her kits the prey.

The civet and her kits melted away into the shadows, and the owl flew away. All was silent and still. The last light of the setting moon reflected off something that had been uncovered when the civet tumbled stones from the pile. Gleaming white, and reaching out of the rocky cairn as if in a last desperate bid for attention, was the skeleton of a human hand.

DEPUTY SHERIFF THARON TATE left this life at eighty miles an hour. On an autumn afternoon in 1992 he smashed his patrol car straight into a rocky canyon wall at a curve in the road between Caliente and Panaca, Nevada. Deputy Tate had been on his way home for supper, but he didn't make it past the Devil's Elbow.

Before the tuna casserole was cold on the countertop, the awful news had been passed along the local network of telephones and backyard fences to half the sparsely populated county. The men who'd raced to the canyon to help stood around in awkward clumps. The one who usually directed their emergency efforts was compressed inside the twisted cage of his white cruiser, cradling a hot, greasy Chevrolet 350 in his lap.

Sheriff Dan Brown arrived last and marched around like a banty rooster, greeting those assembled with a grim, take-charge tone that fooled no one. Then he stood with the rest, mutely staring at the driver's side door, buckled to a quarter of its normal width and welded shut with the force of impact.

Behind the sheriff, a grizzled rancher spoke to the man standing beside him. "So, what you think, Spider?"

"I dunno, Bud. There's no gas leak. It'd be safe to use a cutting torch. Maybe I'll go home, get my outfit, and we'll get him out of there."

Sheriff Brown seized upon this plan, fraying nerves and losing next-election votes as he reframed each of Spider Latham's suggestions in the form of an order.

It took time to get the oxyacetylene rig and time to engineer an opening, using pry bars and come-alongs, that would let them safely remove the body while keeping it intact. The men worked steadily in tight-jawed concentration, illuminated by a ring of headlights when it got too dark to see. It was ten o'clock by the time they had cut their way in to the deputy, and midnight before they had gotten him out and the tow truck had hauled away the deputy's cruiser. One by one the emergency crew went soberly home, leaving only three standing in the night.

A full moon hung directly above them, casting the canyon into geometric planes of blue light and blue shadow, and illuminating the ghost of a smile on Bud Hefernan's lips. He stood with Spider Latham and Spider's neighbor, Murray Sapp, watching Sheriff Brown follow the tow truck down the canyon toward Caliente. "That ought to be one worried man," he said. "What's he going to do without old Tharon Tate?"

"Why, he's gonna deputize Spider!" said Murray. "I'm sure glad you mentioned that he ought to go with the tow truck, Spider," he added. "He was wearing awful thin."

Spider nodded, coiling up the hoses to his cutting torch.

Pausing a moment, he looked back down the last road that Tharon Tate had traveled.

"Was Tharon a Mormon?" Bud asked Spider. "Are you going to have to go comfort LaVida tonight after pulling the pieces of her husband out of the wreck? Oh, I forgot. You're not bishop anymore, are you?"

"Naw, not for a year now. I'm sure Bishop Stowe's already been to see her."

"Darned if that ain't worse. First he's going to offer comfort and then he's going to offer to sell her a coffin! Whyn't you Mormons do like the rest of us and hire a preacher?"

"Why pay for something you can get for free?" asked Murray.

"You get what you pay for," Spider grunted as he hoisted the heavy gas bottles into the back of his pickup. "I never was much good at comforting widows." He shook his head. "Poor old LaVida."

"Poor Lincoln County," said Bud. "Tharon was a good man to have around."

Murray tossed a crowbar into the pickup bed, slammed the tailgate shut and leaned on it. "My daddy used to say that old Tharon Tate was the one that kept this county safe. Didn't matter who the sheriff was, Deputy Tate was the law in Lincoln County."

The three men stood silently for a moment. Off in the distance a train whistle wailed. A crisp October night-breeze rattled the dried grasses along the roadway and laid a chilly finger on the back of Spider Latham's neck. He shivered and hunched his shoulders and said, "I'll see you guys tomorrow. I'm going home."

The moon cast the shadow of a phantom pickup on the

ground. It kept pace alongside Spider as he drove along the narrow highway to Panaca. When he angled off onto a gravel road, the shadow nosed ahead. When he turned into his own driveway, it fell abreast again, rippling silently over the cattle guard. Long after Spider had gone to bed and lay trying to erase the images of the evening from his mind, the shadow stood sentinel beside his pickup in the dooryard.

NEWLY SWORN-IN DEPUTY Sheriff Spider Latham ambled through the Las Vegas Municipal Motor Pool storage lot with a key in his hand, searching for a unit with a number matching the red plastic tag on the key ring. He headed first toward a shiny new muscle car, a police cruiser with brute power under the hood and banks of switches and dials in the cockpit. Entertaining a mental picture of himself behind the wheel, streaking down Highway 93 with lights flashing and siren wailing, Spider checked the tag. No match. Further down the row he spied a couple of sturdy workhorses—muscle has-beens. Expecting to inherit one of these metropolitan hand-me-down cruisers, he walked over to check the number. No match.

Spider looked over the remaining cars. His swearing-in should have prepared him for this.

He had taken the deputy sheriff's oath in Judge Philmont's chambers at the county courthouse in Pioche after cooling his heels on a straight-backed chair in the hall for twenty minutes. When the judge finally appeared, hazed to his chambers by the sheriff's clerk and looking like a thundercloud, Spider began to be glad he hadn't let Laurie come with him. It took all of two minutes for the judge to jerk on his robe and bark out the oath. Though Spider repeated, "I, Quimby Latham, do solemnly swear . . ." with as much dignity as he could muster, he found himself standing back in the dingy hallway, hat in hand, with unceremonious speed.

Randi Lee, the sheriff's clerk, led him back to her office and adroitly apologized for the delay without criticizing the judge. She was tall and rawboned, with an honest face and a no-nonsense air. She asked Spider to sit down, then opened a drawer and took out a gun in a holster on a belt, a badge, and the red-tagged key.

"The county got some emergency funds from the state to replace Deputy Tate's cruiser." She gave him the key. "We bought one from the city of Las Vegas. You got someone can take you over to get it?"

"Laurie can take me."

"Great. Sign here, please, for the gun. Here for the badge. Thank you. Now, we have a new regulation that assigns all deputies to plain-clothes duty."

"You got other deputies?"

"Nope. You're the only one."

"I notice old Tharon always wore a uniform."

"And not one of them less than five years old. You're a good five inches taller than he was, so forget about inheriting any of his."

Spider smiled. "In other words, there's no money for uniforms."

She answered his smile. "Not since the mines closed." She slid a piece of paper over to him. It was covered with columns of figures. "This is your budget. It's very simple: You got your salary, your mileage allowance, your phone allowance, and your miscellaneous fund."

"What's the miscellaneous fund for?"

"Anything that's not covered in the other columns. Like if you had to have a tire fixed. Or maybe there was a disaster and you had to hire a piece of special equipment to come in. Anything extra you do has to come out of that fund."

Spider eyed the figures. "Looks to me like a flat tire would be about as big a disaster as I could handle."

Randi laughed. "That's about it. If you get in a bind, call me. Sometimes I can wangle funds from the state to cover extra costs. But if not, you'll just have to make do. Since the mines closed . . ." She shrugged.

Spider knew about making do. After twenty years as millwright at Keystone Mines and two years of scraping by on unemployment and odd jobs, Spider was making do with a job as deputy sheriff.

"Handbook of Procedures," Randi went on, laying a three-ring binder down on the desk by his badge. "And here is what we call the Triple L. *Law in Layman's Language.* Your job is to enforce the law. But you gotta know what the law is. This puts it down in easy-to-read form. Make sure you study these real closely."

Spider lifted the cover of the top notebook and peeked inside. "And how about training? Do I go to school somewhere or follow someone around for a few days to learn the ropes?"

Randi shook her head. "Not—"

"—since the mines closed," Spider finished the sentence. "I see. Do I talk to the sheriff?"

"He's out of town."

"So this is it? I'm the deputy? I just go out and start deputying?"

"Read your books. You'll do fine. From what I hear, you're a good man to have around in a crisis."

Three hours later, standing in the Las Vegas motor pool parking lot, Spider grunted, "I might be a good man in a crisis, but I sure don't know my way around a parking lot."

Strolling over to the last row of cars, Spider looked over the compact-sized hoods lined up in front of him. "Guess I know how Laurie's bull calf felt when we made a steer out of him," he muttered. "I think I'm about to lose my manhood."

Steeling himself for the worst, Spider began checking the numbers. He was relieved to find that his match was a newer model, equipped with lights, siren, and an engine that would do. When he folded his long, lanky frame into the driver's seat and adjusted it, he found that it was comfortable enough. Putting the gun in the glove compartment, he locked it. Then he started the car and revved the engine, smiling with satisfaction as the torque rocked the car each time he stepped on the accelerator. "Could have been worse." He pulled down on the gearshift and prepared to make his first official trip as deputy sheriff of Lincoln County.

Instead, he washed the windows of the deputy's official car. "Great Suffering Zot!" he sputtered. Finally he figured out that the gearshift was on the floor, and the windshield wiper lever was on the steering column.

"All right, Inspector Clouseau," Spider chided. "Let's get it together now and see if we can make it out of the parking lot without embarrassing ourselves." He managed to do that. Then he threaded his way through city traffic until he found the freeway and headed north.

After the turnoff to Highway 93, where the road lay flat and straight for twenty miles, Spider pulled off to the side and spent ten minutes flipping switches, finding the siren and lights, practicing until he could turn them on with his eyes closed. Then, after mistakenly washing the windows again, he put the car in gear, pulled onto the road, and pushed the accelerator to the floor.

Two hours later, when Spider turned off the highway onto the gravel road that led to his house, he knew what his county car would do and what it wouldn't. "One thing it won't do," he said to himself, "is handle these washboard roads very well." Slowing down, he spied his neighbor's brown Ford 4x4 coming toward him, so he hit the flashing lights and slowed to a stop. Rolling down his window, he waited for Murray Sapp to come abreast.

"That you, Spider?" Murray asked, and Spider was surprised to see tenseness in the weather-beaten face.

"Deputy Spider, to you," he said.

"You scared the pea-waddin' out of me! What're you doing flashing those lights at me?"

Spider grinned. "What's the matter, Murray? Got a guilty conscience?"

But Murray didn't smile back. He stared at Spider with dark eyes. Finally he pushed back his battered Stetson. "The tabs on my truck have expired. I didn't know it was you. Thought I was caught for sure."

"Uh-uh. I was wondering if we could get the road graded again. If you don't have time, I could do it. But it's getting pretty bad. Especially back there along by the wash. I was going a little fast and almost lost it on the approach to the bridge. What d'ya think? Want me to do it?"

"Naw. I don't have anything going. I'll do it tomorrow."

"Thanks. And Mur?"

"Yeah?"

"Your tabs are expired. I'd get that taken care of, if I were you." He waited for Murray to laugh at the joke. Finally he was rewarded with a tentative smile. Spider waved at Murray, called "See ya," and drove on, wondering what kind of a wedge the badge on his shirt was going to drive between him and his friends in the county.

CHAPTER

3

ANY SECOND THOUGHTS SPIDER might have had about taking the job of deputy sheriff left him as he turned off the gravel
road and drove over the cattle guard onto his own place. He
and Laurie owned a hundred and twenty acres of prime grazing land with a year-round spring bubbling up through a rocky
outcropping half a mile from the house. They had spent the last
twenty-five years building a house, raising two boys, and building up a herd to ensure each of their sons a mission for the
Church and a college education. The mines had closed before
the second son was through, but beef prices were up and there
was lots of rain, and the sleek red Herefords that Laurie sent to
market brought enough to pay for the last two years. Now their
savings were gone, and all but six heifers were gone; there were
no jobs in the county and no hope of the mines reopening.
Selling out and moving had been inevitable until Spider was
offered the job of deputy.

He parked the county car in the empty dooryard. Laurie wasn't home from Vegas yet. Carrying the notebooks Randi had given him, he entered the house through the back door, pausing to hang his Stetson on a peg on the service porch before he dumped the notebooks on the kitchen table. Opening the fridge, he looked inside, closed it, and opened the bread drawer.

Five minutes later, as he sat with a slab of homemade bread and jam and the Triple L opened in front of him, he heard the pickup cross the cattle guard and looked up to see Laurie park and jump down with a bag of groceries in her arm. At forty, she was five years younger than Spider. Trim and energetic, she had dark eyes and a dusting of freckles across her nose. Her expressive face was just beginning to set into creases at the eyes and corners of her mouth. She wore her auburn hair long and pulled back in a ponytail.

"Nice car," she said as she breezed in and set the sack on the counter.

Spider turned in his chair and smiled at her. "It'll do. I expected you'd be home before me."

"I wasn't driving a patrol car. And I did a few errands. It's so nice to have a car of my own again. I didn't realize how much I missed it."

"Yeah. I figured the deputy's job doesn't pay much, but it gets us back to being a two-car family again."

Laurie began unpacking groceries. "It's been so long since I drove anywhere, I took the curve too fast over by the wash and started fishtailing." She bent over to put some apples in the fridge.

Admiring the view, Spider said, "I stopped Murray on the

way home and asked him to grade the road. Flashed the lights at him, and he thought I was a policeman."

Laurie straightened. "You are a policeman."

"Yeah. But you know what I mean. He didn't take kindly to it. You get any Pepsis?"

"Not until you get your first check," she said. "I'll get you some milk."

"You know, ole Murray hasn't been the same since Missy left."

"That's because she keeps coming back to remind him what a mistake he made to marry her in the first place. Actually, I thought that he perked up noticeably when she first went away."

Spider shook his head. "He's letting his place go to seed. And things like grading the road. I've never had to remind him it needed to be done."

"Yes you did. That time, remember, last spring? We were on our way home from Bobby's graduation and Murray was on his front-end loader. Remember, that rainstorm was so bad we had to pull off the side of the road out on the flat because the wipers wouldn't go fast enough. And then when we got to this side of the wash, it was still raining some, and there was Murray on his loader."

"Yeah, I remember. He looked like something the cat drug in."

"And you asked him to grade the road. Or at least volunteered to do it if he was too busy."

"Huh! I knew he wasn't too busy. Only thing keeps him from starving is that piddling little contract he's got over at the landfill. If he didn't have his machinery paid for, he'd go under for sure. Did you bring in the paper?"

Laurie fished the paper out of the shopping bag and handed it to Spider. "Looks like they've found another body up by Tahoe. What does that make, five?"

Spider took the paper and placed it over the open notebook. He took a bite of his bread and read the lead article as he chewed slowly. "Yeah," he answered finally. "Five. California cops are champing at the bit to get in on it. Nevada police are scratching their heads."

"Or their backsides." Laurie sat down opposite Spider with a bread-and-jam sandwich and a glass of milk. "Does this one fit the pattern?"

"I dunno. I haven't been following this like you have."

"That's because you're not a woman. So far they've all been brunettes, around thirty-five or forty years old, and they've all been prostitutes."

Spider studied the article. "Looks like she was dark haired, forty or so. They can tell that from looking at the body. What's left of it, anyway. She's been dead quite a while. Body was dumped out in the middle of nowhere. They haven't identified her yet. But it says here that they think they're dealing with a serial killer."

Laurie shivered. "It gives me the creeps just thinking about it. Maybe we ought to start locking our doors."

Spider leaned back in his chair. "Look, Darlin', Tahoe is way across the state. And they're all prostitutes. We've only got one lady of the night in the county, and that's Twila Keeley. If old Twila disappears, we'll start locking the doors."

The telephone rang, and Laurie went to answer it.

She listened. "No," she said, winking at Spider, "he's here. Matter of fact, he was just sworn in this morning." She paused, listening again. "What!" The freckles on Laurie's nose stood out as the blood drained from her face. Her eyes widened.

"What's the matter?" Spider asked, sitting up straight.

"Wait," she croaked into the receiver. She thrust the instrument toward Spider. "It's Kyle Bates calling for the deputy sheriff," she rasped. "His son was out rabbit hunting with Cody Larsen this afternoon, and they found a body."

AN HOUR LATER, SPIDER was five miles up the valley, hunkered down on a hillside with Kyle Bates. Fourteen-year-old Junior Bates and Cody Larsen were telling about finding the body.

"And you were coming from where?" Spider asked.

"We come over this ridge, right down this little draw," said Junior.

"Our bikes was a mile or so down the road," Cody offered. "No sign of rabbits. Thought we'd get our bikes and go back to our regular hunting ground."

"So you don't usually hunt here?"

Both boys shook their heads.

"What made you come here today?"

Cody looked at his feet and shrugged his shoulders, but Junior said, "My mom made us each a harness so we could put our guns on our backs and ride our bikes out further to go hunting. Always before we just hiked to the foothills behind our place. I knew there was a spring out here somewhere. Thought we'd see if we could find it."

"Did you find it?"

"Yeah. But it was more of a seep than a spring. We thought we'd just cut straight out to the road. Be easier walking to get back to our bikes. We come over the ridge right about there, and climbed under the fence here where it crosses the draw. I just got under, was still on my hands and knees, when I seen the . . . seen the . . ."

Junior Bates couldn't say the words, but he had his arm held out in front of him with his fingers spread wide, and Spider understood. *Arm* wasn't the right word. And neither was *skeleton*. What was sticking out of the old CCC flood-control dam had once been an arm. When the scavengers had finished picking the dried skin and flesh off the bones, it would be a skeleton. But right now it was halfway between. It looked pretty gruesome.

Spider patted Junior on the shoulder. "Thanks, boys," he said. "You did just as you ought. You didn't disturb anything here, and you went home and told your daddy. I appreciate it."

He turned and offered his hand to Kyle. "Thanks, Kyle. You'd better take the boys on home now."

"That's okay, Bishop. We'll stay if you need us, help you get it all uncovered."

"Naw. That old boy's been in there for a while now. He can stay for a little longer while I figure out what I've got to do."

"Well, call me if you need me. Come on, boys." Kyle put his hand on Junior's shoulder and started down the slope to where his pickup truck sat by the deputy's car. Pausing, he sent the two boys on ahead and came back to speak to Spider.

"This may not be the time to talk about this, Bishop, but Rose Markey is back in town."

"Is that so!"

"She and Gilbert divorced, and she moved back here."

"Huh! So much for revelation. Remember, he said he saw her across the dance floor at the single-adult dance, and right then the Lord revealed to him that she was the one he should marry."

"I remember you told him you thought it was his hormones speaking to him and not the Spirit."

"Did I say that? I was sure a tactless son-of-a-gun, wasn't I? No wonder they released me early as bishop."

Kyle made a helpless gesture and plowed on. "The thing about it is, Rose is back."

Spider smiled wickedly. "Looks like the new bishop is going to earn his wings now."

Kyle cleared his throat. "Well, the thing is, I told Bishop Stowe about how, when you were bishop and I was counselor to you, you did lots of counseling with Rose. He feels, since you had experience with her, that you should be her home teacher."

"Great Suffering Zot, Kyle! You wouldn't do that to me!"

"We're taking everyone else off your route, except Murray. You just continue to be his friend and count him as visited." Kyle stuck out his hand. "Sorry to complicate your day," he said, indicating the pile of rocks behind Spider.

"Yeah, well, this one I can deal with. But Rose . . ." Spider shook his head.

Kyle nodded sympathetically as he turned downhill. The boys were waiting in the pickup, and as they drove away Cody Larsen leaned out the window, looking back to learn what happens when an officer of the law is left in charge of a body found in suspicious circumstances.

Spider didn't know much more than Cody, but he wasn't going to let on. After waving good-bye, he stood with his hands on his hips. His eyes crinkled at the corners and his lips drew back in a grimace as he surveyed the surrounding area. The road below him was a little-used secondary road that ran from the highway to a mine shaft in the hills across the narrow valley. It was named the Lucy Roberts. Before the mines shut down there had been fifty men working this shaft, and trucks had rumbled over this road night and day, carrying ore to the mills in Castleton. Murray Sapp had been one of those truck drivers after he quit rodeoing. When his dad died, he inherited a bit of money and bought some heavy equipment. From then on he contracted with the mines to maintain their gravel roads. But now the mines were closed, and Murray was lucky to be covering garbage out at the landfill. And his place, his great-grandfather's homestead, was going to seed. "And I'm working as deputy sheriff," Spider muttered, "and I don't know what the dickens I'm doing."

He turned back to look more closely at the rocky grave.

In 1893 and again in 1920, the village of Panaca, farther down the valley, had been all but swept away. A muddy wall of water, the result of hundreds of little draws funneling their runoff into the valley all at once, caught the townspeople unaware. There were no lives lost, but there was considerable property damage and loss of livestock. Congressman Rupert Hughes lost a barn and a hundred head of breeding stock in the second flood. Years later, when Congressman Hughes had become a power to be reckoned with in Washington, no one was surprised when a group of President Roosevelt's Civilian

Conservation Corps spent some time in Lincoln County building flood control dams and dikes.

Growing up in this area, ranging across the countryside like Junior Bates and Cody, Spider had always taken the little rocky dams for granted. There were hundreds of them in the county, thrown across the creases in the hills. Spider squatted on his heels and examined this particular dam more closely. Then he grunted to himself, stood, and headed back to his car. He needed to make a call to Randi Lee.

Randi wasn't much help. Spider stood in a phone booth at the Texaco station in Panaca and stuck a finger in his ear to drown out the sound of a semi going by.

"No, the sheriff's on his way to Tahoe," Randi said.

"What's he doing up there?"

"He's offering his services as a tracker."

"You're not serious!"

"Election year coming up. There's a chance for some publicity."

"Only if they don't ask him to do any tracking. So what do I do?"

"Did you read your handbook of procedures?"

"I just got it this morning. I looked to see if there was anything to cover this situation. I didn't seem to find anything."

"Well, the coroner will have to have a look at the body. But that will be after you bring it in."

"Bring it in where?"

"Stowe's Mortuary."

"Can the coroner help with the cause of death and stuff like that?

"I don't know. If it's pretty obvious, he can. It's old Dr. Goldberg. If it's tricky, we call in a forensic pathologist."

"I think it's going to be tricky."

"The only thing is . . ."

"This doesn't have anything to do with the mines closing, does it?"

"Well, in a way. The state has one we can call in, but he'd be up in Tahoe right now, too. If you're in a hurry, you can hire one, but it comes out of your budget."

"I'll wait."

"When you want the coroner, you'll have to drive him out. His palsy is so bad they wouldn't renew his license. I'll send you the forms for requesting the forensic pathologist."

"Thanks, Randi."

"Don't mention it. 'Bye."

Spider hung up the phone and stood for a moment, thinking. Then he opened the county phone book. White and yellow pages together numbered no more than thirty. He found the number he wanted and dialed.

"Myrna," he said, when his party answered, "where is Bud working today? He is? Well, let me talk to him, will you? Thanks."

Spider listened to Myrna Hefernan's retreating footsteps, picturing the shiny hardwood floor of their comfortable ranch house. He heard the squeaking of the door as she opened it and the banging of the screen as she went outside. Then he heard her call her husband's name, hallooing through cupped hands to get his attention. "Telephone!" she called. Then bang went the screen and tap tap tap on the floor. "He's coming."

"Thanks, Myrna."

"How's Laurie?"

"Good, good."

"How many cattle did you end up keeping?"

"We've got six heifers that should calve this spring. Double our herd."

"Tell Laurie that if she wants to she can put them in that section next to your place with our bull. It'll save you the A.I. fees."

Before Spider had a chance to say thanks, Myrna said, "Here's Bud," and Spider heard the booming voice of the manager of the Lazy H, principal holding of the Hughes family corporation.

"That you, Spider?"

"Yeah, Bud."

"What can I do for you?"

"You doing something right now you can't leave?"

"Shoot, no! I'm getting the hay baler greased up and ready to store for the winter. Been putting it off till now. Guess I can put it off a little longer. What d'you need?"

"Can you meet me on the road to the Lucy Roberts?"

"Right now?"

"If you can."

"I'm on my way." Click.

Spider detoured by his place, parking the county car and backing his pickup over to the barn. He got down an old plywood door that had been stored up in the rafters. After blowing off the accumulated dust with the air compressor, he removed the hinges and handle. He had just put it in the back of the pickup when Laurie came out of the house.

"How's it going?" she called.

"All right." He walked over to where she stood at the end of the sidewalk. "You got an old sheet I could use?"

"Yeah. I'll get it."

"How about some safety pins?"

"I'll get those too." She disappeared into the house.

Spider glanced at the sun and judged it to be about five o'clock. Though it was shirtsleeve weather now, he knew that close to sundown it would get chilly, so he went to the back door and got his jacket off the service porch. When he got back in the pickup, he made sure his work gloves were there. Then he backed around to meet Laurie as she came out with the sheet and pins.

"Can I use your car?" he asked.

"Only if you tell me about it when you get home."

"I'll tell you what I can," he said.

"Is it awful?"

"It's not pretty."

"Well, here." She handed the sheet in through the window. "I could only find five safety pins. Some of them are pretty small."

"That's fine." Spider slipped them into his shirt pocket, waved to Laurie, and drove away to meet Bud Hefernan on the road to the Lucy Roberts.

Bud's brown Chevy pickup was sitting at the turnoff, and he was inside, practicing his harmonica. He stashed his harmonica in his pocket and joined Spider. As they drove the final mile and a half, Spider explained about the two boys finding the body.

Bud whistled softly. "Boy, howdy! That'd be something for a young'un to come upon."

Spider parked the pickup and went around to let the tailgate down. Remembering the sheet, he went back to get it. When he finally had the door under one arm and the sheet in the other hand, he looked around. Bud was already up the hill squatting by the little CCC dam.

"How'd you know where it was?" he called.

"Shoot, Spider, there was plenty of tracks leading right up to it. Isn't that what you brought me for, to read sign?"

Spider waited to answer until he reached the rocky pile. "Yeah, it is," he said, squatting by Bud. "What d'you think?"

Bud didn't answer right away. Spider waited while the older man studied the puzzle in front of them.

Finally he spoke. "I'd say that you've got a woman buried there. And I'd say that she was beat up pretty bad before she was put there. And I'd say that whoever did it was either plenty scared or in a hurry. Or both."

"So, how do you tell that?"

"Well, lookit there. First thing is, the rocks were piled on top of her all no-how. Person's in a hurry, doesn't want to take time to do it right. Just get the body covered and get out of there. Shows panic. Naturally, as the little floods come down, it's going to move the rocks that aren't placed well, and some are going to fall down. That's what's happened. And the little critters that have been crawling in and nibbling away at the carcass are joined by larger critters. They disturbed that arm, pulled it out of the pile. That probably loosened the ring, made it fall off the hand. That was possible because as the flesh dried out it shrank, and the ring just slipped off."

"Where's the ring?"

"See, there in the crevice between the bottom two stones." Bud picked it up and handed it to Spider. "It's a woman's ring."

Spider held the ring between thumb and forefinger. It was silver and turquoise. "Huh," he grunted, and put the ring in his pocket. "So what about being beat up?"

"Well, do you notice where the arm bends?"

"Yeah."

"Arm don't naturally bend there. Look at the way the bone is slivered out. I'll bet that was one of them—what do you call it when the bone sticks out of the skin?"

"Compound fracture?"

"Yeah. Compound fracture."

"Maybe one of the critters broke the bone worrying it, trying to get it out."

"Naw. It's all the same color. No large teeth marks like a coyote would make. I think that arm was broke before the flesh disappeared. You got a medical man gonna look at this?"

"Old Doc Goldberg."

"Well, I'll tell ya, he's old, and his hands shake like the dickens," Bud imitated the doctor's palsy, "but his eyes are sharp, and there's nothing wrong with his head. You could do worse. You ready to uncover the rest of her?"

"If you don't think there's anything else we can learn before we disturb it."

"Like tracks or sign? Naw. The water that washed those stones away would have washed away any tracks. Let's see what she looks like."

Bud pulled his gloves out of his back pocket and put them on. Then he commenced lifting off stones and dropping them on the upstream side. Spider remembered his gloves in the pickup and strode down the hill to get them. One had fallen on the floor, apparently knocked off when he reached in for the sheet, and it took a moment of searching to find it. As he climbed back up the slope, he noticed Bud was putting something in his shirt pocket.

"We got to be careful to put all these rocks back just as we found them," Bud called to him, buttoning his pocket shut.

"Otherwise, we might be guilty of disturbing the ee-co-logical balance of the ee-co-system."

Spider grinned, remembering the run-ins Bud had had with radical environmental groups over grazing rights. But the grin faded as he looked down and saw what Bud had uncovered.

It hardly looked human. Certainly there were two arms and two legs, but they rested awkwardly on the rocky bed, dipping and hooving in unlikely places. The skeleton was still held together with sinew, but it was evident that the small carnivore population of the area had been dining here regularly for some time. The muscle and skin that was left was in patches and an ugly brown color. The head was twisted too far around so the eyes stared down into the cracks between the rocks, and wispy hanks of dark brown hair fluttered in the breeze. Spider felt his gorge rise and was thankful he couldn't see the face, turned down like it was. He looked away and made himself breathe deeply. Finally he looked at Bud.

Bud was staring intently down at the remains. "I'll bet she ain't from around here," he said.

"Why do you say that?"

"Well, first off, ain't nobody missing. This lady's been lying here at least four, five months. Long enough for the deep flesh around her middle and rump to turn to jerky—see where the skirt has been eaten away there by her backside. 'Course, lying in rocks like she was, they'd heat up and speed the process, but I'd say four, five months. If it'd been a year, now, the critters would probably have picked the bones clean. You know of anyone who left this spring and didn't come back?"

"Not right off. But there might be someone we didn't remember."

"All right. But what about those clothes. They ain't much of them left. Critters been cartin' 'em down to their burrows in pieces, I suppose. But lookit here." Bud bent down and pushed a piece of what had been a blue wool jacket aside and revealed a black and white Saks Fifth Avenue label. "You know anyone can afford to shop at Saks Fifth Avenue?" he asked.

"Not since the mines closed," Spider replied in a grim attempt at humor.

"Check the watch."

Spider gingerly turned the stainless steel expansion bracelet around so the watch face sat in place on top of the exposed arm bones. It was a macabre sight, and Spider found that he was sweating. He wiped his hands on his pants and looked away.

Bud bent down to peer at the watch. "It's a Timex. Has a regular face on it, and the crystal's been smashed."

"What time does it say?"

"Four forty-five. But that don't mean nothing. Without a crystal those hands could have been moved anytime something pushed against them. Or maybe the watch kept on running, turning the hands around, until it ran down. Funny thing, though."

"What?"

"Timex watch and a Saks Fifth Avenue outfit. Let me check one last thing."

"What's that?"

"The shoes. Or I guess I should say shoe. Where did she buy it?"

Bud bent down to take the shoe off, but it seemed to be stuck on. As he worked it back and forth, it finally came free, but the toe bones were welded into the bottom of the shoe by the dried flesh and came away from the foot. Bud made a face as he peered inside for the brand name.

"Wonder where the other shoe is," said Spider.

"I dunno. I can't read the name on the bottom. But on the side here it says, 'All manmade materials. Made in China.'"

"Huh," Spider grunted again. "So, what d'ya think? You ready to get her out of here?"

"You fixing to put her on that board?"

"Figured to. Then I'll wrap the whole thing up in a sheet."

"Tell you what. If you'll lift her feet and legs, I'll slide it under her. Then you can lift the hips, then shoulders, and on up. Be easier than trying to lift the whole carcass, don't you think?"

"Probably so." Spider put on his gloves and pushed a couple of rocks away from the feet to allow access as Bud set the shoe down on a rock and got the piece of plywood. "Ready?"

"Yeah, go ahead."

Spider put his hands under the feet and lifted, glad he had on his gloves so he couldn't feel the brittleness of dried skin and flesh that clung to the bone in knobby brown patches.

"All right, now the knees," coached Bud.

Spider lifted the knees and tried to ignore the sound of the board as it scraped on the rocks. It was a fingernail-on-the-blackboard kind of a sound that sent the flesh crawling.

"Okay. Now the hips. Uh . . . Spider, I wonder, d'you want to see if you can pull her skirt down, what's left of it, anyway? The board's caught it in back. Here, see if you can get it free. There! Don't seem right to have her exposed like that, d'ya think?"

Spider finished pulling the ragged piece of blue wool back down over the ropes of jerky that had been the woman's thighs and got his hands under to lift so that the board wouldn't catch again.

"Now," Bud said, "under the rib cage. Now the shoulders."

"She's very light," Spider said as he eased her broken arm up on the board.

"That's 'cause she's all dried out. All right, now for the head. When you pick it up, why don't you twist it around so she's lying natural. I'd feel better about looking at her if she looked more comfortable."

Spider looked down at the dirty brown skull with its crusty leather patches sprouting meager tufts of dark, dull hair. He had no desire to touch it, much less turn it around to reveal what had once been the face. He felt his palms start to sweat inside his gloves, and his face began to feel warm.

"They paying you enough for this kind of work?" Bud asked.

"I don't think so," Spider said in a strangled voice. He took a breath and closed his eyes, grabbing blindly at the head and twisting. He felt resistance for a moment, and then suddenly there was a snapping noise and the head turned freely in his hands.

Spider heard an "Uhhh . . ." from Bud, an exhaling of air, and he opened his eyes to see what was the matter. Bud was staring at what he had in his hands. Looking down, Spider saw that the head had come loose from the body. He was holding the severed skull, face up, with shriveled eyeballs lying in the sockets and partial lips dried into a leathery half-smile, revealing a gap where the two front teeth had been. There were brown patches of cheek, brow, and chin stuck here and there. Of nose and ears there was not one vestige.

Spider stared for a moment at what he had in his hands;

then he dropped it on the board and took off up the hill. Stumbling over rocks and bushes, he headed for the support of the fence post, keeping that goal uppermost in his mind as saliva poured into his mouth and spasms began racking his midsection. He reached the fence and, grateful for its support, leaned against the top strand of barbed wire and vomited.

★   ★   ★

Half an hour later, as he dropped Bud off at his pickup, Spider reached his hand out the window to shake the older man's hand. "Thanks, Bud," he said. "Don't know what I'd have done without you."

"Oh, you'd have managed. Let me know when you're ready to put that dam back together. I'll come and help you. Got to preserve our ee-co-system, you know."

Spider laughed and waved at Bud. Then he took off for Stowe's funeral home.

THE SQUARE, RED-BRICK funeral home sat on a patch of lawn nestled in the protection of some stumpy gray hills on Highway 93, a mile north of the Panaca junction. Spider had been here more than once, most recently as bishop, slowly shepherding Nephi Wentworth through the double row of caskets on display. Nephi's wife had been dear, but his pension was slender. It had been a hard choice.

Spider drove around to the back, parked near a set of double doors, and got out of the pickup. Pulling on his gloves as he walked to the tailgate, he was startled when one of the doors exploded outward and a grizzled, gnarled figure came rocking out. It was Shorty Rhodes, and he was livid.

Shorty's ungainly gait was caused by one leg being shorter than the other. His gray head was down and his hands, knotted from arthritis, were pumping the air, punctuating the epithets he was voicing in venomous sibilants.

"Short-sighted scum-sucker! Sorry, snatch-fisted, snaky so-and-so."

"Hello, Shorty. What's going on?"

"What? Oh, hello, Spider. I didn't see you. I've just been in to see the Favorite Son. He may own the business now, but I'll tell you something: He's got a ways to go to be the man his father was!"

Spider folded his arms and leaned against the tailgate. "Oh?"

"Yes sir, he's got a ways to go."

"You haven't lost anyone, have you, Shorty? I mean, what're you doing here?'

Glancing angrily at the double doors, Shorty didn't need more of an invitation to begin venting. "Old Mr. Stowe and I had an arrangement—a business arrangement. He wanted to make sure that if anything happened to his refrigeration system, night or day, he could get it fixed. So, he paid me a retainer. Paid me twenty-five dollars a week, cash, so he'd have the service. Then, when anything happened, I just fixed it. Didn't charge him."

"Sounds good to me."

"Old Mr. Stowe paid me in cash. He'd leave the money on the corner of the table in the back room, and I'd come in and pick it up. That way I didn't have to report it as wages earned, and it didn't affect my disability pension. It made it so I could live, y'see? It didn't buy me any extras. Just made it so I could survive."

"I see."

"Well, the Favorite Son doesn't see. He says his dad was foolish to spend the money if no service was rendered. Says leaving cash on the corner of the table is an unforgivable way to run a business. I'll tell *him* unforgivable! Low-down, snaky scum-sucker!"

"He's young, Shorty. He's got a lot to learn."

"Well, let him learn on someone else. What'm I gonna do for money to buy groceries? How do I pay for my Tylenol?"

"I don't know, Shorty."

"I don't want charity, you know. Mr. Stowe got good value for his money." Shorty turned away muttering, "I don't know what I'm going to do."

Spider watched the old man's rolling progress toward a weathered 1963 International pickup. Then he turned to unlatch his tailgate.

"What's an embeeay?" Shorty had stopped halfway to his truck.

"Beg pardon?"

"What's an embeeay?"

"Well, I don't know, Shorty." Spider strolled over. "Where'd you hear about one?"

Shorty wagged his thumb toward the double doors. "Favorite Son in there. Said he had one and that's why he didn't need me anymore." He looked down at his feet for a moment; then he held up the two knotted lumps that were his hands. "I can fix anything in my head. It's getting these to do the work, anymore. Picking up a screw is painful. Turning a dial hurts like blazes. But I do it. I give good value. Now I'm done in by an embeeay."

Shorty let his hands flop to his sides. He shook his head and turned. Slump-shoulders dipped with each disappointed step as he trudged to the cab of his truck and climbed in.

Spider pulled down the brim of his Stetson to keep the rays of the late afternoon sun out of his eyes. He watched Shorty's pickup until it disappeared around the side of the building. Then he turned back to let down the tailgate before entering the mortuary through the double doors in the back.

He found himself in a wide passageway with a set of double doors immediately in front of him and another set to his right. To his left was a single door. Spider opened it and peeked in.

Richie Stowe, Favorite Son, was in his office. Dressed in a dark suit and a tie of muted and somber stripes, he raised his eyes as Spider opened the door, and a look of concern came over his face. "Spider . . . hello. Can I help you? Come in."

Spider removed his hat and stepped in. "I think so." The office was small and comfortably old-fashioned, still carrying the aura of the man who had sat at the desk for so many years.

"Sit down." Richie Stowe indicated a nearby chair. "Has there been a death in your family, Spider? Your mother?"

Spider sat. "No, no, Bishop. Everyone is fine. This is county business. Randi Lee told me—you know Randi? Works in the sheriff's office? She told me that the mortuary here keeps bodies for the county—stores them, you might say. I've got a body that I need you to hold on to for a few days for me."

Bishop Stowe frowned. He lowered his eyes and pulled at his lower lip. He said nothing.

Spider stirred in his chair. "Ah, have I come at a bad time?"

Bishop Stowe looked up. "No, this is as good a time as any to clear this up." He stood and began to pace. The size of the room limited his steps in either direction, but it also amplified the feelings of agitation that emanated from the tightened jaw, the clenched fists, the clipped syllables.

Spider stood as well and moved over to the doorway. He let the hand that held his hat hang loose at his side, and he leaned a shoulder against the doorjamb, but his eyes followed as the other man paced back and forth.

Richie Stowe stopped and jerked open a desk drawer. He pulled a manila folder from a hanging file and threw it on the desk. "This is my deadbeat drawer—people who owe money and won't pay. The county is the biggest deadbeat in here. They owe the mortuary $2,400. Until they pay, I'm not storing any more bodies."

Spider whistled. "That's quite a bit of money. How'd they run up such a bill? I didn't think there were that many people that the county'd have to take care of."

"They haven't paid anything for five years. The interest adds up."

"Bishop, you know the county doesn't have that kind of money."

"They have the money. I pay half that in taxes every year."

"Randi said something about a contract. If your dad had a contract with the county, can you just quit taking the bodies?"

"Contract? My dad had a contract?" Patches of color appeared on Richie Stowe's cheeks. "The man didn't know the word. Come and look at this!" There was a set of cupboards built into the wall by the door. The varnish was cracking and the dark stain had worn away around the handles. Richie opened one of the doors and held out his hand to display the contents.

Spider pushed away from the doorjamb and moved to gain a view of the cupboard. Inside were two rows of empty gallon jars with wide slots in the lids. There was also a large index-card file box.

"This was my father's bookkeeping system." Richie Stowe jabbed at the labels on the jars: Caskets. Supplies. Office. Taxes.

Household. College. Mission. Tithing. Vacation. Retirement. Unexpected. The plastic box was labeled *Receipts*.

Spider surveyed the contents of the cupboard and then looked at Richie, raising his brows in question.

"He didn't keep a set of books. It's a nightmare."

"He didn't have any records at all? How'd he manage that?"

"Oh, he kept the rudiments. He had a ledger where he wrote down what people paid him. He had a formula that he followed with anything that came in: a certain percent to one jar, a certain percent to another."

"In cash?"

"In cash. He operated a cash business."

Spider whistled. "And the receipt box?"

"The history of his business is in that receipt box. That one and forty others like it in the storeroom. I mean, you talk about contracts! The man didn't have the least idea about how to run a business."

Spider eyed the jars. "Oh, I don't know. Your dad sent you and your brother on missions, didn't he?"

"Yes."

"Sent you and your brother to college?"

"I went to Stanford. He helped with my bachelor's, but I got my MBA by myself."

"And your dad and mom have a condo over in St. George on the golf course?" Spider shrugged. "Seems to me like he didn't do too bad."

"Maybe he didn't know any better. But I have an MBA and I do. I'm going to run this business the right way." Richie Stowe closed the cupboard doors with a snap.

"And is the right way to deny a decent place for somebody's

last mortal remains to rest while folks are being notified?" There was an edge to Spider's voice.

There was an answering edge when the younger man spoke. "I'm not the one responsible for that. The county is. If they want to negotiate a contract with me, I'll be glad to provide that service for them, after they pay what they owe."

"I've got a body out in the back of my truck, Bishop. I need a place to leave her."

"Talk to the county. They are responsible, not me."

"But you *are* responsible. You're the bishop of this area. That means that everyone, member and nonmember alike, is part of your temporal stewardship. You can't get much more temporal than this."

The red patches on Bishop Stowe's cheeks intensified and his eyes flashed. "You're not going to lay that on me, Spider! We're talking business here, and whether or not I'm the bishop has nothing to do with it! You take the county's problem someplace else. It has nothing to do with me."

"Now, there you're wrong." Spider jammed his hat on his head and turned on his heel. He wrenched open the door and stalked out of the office, exiting through the double doors with the same force and sibilant mutterings that Shorty had used a short time before.

Slamming the tailgate, he got in the pickup and burned rubber when he left. He had to brake before getting on the highway, but he laid another strip of rubber on the driveway as he turned south toward home.

Back in the mortuary parking lot, after the sound of his engine faded away, the last rays of a setting sun highlighted those tire marks: a double black line underscoring the ugly thoughts Spider was harboring when he left.

TEN MINUTES LATER, when Spider drove over the cattle guard to his own place, the dried-up corpse was still on its shed-door bier, swathed in a sheet and rattling around in the back of his pickup. Swinging in a wide arc, Spider slammed the gearshift into reverse and, with a spray of gravel, backed into the barn.

Laurie found him there a bit later, standing at the tailgate of his pickup, working with a roll of rabbit wire and a pair of tin snips. "Spider?" she ventured.

"Yeah?" His reply was terse.

"What are you doing?"

"I'm fixing to store a body."

Laurie leaned up against the pickup bed and looked over the side at the lumpy mound under the printed floral sheet. "Can you do that?"

"I don't know what else to do. Our good bishop says the county owes him for the last bodies they stored. He's not going to accept any more until the county pays its bill." Spider turned away, muttering, "That's what comes from calling twenty-nine-year-old bishops!"

"Spider . . ." Laurie's tone was admonishing.

Spider looked defiantly over his shoulder at her from the doorway to his shop.

"You're sounding like a former bishop," she chided.

He came back with a staple gun in his hand. "I'm sounding like someone who's just seen his bishop faced with a choice between a Christian duty and the almighty dollar, and he chose the dollar." Whack! Spider stapled the wire to the door. Whack! Whack!

"Are you sure that's all this is about?"

"What do you mean? Am I still smarting because when I lost my job and started showing signs of poverty, they released me as bishop to call the one prosperous person in the whole ward?" Whack! Whack!

"That wasn't the way I was going to put it, but, yes, I guess that's what I mean."

Whack! Whack! "I'll tell you something, Laurie, it'll take a while to work through that one! Here I finally get time to do the job of bishop the way it needs to be done, and I am able to think that there's one positive thing about not working, and whsst, it's gone. It's not that there weren't seven other guys who could have done better than me. There were. 'Course, they were all in the same boat I was. Poor." Whack! Whack!

"Spider . . ." Again the tone was admonishing.

"No, I mean it. Have you ever seen a poor bishop?" Whack! Whack! "Or better than that. Have you ever seen a poor stake president?"

"Your daddy never had much money."

"Ah, but that was different. My dad was a patriarch. The question for that one is: Have you ever seen a rich patriarch?"

"I don't like it when you talk like this! We're not poor! The people down in Chiapas where Kevin is are poor. Those starving Africans that we see on the news are poor. We've got a home and plenty to eat. There are lots of people in the world who don't have that. We're broke, maybe, but not poor."

"Not everyone sees it that way. People think that if you are righteous you'll be blessed with material things. So, if you're poor, you're not righteous. There's not a one of us that doesn't judge another by what he drives and wears and lives in. Me included." Whack! Whack! Spider looked at Laurie's troubled face and his eyes softened. "Except for you, Darlin'. You look on the heart. Don't worry. I don't know that I really mean what I say. It's just feelings that come out when I get angry. I don't say this to anyone but you. You're my safety valve."

"I don't much like being your safety valve."

Spider laid his tools aside and regarded his handiwork, testing a metal seam at the corner. "Yeah, I know. I guess what set me off was thinking about her." He nodded at the shrouded figure in the wire cage. "I keep thinking about the line, *I was a stranger and ye took me in* . . ." He shrugged.

"So, if Bishop Stowe won't take the body, what are you going to do?"

"Well, I've fixed it so the birds and mice can't get to it. If you'll help me, we'll just put it up in the rafters."

Laurie shivered. "I'll help you," she said, "but let me go in and get a jacket first."

When she returned, Spider had rigged the wire cage up to a block and tackle. As he raised the gruesome burden in its Springmaid shroud and rabbit-wire sepulcher, Laurie stood in the pickup bed and guided it sideways to allow it to pass through the rafters, then turned it crossways so it would lie across them. She looked down at her husband as he tied the rope off to a staple hammered into the barn wall.

Spider picked up the tin snips and rabbit wire and carried them through the door into his shop as Laurie climbed down from the pickup bed. "Dinner's almost ready," she called.

Pause. Then Spider appeared in the doorway. The dim lights hanging high in the barn cast his craggy face in shadow, making his eyes look dark as flint. "You go on in, Laurie," he said. "I don't believe I'm hungry right now."

Laurie went back to the house and ate a solitary supper, keeping a plate warm for Spider. When he finally came through the back door, she looked up from the book she was reading at the table. "It's on the stove," she said.

Spider stood and stared at the meal Laurie had saved for him. It was his favorite: fried chicken, mashed potatoes, and cream gravy. "Maybe later," he said.

When they knelt for family prayer that night, the chicken and mashed potatoes still sat on the stove. They were cold, and the gravy had congealed. Laurie threw everything to the chickens the next morning, who cackled over their bonus from the deputy's first day.

7

WITH THE TURNING OF the earth, Spider was able to leave yesterday behind him, and he came whistling into the kitchen for breakfast. Laurie stood over the griddle with a dish towel over her shoulder and a pancake turner in her hand, smiling at him as he poured a glass of milk. "You had quite a day yesterday," she observed.

"Yeah. I've always liked a job where they break you in easy." He drank half his glass of milk, filled it up again, and sat down at the table.

Laurie set a stack of pancakes in front of him. "So what're you going to do today?" She took the butter dish out of the cupboard and set it, along with the syrup pitcher, beside the pancakes.

"Got any cold butter?"

"It's going to melt anyway. Why not start with it soft so it can melt faster?"

"I don't like it all to melt. I like the feel of the lumps in my mouth. It goes down real smooth."

"Ugh!" Laurie made a face as she took a cube of margarine from the refrigerator door. "It probably goes right to your arteries."

"Uh-uh. They checked my cholesterol when I had my physical for the deputy's job. The doctor said he'd sell his soul for a number that low. Thank you." And he began dotting pats of margarine over his steaming hotcakes.

Laurie poured herself a glass of milk and sat down opposite Spider with one leg tucked under her. "I'd better pray," she said. "You already drank some milk."

"Yeah, go ahead." Spider folded his arms and bowed his head.

Laurie said a short blessing, and as she speared a single pancake with her fork, she asked again, "So, what're you doing today?"

"I'm going to go get old Doc Goldberg to come out and look at our new lodger." Spider jerked his thumb toward the barn. "And then I think I'll go see old Bucketa Blood."

Laurie drizzled syrup over her pancake. "We got a letter from Bobby yesterday."

"Oh?"

"Yeah. It's kind of bad news, and I didn't think you were in any shape for bad news last night."

"What kind of bad news?"

"He's not coming home for Thanksgiving."

Spider chewed meditatively for a moment, frowning at his plate. "He's going to her house, then?" he asked, fixing Laurie with an accusing stare. "That girl's?"

"Her name's Wendy. Yes."

"I'm not surprised. Look at the way he did at his graduation, pulling out and leaving us standing at the auditorium door right after the ceremony."

"He had a plane to catch. His new employer bought the ticket. He didn't think he should quibble about the time. Besides," and she smiled knowingly over her milk glass, "he's in love. I don't remember you being too anxious to hang around your mom and dad when you were courting me."

"Dang right I wasn't! One look at your brown eyes and I was ready to do what the Bible says, leave my mom and dad and cleave unto you."

"Is that what you were doing?" she asked, eyes twinkling. "Cleaving?"

"Just trying to do what the scriptures say," Spider pronounced piously.

Laurie laughed out loud. "That's what all the returned missionaries used to say. They were the biggest make-outs, and always with chapter and verse to justify parking at the Court Rock."

"I never took you to the Court Rock!"

"I know," she said. "I began to wonder if you were ever going to kiss me. I think that's what made me fall for you." She reached across the table and squeezed his hand. He returned the pressure.

"So what about Thanksgiving?" she asked, getting back to the matter at hand.

"What about it?"

"Well, with Bobby in Seattle and Kevin in Chiapas, it looks like we'll be alone. Shall we ask Murray over?"

"Not if there's any chance of Missy showing up again this

year! That woman's got a tongue on her that could shave the hide off a rhino. That show she put on last year about did me in."

"Oh, she won't be back. I think she remarried."

"How do you know?"

"She told me so."

"When?"

"When we were in Vegas for Bobby's graduation. It was the day before. Remember, when you and Bobby were helping Wendy move, and I went shopping at the thrift stores? I ran into Missy at Sally Ann's. I told you all about it."

"You sure about that?"

"Yes. But you were on the prod about something and probably didn't remember."

"Oh, I remember about being on the prod. I was wondering what I was doing breaking my back hauling furniture that was better than any I'd ever paid money for. Seems to me if she could afford furniture like that, she could afford to hire someone to move it for her."

"I think you were just uncomfortable with the idea that Bobby's girlfriend comes from a wealthy family."

"Dang right I was! And I don't much like it that he'd rather spend Thanksgiving with her rich folks than with his own poor ones."

"Never mind they're right there in Seattle."

"Yeah, well . . ."

"And her dad's been called as a mission president. This will be the family's last Thanksgiving together for a while."

"Well, he's not part of that family yet."

"You know, Spider, last night you were talking about people judging other people on money or status. You say people tend to be called to positions—"

"Like mission president?"

Laurie ignored him. "—but I wonder if you're not just as quick to judge as anyone else. The only thing is, you judge the other way. It sounds like you think someone with money is automatically undeserving of the call. I think we've got a mote-beam situation here."

Spider paused with a forkful of pancakes halfway to his mouth. "Huh!" he grunted. Taking the bite, he chewed slowly, staring in front of him. "Huh!" he grunted again.

"And while we're on the subject, if we're poor, we've done it to ourselves. We had enough money on the hoof—the cattle that we sold to do college for the boys—that we could have bought a small business for ourselves. We beggared ourselves to give them an education. I don't begrudge it to them—at least I don't think I do . . ."

"I don't. I never had the chance to go to college. None of my people ever went to college. It wasn't until a few years ago that I look back and see that I could have gone. I was determined that my boys were going to have the chance that I never had."

"Well, they got it."

"Yeah, they did."

Laurie got up and dumped her dishes in the sink. She turned the faucet on full blast and shot a stream of detergent into the water. She scrubbed furiously at a dish for a moment, then stopped and, without turning around, asked, "So, shall I invite Murray for Thanksgiving?"

"Beg pardon?"

"Shall I invite Murray for Thanksgiving?"

"Um . . . tell me again what Missy said."

Laurie sighed and turned around, drying her hands on the

dish towel. She folded her arms and leaned against the sink. "Let's see. She'd been working as a bookkeeper at the Salvation Army Thrift Store. I was coming in as she was leaving, and she said that was her last day there, and the next day was the beginning of the rest of her life, something like that. Something about meeting a lawyer and lots of money and lots of changes in her life and tomorrow was *the* day. I didn't listen too closely, because I didn't want to encourage her. She said she had taken back her maiden name, I remember that. Said the name *Sapp* fit Murray, but she was nobody's fool. When I left she kissed my cheek and said I'd been a good friend, and she probably would never see me again." Laurie straightened up and took Spider's plate. "And that's it. Here, drink the rest of your milk. I've got chores to do."

Spider obliged and handed her his glass. "So she said she's never coming back?"

"I'm sure that's what she said."

"Well then, invite old Murray to Thanksgiving, and we'll give thanks!" Spider stood up and pushed in his chair. "And I thank you for the pancakes. They sure hit the spot. Now, if you'll excuse me, I'll be in my office. I have some important calls to make." Ignoring the swat Laurie gave him with her dish towel, Spider walked solemnly past her to the phone on the wall by the microwave.

DOCTOR GOLDBERG ANSWERED on the second ring. His voice had the reedy sound of age and echoed like he was speaking from the depths of a well.

"I think we've got a bad connection," Spider said. "I'll call you back."

"No, don't do that. I'm using a speakerphone. What can I do for you?"

"This is Spider Latham. I'm the new deputy sheriff, took Tharon Tate's place. I need you to come and look at a body we brought in yesterday."

"Who is it?"

"I don't know. A couple of boys found it out on the road to the Lucy Roberts."

"Been dead long?"

"I don't know. I think so."

"You don't know much, do you?"

"Boy, you can say that again! How about it? Can you come?"

"I don't drive anymore, you know."

"That's all right. I can come and get you."

"Then come ahead."

Spider hung up and called out, "I'm going." He had just reached the service porch and was taking his jacket off the peg by the door when Laurie appeared in the hallway with a load of rumpled sheets in her arms. "I'll be back in a while with the doc, and then I'm gone again," he said, shrugging himself into his coat.

"Are you going to have to look at her again? Our lodger?"

"Yeah, I'm afraid so." Spider grabbed his hat off the peg, said, "'Bye," and was out the door, conscious of Laurie's troubled eyes staring at him through the back-door window as he walked to the county car.

Doc Goldberg lived in the hamlet of Panaca. Settled by Mormon pioneers in 1864, Panaca sat in the middle of Meadow Valley where west-running Highway 319 teed into north-south-running Highway 93. It had changed little in its hundred and thirty years of existence. Water still flowed from the warm spring on the north end of the valley through irrigation ditches to fields and gardens and lawns. The same surnames were evident: Fox, Wentworth, Hughes, Sapp, Latham. Even the population had remained constant, hovering around five hundred.

The morning was bright and crisp. Driving along, Spider could see that a mountain range in the distance had a dusting of snow on the top. Living forever, as he did, in the presence of mountains, still Spider never felt hemmed in. The valleys between the north-south-running ranges were broad and long and gave a feeling of openness. Spider wondered how Bobby was faring in Seattle.

He slowed down as he approached the junction. Panaca had never been more than a wide spot in the road, so it hadn't suffered as noticeably when the mines shut down as had Pioche, eleven miles north, or Castleton, on the other side of the hill from Pioche, where the mill had been located. Panaca didn't have stores and houses with boarded-up windows, or industrial-size, hulking, rusty tin shells. Castleton was depressing. Spider was glad he didn't live there.

He drove past the Texaco station and turned at the first street past La Vonda's Café. At the end of the short block, the last house before the village petered out was Doc Goldberg's place. The old man was standing in the yard, picking spent blossoms from his rosebushes with shaking hands. There was a worn black satchel sitting on the fence post.

Spider pulled up at the gate and got out. "Morning, Doc," he greeted. "It's been a long time since I was here last."

The doctor began a slow but steady progress toward the gate. "Good morning, Spider. Would that have been the time that I pulled that piece of shrapnel out of your backside?"

Spider smiled as he lifted the satchel from the post and held open the gate. "I think it was."

"I don't know what that jackass thought he was doing, trying to weld a gas tank!"

"He said he was going to save the company some money. Save them the price of a new gas tank. Finance never was Monty's strong point." Spider let the gate swing shut and opened the car door.

Doc Goldberg's eyes twinkled in amusement as he gingerly settled his old bones on the seat. "So how was he as a welder?"

"Oh, he never much wanted to weld after that." Spider set the black bag on the floor beside the doctor's feet, closed the door, and walked around to the driver's side.

"And how is Rachel, your mother?" the old gentleman inquired as Spider slid beneath the wheel. "Is she still in Las Vegas with your sister?"

Spider started the engine and fastened his seat belt. After mistakenly washing the windows, he yanked on the floorshift in annoyance and made a U-turn, heading back to the highway.

"Mother is fine," he said. "It's my sister I'm worried about."

"What's the matter with Debbie?"

"She's become a tyrant. She's cross with Mother and treats her like a child, orders her around. She never calls but what she complains about something new that Mother's done to put her in a tizzy."

"Has your mother become forgetful?"

"I suppose. Some. But I hope that when I'm her age my memory is as good as hers. Why, she can remember things that happened forty, fifty years ago like it was yesterday."

"And how about things that happened yesterday?"

Spider glanced over and saw the sharp old eyes watching him. He shrugged and grimaced.

"Life is funny," Doc Goldberg said. "You make it through the times when you've got no sense and you've got no money. You make it on pure energy and youth. And when youth starts to fade, why, you don't have to work so hard because you can work smart. And you've got a bit of jingle to pay some young buck to tote the heavy stuff."

Spider nodded, remembering the summer he spent toting cement blocks and carrying hod for the man who was building an addition to the doctor's house.

"And just as you get it all figured out, just when you're wise as a tree full of owls and you've got a nest egg tucked away and it's all smooth sailing, why . . ." the old man held up his shaking hands as evidence, " . . . your body betrays you. It's a chintzy deal."

Spider nodded in sympathetic agreement, and they drove in silence the four miles to the turnoff to Spider's road. He adjusted his speed for the bumpy surface.

"Did your mother ever tell you I wanted to marry her?" Doc Goldberg asked.

Spider looked at him in amazement. "No, she didn't."

"I already had a practice. I could have given her an easy life. Instead she chose to live out at Jackrabbit in a house without electricity or indoor plumbing." The old man shook his head. "It's not that she didn't care. I think if things had been different . . ." His voice trailed off and he shrugged. "But she was a good Mormon girl. She called me a gentile. Hah! Me, a gentile! She wouldn't marry me because I wasn't a Mormon."

"Huh!" Spider grunted. "I never knew anything about that." He could see Murray Sapp's windmill glinting in the sun, and below it, clustered around a pole barn, the bright patches of yellow that, as they neared, grew into the massive earth movers that eked out Murray's existence: bulldozer, road grader, front-end loader, and dump truck.

As they passed, Murray stepped out the back door and stood with his hands in his back pockets, gazing off to the south. Spider tooted and waved. Murray turned his head to look at them and, after a moment's hesitation, waved back.

"That's a fellow I've had in my surgery more than once," said the doctor. "Rodeo cowboys! I'll never understand them."

"What's to understand? They love to rodeo."

"I remember once Murray broke his arm up in Idaho, and he drove all night pulling a horse trailer so I could set it for him. He was in a bad way. Shocky, you know, and raving about how he had to be able to ride in the next rodeo six weeks away."

"I remember that. You told him no way would the cast be off by then, and he came over and had *me* cut it off for him."

"Crazy!"

"Yeah, I guess. But if I hadn't done it, he'd a done it himself and butchered himself in the process."

"Boy, that wife of his sure clipped his wings!" Doc observed. "She settled him down right now."

"Yeah, old Missy didn't hold with rodeoing."

"Too dangerous, eh?"

"Uh-uh," said Spider. "Too expensive."

"She cut him off at the pockets, eh? Well, there's many a marriage that foundered because the fellow supported his hobby rather than his family."

"Yeah. 'Course, Murray gave up rodeoing for her, got a regular job, built up a business. Then it turned out she couldn't have kids. The work all dried up, and she left him. Makes you wonder."

Spider slowed down to make the turn off the gravel road and over the cattle guard onto his place, noticing as he pulled back to the barn that the pickup was gone. He was glad Laurie wouldn't be here when he brought their lodger down from the rafters.

Doc Goldberg's reedy voice broke into his musing. "What does it make you wonder?"

"What? Oh." Spider parked in front of the open barn door, in shade cast by the morning sun. He turned off the key and leaned back in his seat. "Well, when a fellow goes rodeoing, he gives his life to it. He knows it'll take all his time and all his money and all his loyalty. He knows there'll be hard times and flying-high times. He'll have a bit of fun, and he'll have some grief, too. He knows he'll get hurt probably worse than he's ever been hurt before. If he's a Mormon, like old Murray, he usually gives up his activity in the Church, and he knows that when it's over he'll probably have no job and no money, and he'll be all busted up so he can't do much, and he won't have a ward family to give him any support. But he knows all that going in. It's no surprise when he ends up with no wife and no kids, no faith, no job, and no money. But he's got a few belt buckles and some pretty good memories."

"And Murray?"

"Well, I think he'd a felt that giving up rodeoing was worth it if he'd ended up with something. Maybe a wife and a kid or a job and a wife, or even just a wife or a just a kid. But he's ended up just like rodeoing—no wife, no family, no job, no money, no faith. Only he hasn't got the belt buckles and memories. Like you said, it's a chintzy deal. You ready to go to work?"

Doc Goldberg drew his old black satchel onto his lap and declared, "All my knowledge and expertise are at the disposal of the fine government of our fair Lincoln County."

Spider glanced through the windshield to where he could see, in the dim interior of the barn, Laurie's bedsheet looking like a ghost hovering in the rafters. Then he turned and looked at the shriveled husk of a man beside him, at the trembling hands and the involuntary nodding of the head, at the thin, white, flyaway hair and the liver spots on parchment skin.

The old man's pale blue eyes met Spider's, and he gave voice to what they both were thinking. "God help us."

Spider threw back his head and laughed. "God help the county. We're a pair, Doc. The blind leading the blind. Let's go to work."

LATER THAT AFTERNOON, after a grim but informative session in the barn with Dr. Goldberg, Spider drove to Pioche.

Pioche was the county seat. It consisted of a dozen streets stacked untidily on the side of a hill that was riddled with mine shafts. The silver that had been hauled from the earth to jingle freely in its pockets at the turn of the century had all run out. The lead, less flashy but profitable during the war years, had run out too. The last of the minerals to come out of the mines had been perlite, a humble additive to potting soil. The young-man swagger of Pioche had turned into a broken-down miner's shamble. Sun and wind had worried away most of the paint from the downtown buildings, and bare wood was weathered gray as the stubble on an old man's chin.

Spider drove down the steep incline of Main Street and angled in to park in front of the *Sentinel* building. The square white office building was freshly painted white, with sparkling windows and a screen door with the screen stretched as tight as a drumhead. Spider opened the screen, but stepped back before entering as Sally Hughes opened the office door and met him in the doorway.

"Hello, Sally," he said, touching his hat. "Turning in your column?"

"Hello, Bishop," she smiled. "Yes. I thought I had a scoop when I wrote about the new deputy sheriff being from Panaca, but Mr. Higarten says that's not Panaca news. That's county news, and he gets to write about it."

"You can write that Rose Markey has moved back to town."

"No! Who told you?"

"Kyle Bates."

"She's already been in to see the bishop, I guess. Well," Sally's smile turned to a grin. "I'm not Relief Society president anymore. I won't have to deal with it. But I'll write about it. I can see the headline now: Huge Mass of Pink Fluff Invades Panaca, Found to Be the Markey Family."

Spider laughed, and then waggled a finger at Sally. "Now, Sally, that's not Christian."

"I'm a newspaper reporter," she shot back as she stepped past him. "I write what I see."

"Well, keep your eyes open!" Spider called after her. Still smiling, he entered the small, neat office and greeted the man standing behind the counter.

Oliver Higarten was tall and thin, with silvery hair and an elegance of manner that belied a crusty disposition. A successful aerospace engineer in the heyday of space exploration, he had retired early with a generous pension and purchased the Lincoln County *Sentinel*. As editor, once a week he took issue with government incompetence and liberal politicians. His prose was florid, his views outrageous, but he was evenhanded enough to print every irate letter sent to the editor, and his business was thriving. Everyone called him Mr. Higarten to his face, but behind his back they called him Bucketa Blood. It was a name tacked on by someone who had never read Shakespeare and misremembered Mr. Higarten's reference to a pound of flesh.

"Afternoon, Mr. Higarten."

"Now why," mused the older man, "did Sally call you bishop? According to her own column, published, oh, a year ago, you were supplanted by Bishop Stowe."

"I'm still a bishop," replied Spider. He took off his hat and laid it on the counter; then he took a folded-up piece of paper out of his shirt pocket. "Just like you're still an engineer. You're not working as an engineer right now, but you still have the diplomas and know-how, and could go back to work anytime without having to be re-certified. Same here. I've been ordained a bishop. I just don't have a congregation to be responsible for right now."

"Ah, yes. I've been wanting to discuss that with someone who can enlighten me."

"Beg pardon?"

"Well, I'm somewhat of a Mormon watcher. I'm interested in your cultural patterns, your general traits."

"You make us sound like some back-country tribe."

"Ah . . . yes. As I was saying, when you were turned out after only two years as bishop, when the norm is usually four to six years . . ."

"Yes?"

"I predicted it."

Spider could only stare.

"As I read the *Church News*—and I do, you know, and will express my journalistic opinions later—but as I watch the column about new Church leaders—seventies and mission presidents, bishops and stake presidents—I see that there aren't many blue collars among them. I read about dentists and lawyers, successful businessmen, professional men. Why do you suppose that is?"

Spider paused a moment to frame a reply, but Mr. Higarten went smoothly on. "It has to do with comfort level. Somewhere in this century the leaders of the Mormon Church changed from being farmers and glaziers—did you know that Brigham Young was a glazier?—to being educated, professional men. Now, educated, professional men are going to call as leaders others with whom they're comfortable—other professional men, successful businessmen. Not going to trust the flocks to any common men. Now, the exception to prove that rule was the man who called you as bishop. Your stake president was a farmer. He's comfortable with someone who works with his hands, so he calls a millwright as a bishop. But when he is released and a young dentist—not a struggling young dentist, but one who stepped into his father's practice—is called as stake president, the millwright is history."

Spider listened intently to what Mr. Higarten was saying, eyes on the paper in his hand that he slowly creased over and over.

When he didn't answer right away, Mr. Higarten went on, "I haven't seen any fishermen among the leaders, great or small, of your church. No carpenters, either."

Spider took a moment to unfold the paper he had in his hand, laying it on the counter and smoothing out the creases.

"Well, I tell you, Mr. Higarten. It's easy to sit on the outside and judge. But it looks different on the inside. Let's talk about our young stake president. He's ten years younger than I am—I guess that's young. I know him, know his family. His oldest brother was a friend of mine. President Fox may be just thirty-five, but he's mature in spirit. He had cancer as a young man, lost a leg. He was called to the same mission in Mexico where I served and had to wait to go until he'd got his leg sawed off and could walk on a wooden one. I know how many dusty roads he walked on that wooden leg, knocking on doors same as any Mormon missionary. And as far as comfort—I don't know how it is anywhere else in the Church. But here in Lincoln County, a fellow that's looking for work has enough on his plate without the problems of a ward to think about. Especially when half the ward has the same problem. A stake president would feel extremely uncomfortable holding such a bishop accountable for his full stewardship. Releasing him under those circumstances would be an act of compassion." Spider pushed the paper toward Mr. Higarten.

"Compassion, huh? What have you got here?" he asked, putting on a pair of black-rimmed reading glasses.

"Some notes Doc Goldberg made. We found a body buried in a CCC dam up by the Lucy Roberts. It had been there long enough to become mummified. We need to find out if there's anyone in the county knows anything about it."

"A body! That's certainly news. Let's see. Doc write this? It's pretty good. I can almost make it out. Says it was a woman, somewhere around forty or forty-five years old. How could he tell?"

"Well, it was obviously a woman—long hair, dressed in a skirt and jacket and patent leather pumps."

"Anymore, that doesn't necessarily follow."

"Well, maybe not in San Francisco, or even Vegas. But in Lincoln County it's a pretty good bet. Besides that, she had . . ." Spider cupped his hands over his chest, indicating a woman's bosom. "They were all dried up, but that and the rest of the anatomy—it was a woman."

"And the age? How did he peg that?"

"He looked at her teeth. Something about the wisdom teeth and how worn they were."

"But the man's not a dentist. How is he qualified to speak about teeth?"

"Well, I figure he's spent fifty-five years looking into people's mouths asking them to say aah. I imagine he's got a pretty good notion of how teeth wear. He spoke about some other things too, something about the bones and things he's learned from reading about the skeleton detective."

"He's not turning senile, is he?"

"He made pretty good sense to me. Acted like he knew what he was talking about. Said at the time of death she had a broken collarbone, a compound fracture of the right arm, and a broken neck."

"So what do you want me to do?"

"Go ahead and print that we found the body. Shoot, it's probably all over the county now anyway. But say that we're interested in any information about anyone who might have turned up missing several months ago."

Mr. Higarten directed a piercing stare at Spider over his reading glasses. "What if it isn't anyone from the county? What if it were someone who came from outside?"

"Could be. Bud Hefernan didn't think it was anyone from here because of the Saks Fifth Avenue label on the jacket. What're you thinking?"

"Bud Hefernan, eh? Funny, I just remember that this spring we had a visit from a most obnoxious woman. She was a journalist working for some lunatic-fringe group that was intent on getting all the cattle off the range and tearing down all the fences and letting the elk have it back so all the tree-huggers could visit and enjoy the area as it used to be."

"I remember reading about it in the *Sentinel*. I thought you were being humorous. You mean there really was someone here who wanted to do that?"

"Oh yes! Foolhardy, I called it, to come out here and express those ideas openly. She was from Back East where fellows have learned to eat quiche and pasta instead of beefsteak. She didn't understand about people who live around cattle and coyotes."

"So what happened?"

"She had a run-in with Bud Hefernan. He asked her how the people who made their living running cattle were supposed to support themselves after they gave the range back to the elk, and she said there was money to be made from tourism. He told her that if she wanted to see elk, he'd take her to see some. He said it was a dangerous trip, though, and he couldn't guarantee that she'd come back alive."

"Anyone else there when this happened?"

"Most certainly. It was at the meeting of the Cattleman's Association. She was what is called, in common parlance, a pushy broad."

"What did she look like?"

"Fortyish. Dark hair. Ugly."

"Ugly? How?"

"She had crooked teeth, a big hook nose. Ugly."

"Do you remember her name?"

"No. But I could probably find it out for you."

"Could you do that?" Spider put his hat on. "I appreciate your help. If you think of anything else, will you let me know?"

"Have you wondered if this could be tied to that business up in Reno?"

"I dunno. The sheriff's up there right now. When he gets back, I'll talk to him about it."

Spider shook hands with Mr. Higarten and received his assurances of help, and then he walked with purposeful steps out the door and over to his car, wondering just what he was supposed to do next. Deciding that he should study his handbook of procedures, he drove home to pick it up, musing on the way about whether his release as bishop could have been an act of compassion.

SPIDER WAS JUST DRIVING over the cattle guard into his place when he spied Laurie coming across the home pasture on her three-wheeler, driving her six heifers in front of her. She saw him, waved excitedly, and headed toward the gate.

Spider strolled to meet her.

"I've got business with the deputy sheriff!" she called even before she reached him.

"What's going on?"

"That's what I don't know. I've just been out chasing cows. They didn't come in for water, so I rode the fence line and found a place where it was down and they had got over into Bud's pasture. I followed their tracks and found that they were down in the wash almost to the bridge."

"Yeah?" said Spider. "So why do you need a deputy? Someone been messing with your fence?"

"No, it was something I found in the wash. It's around the

66

corner so you can't see it from the road, and the bank's caved in over it so there's just a rear fender sticking out."

"A rear fender?"

"It's a car, Spider! There's a car buried in the wash. Hop on back and I'll take you to see it."

"Let me get a shovel."

Spider walked to the barn to get a shovel as Laurie sat just inside the gate, impatiently revving her engine. Detouring by the pickup to get his gloves, Spider smiled at Laurie as he opened the gate. "You're mighty impatient," he said. "You sure this isn't just a ruse to get me off in the bushes and ravish my body?"

She grinned back at him. "That's not a bad idea. But this is official deputy business. Get on."

Spider latched the gate behind him and swung on behind Laurie. She scarcely left him time to get settled before she was off, bouncing over hillocks of bunchgrass and sage as she cut across the pasture to the south. When they came to a gate, Spider got off and opened it, grousing as he did so about a deputy's dignity. Laurie answered a small smile, but didn't speak, waiting only until he was seated again before she roared off toward the wash. She barely slackened her speed going down the embankment. Spider held on tight with one hand, balanced himself by holding the shovel out, and whooped at the butterflies in his stomach. When Laurie finally stopped a half-mile down the draw, Spider got off, muttering something about danger in the line of duty.

"What did you say?"

"Nothing. Nothing." He suddenly spied the red taillight winking in the November sun from the brown clay bank of the wash. "Great Suffering Zot!"

"See?"

"Yeah! Isn't that something!"

"So what do you think?"

"Whoa, Darlin', I just got here. In fact, I haven't yet recovered from the ride. But I would say . . ." His voice trailed off as he stood, hands on hips, and studied the area.

"You would say what?"

"Well, I might ask some questions. Like, what are all these bushes doing here?"

"What do you mean?"

"Look here." Spider stuck the shovel in a large, bushy clump of bare branches that lay beneath the spot where the fender protruded. He lifted them off the ground. "Would you say that it's a natural thing to have this many dead branches lying here, stacked up like this?"

"Well, sure. A flood is always carrying bushes down and stacking them in places where it eddies around."

"Yes, but usually they're bushes that have been pulled up by the roots or broken off. Look at these."

"They've been cut!"

"Yeah."

"Spider, you don't mean . . ."

"That somebody wanted to hide the car? Maybe."

"But why not just throw more dirt over it?"

"Has to do with the steepest angle of repose. You can't throw any more dirt on without building the bank way out, and you'd need a piece of heavy equipment to do that. Besides, the first good rain we had would wash it away."

"So what are you going to do?"

"Well, first I'm going to fix your fence."

"I mean about this."

"I don't know. I'll think about it while I'm fixing the fence."

He did. Thrusting a post-hole digger again and again into an ever-deeper hole, Spider was working as hard with his mind as with his muscular arms. "So, is the car there accidentally or on purpose?" he asked himself.

Spider broke his train of thought long enough to consider the site of his next hole. Then the post-hole digger was working again. So was his mind. "And what do I do? Report this? Who to? Last year I would have called Tharon Tate. But now *I'm* Tharon Tate. What does the deputy do? Call the sheriff, or investigate first?"

Thrust, lift. Thrust, lift.

"If I call the sheriff, he's going to ask me some questions. Is there anyone in it? Was there a registration in it? Is there anything to show that this was done on purpose?"

Spider paused, leaning on the post-hole digger with both hands, breathing hard. He stared over the horizon in the direction of the wash.

"How do I know there is a car? What if it's just some old fender that floated down and got lodged in the bank? Wouldn't my face be red if I got all excited about two feet of fender and a taillight!" Spider shook his head and smiled ruefully at the prospective embarrassment. Then he attacked the post hole with renewed vigor, reflecting that he had a bit of solitary digging to do down in the wash.

CHAPTER

11

THE FIRST TWO DAYS after the Lincoln County *Sentinel* came out with the story about the body found in the desert, Spider spent a lot of time maintaining a high profile. He made the rounds of the three towns in the county, dropping in at feed stores, gas stations, drive-ins, anyplace where he saw several cars parked together. He even visited a couple of taverns, one in Pioche and the one at The Junction. Everyone had the same questions to ask: Who was it? How long had it been there? Is this connected to the bodies being found up in Reno? And everyone had the same answers to Spider's questions: nope, nope, nope.

Friday afternoon, Spider stopped at the Texaco station in Panaca. As he drove up to the pump, Zorm Hughes walked out of the service bay wiping his hands on a rag, kicking a creeper in front of him, and grinning. Tall and strapping, he was a ruggedly handsome twenty-six. He stuffed the rag in his back pocket.

"Hello, Spider. I've been waiting for you to stop by." Zorm lay down on the creeper and slid under the cruiser.

"I just need some gas, Zorm."

"Yeah." The word was muffled.

Spider stared thoughtfully for a moment at the steel-toed work boots sticking out from under his car. He shrugged and began to fill his tank.

"This is great!" Zorm hollered from underneath. "They've beefed up the suspension, put in anti-roll bars. It's got brakes big as Aunt Bertha's backside, and you should see the tread on these tires!" The heels of the work boots grabbed at the concrete and the long legs bent as Zorm worked his way out from beneath the car. "It should corner a lot flatter. Not so much roll. How is it?"

"It sticks to the road pretty good."

"I thought so. Can I drive it?"

"Oh, I don't know, Zorm."

"Well, if you brought it in to have it fixed, I'd have to test drive it."

Spider returned the nozzle to the pump and put his gas cap back on. "Yeah, but I don't need anything fixed."

"Yeah, you do. You don't have the sheriff department decal on your doors."

"Car came from Vegas. I'm lucky it doesn't say Las Vegas Police."

"I have some decals. I can put them on for you."

"Where did you get sheriff department decals?"

Zorm got up from the creeper and gave it a kick to send it hurtling back to the nearest service bay. "Sheriff Brown called around asking for prices for putting them on that new Caprice the department got three years ago. The one old Tharon pasted on the Devil's Elbow. I shot him a good price; he brought it here. The first set of decals had something wrong with it, so he brought me another set. I kept the first one. I still got 'em."

"But if there was something wrong, I don't want them either."

"That's just the thing, Spider. I looked at these decals, and I couldn't see anything wrong. It's like those 'seconds' you buy at the factory stores. Perfectly good, but there's some little something wrong that only the inspector notices. Besides, you know how Sheriff Brown is. He'll make you redo something just to show that he's the one in charge."

Spider considered a moment. "You're sure they're all right?"

Zorm raised his right hand. "I swear."

"How long will it take you to do it?"

"Half hour, max. I won't charge anything for doing it, either."

Spider looked at the plain white door panels. "Okay. While you're doing that, I'm going to go over to the store. Do I need to sign for this or something?"

Zorm took a generic sales book out of his shirt pocket and wrote up an invoice. He gave it to Spider to sign and handed him the original. "Then I'll take it for a test drive and park it for you out front."

"All right, Zorm."

"Keys in it? Fine. See you in a while."

Spider immediately repented. Zorm drove the fifty feet from the gas pumps to the service bay like he had just seen the green flag at Daytona Beach. Spider called, "Hey, watch it!" Then he stalked across the street to the Panaca Emporium, shaking his head and muttering under his breath.

Stepping through the door of the small general store was

like stepping back in time. Nothing much had changed in the last forty years except the owner, Harvey Lentz. He had grown balder and rounder and just a little deaf. He was behind the meat counter right now, cutting some cheese for Hazel Sikes.

Spider wandered into the warren of aisles that was the dry-goods section. He strolled past bolts of cloth and lace edging, past sheets and towels, past cast-iron skillets and electric Crock-Pots to the tools and hardware. There, Sandy Sikes and B. D. Wentworth, two old friends of his father's, were deep in discussion.

"I worked with the CCC boys," Sandy was saying. "I helped build that very dam." Spider paused and leaned his shoulder against the rack of nail bins. He wanted to hear what Sandy had to say.

Sandy's stories beguiled him, and he forgot his unease at letting Zorm take the cruiser. He listened for about half an hour, until the sound of an engine roaring and tires squealing made all three men look out the window. The cruiser flashed past.

"Geez, Zorm," Spider muttered. "It's a school zone."

"That your car, Spider?" asked Sandy.

"Yeah. Zorm fixed something on it, and he's taking it out for a test drive."

"You're being mighty careless of county property, letting Zorm out with it."

"Yeah. I don't know what I was thinking."

Spider drifted over to the window. His gaze followed the cruiser until it became a diminishing white dot that merged with the highway on the horizon. He sighed and turned back, his attention taken by a card table set up next to the window. A vacuum cleaner stood on top. Next to it was a picture of a local girl embracing a young man unknown to Spider. Her cheek was against his chest, his chin against her forehead as they smiled into the camera. Next to the picture was a formal wedding announcement. Patricia Ann Wentworth and William Lee Christensen were marrying December 1 in the St. George Temple. A card saying "Congratulations!" lay open beside a glass gallon jar half full of folding money. Spider examined the vacuum cleaner. He read the tags that were hanging on it describing the powerful motor, the hideaway cord, and the light on the front. He fished his wallet out of his back pocket and looked inside. Ten dollars. He read the names on the card. Then he took out one of the two five-dollar bills, stuffed it through the slot in the jar lid, and wrote *Laurie and Spider Latham* below the last name.

Just as he crossed the *t,* Sally Hughes came quietly up and murmured, "I've got something to tell you."

Spider stuffed his wallet in his back pocket. "Hi, Sally. You read the article in the paper?"

"Yes, but I can't help you there. I wanted to tell you something about your car."

"My car!"

"Yes, it's parked outside."

"I didn't hear it come back. Boy, that was fast. Is it all right? What's wrong?"

"Come and see."

Spider didn't wait for Sally. He strode through the aisles of canned goods to the front door with his heart in his throat. "When I get through with him, it'll be a month before he'll be able to hold a monkey wrench," he said through his teeth. Stiff-arming the screen door, he was down the stairs and over to the cruiser before Sally even made the door.

The front end was intact. The driver's side was fine. No

dents in the rear. The passenger side was unblemished. All the windows were fine. The only difference that Spider could see was that the car had been washed, and the seal of Lincoln County was on each door in black and white. He looked quizzically at Sally as she came down the stairs.

"Notice anything wrong?" She wasn't smiling, but her eyes were dancing.

Spider shook his head. "Old Zorm just took it for a spin. I was afraid he had cratered it."

"Did Zorm have anything to do with the shield on the doors?"

"He put them on. Yes."

"I should have known! I taught that boy in the sixth grade. Did you notice that the word *sheriff* is spelled wrong? It has two *r*s and only one *f*."

Spider stared. "Great Suffering Zot! I knew I should have taken a look at those decals before I let him put them on. What a deal!" He walked over and tested the edge with his fingernail. "I wonder how you get these off."

"Probably with a razor blade."

"That would ruin the paint. Great Suffering Zot! Thanks for telling me, Sally!" Spider set his jaw and walked across the street to the Texaco station, hollering "Zorm!" before he was even halfway there.

Zorm came out of the service bay, rag in hand, still grinning. "That's a sweet-going machine, Spider. Corners like a jackrabbit. Sticks to the road like a cockleburr."

"About those decals, Zorm."

"Went on smooth as Vaseline on a baby's bottom. Not a wrinkle. Not a bubble. I'm getting pretty good at putting on decals."

"Well, I want you to take them off."

"Why?"

"Come over and see." Spider turned on his heel and stalked back across the street, standing beside the cruiser with his arms folded.

Zorm sauntered over, stuffing his rag in his pocket again. He stood by Spider and regarded his handiwork with a look of pride. "I don't see anything wrong, Spider. Looks great to me."

"The word *sheriff* is spelled wrong, Zorm."

"No! Is it?"

"Yeah, it is. I want you to take the decals off."

"I don't know if I can, Spider."

"You have to."

"I don't know if I can," Zorm repeated. "I'll have to find out how to do it."

"Well, I can't drive around with a misspelled word on my car."

"Why not? Who's going to notice?"

"Everyone."

"I didn't notice. I saw five or six people walk by and go into the store. They didn't notice."

"Sally did. She's the one that told me."

"Well, Aunt Sally's a schoolteacher. You mean you didn't notice until she told you? Well, there you go."

"Zorm, I'm not going to drive around the county looking like an idiot."

"I'll take it off just as soon as I know how. And I won't charge you a thing. In the meantime, I'll bet you five dollars there aren't three other people in the county that will even notice."

"You're on." Spider opened the door. "You call me just as soon as you can get these misspelled decals off."

"Sally doesn't count."

"What do you mean?"

"Three besides Sally."

"Fine. You call me." Spider got in and sprayed gravel as he drove away.

Zorm strolled, whistling, back to his work.

WHEN SPIDER WASN'T OUT being visible around the county, he was down in the wash, digging. Laurie's brown eyes grew big as he pledged her to secrecy. She frowned as he appropriated her garden trowel and the brush she used to sweep dirt into her dustpan. She visited him midmorning and afternoon to take him a snack, and fretted that he wasn't moving earth fast enough.

"It's been there a while," Spider said. "It's not going anywhere, and neither am I. I'd a whole lot rather take my time and do it right than slice through something important with the shovel point."

"What do you mean, important?"

"I don't know what I mean."

"But you have a suspicion?"

"What I have," and Spider gestured toward the car, an older gray Chevette sedan with the driver's side revealed, "is a car that was buried in the riverbank. My idea is that it was swept there in a flash flood. See, it's got a foot or so of dirt inside and a watermark higher than that. The driver's door is intact, but you can see through and see that the passenger window is broken, windshield's gone. The front end is smashed—someone must have gone off the road and hit pretty hard."

"Who?"

"I don't know. Whoever it was isn't in the car now."

"Thank the Lord!"

The rectangular lines around Spider's mouth creased into a grim smile. "Yeah, I wasn't looking forward to finding . . ."

" . . . another lodger?"

"Yeah."

"So whose car is it?"

Spider shook his head. "I don't know. There's no registration on the visor. Maybe there's one in the jockey box, if the water didn't ruin it. See, the water line is right about to it."

"Why don't you just get in and get it? You've got the driver's door uncovered."

"Well, I just have a plan that I'm following. I'll get to it."

"But don't you want to know whose it is?"

"Yes. But I don't want to go tromping over an answer to why or when as I'm scrambling to find out who. You need to let me do this my own way."

Laurie wrinkled her freckled nose at him. "Okay. I can take a hint." She picked up an empty sandwich bag that was lying on the ground and went to get on her three-wheeler. "I'm sure Kevin would approve of what you're doing, but I still say there's no reason to shovel away dirt from all around it when you could just hook on with the pickup and pull it out."

"I heard you the first three times you mentioned that."

"Just checking."

"And thanks for the sandwich," he said. She answered with a smile and a wave, and was off. Spider watched as she bounced over a boulder before tearing up the arroyo bank, and he shook his head, muttering, "Neck or nothing," as he turned back to his task.

At midafternoon on Saturday, Spider drove the pickup to the back door of the house and came onto the service porch. "Laurie!" he shouted as he opened the door of her canning cupboard. "Laurie!"

There was no answer.

Impatiently he began rummaging around, moving boxes of lids and rings, colanders, and a pressure cooker. Finally, lifting the lid of a big granite pot, he found what he was looking for: a large sieve. Realizing that Laurie might not appreciate the purpose to which he was about to put her tool, he offered a sop to his conscience by calling, "I'm borrowing your strainer."

He had just pulled the back door closed behind him when a blue pickup bearing the Keystone Mines logo on the door pulled into the yard. Spider walked out to meet his visitor, setting the strainer on the roof of his own pickup as he went by. The man who emerged from the Keystone pickup was older and slight, with a weathered face wrinkled and furrowed from years in the sun.

"Howdy," said the stranger, holding out his hand. "The name's Kurt Wiggins."

"Spider Latham."

"You the deputy?"

"Yeah. You in need of a deputy?"

"Nope, nope. Just read in the *Sentinel* about finding that

body up by the Lucy Roberts, and I thought I'd better tell you that I may have seen whoever put it there."

"Yeah?"

"Yessir. I don't know if you know it, but Keystone still maintains all the systems at the mines, in case it ever becomes profitable to open them up again. I go around and fire up the generators and make sure things are winterized or weatherized. I have a schedule, and I was up at the Lucy Roberts around the middle of May."

"Yeah?"

"Yessir. It must have been early afternoon that I come out of the machine shop, and I looked across the valley and I saw a pickup sitting by the side of the road."

"What kind of pickup?"

"It was too far away to tell."

"New? Old?"

"Newer. Maybe five, six years old."

"Color?"

"You know, I been thinking about that. It was dark."

"You said it was early afternoon."

"No, the color of the pickup was dark. But it wasn't black."

"Dark blue? Dark green? Dark brown?"

"That's the thing. I can't swear to it, but it runs in my mind that it was brown." He shrugged his shoulders. "I never thought it would be important to remember. I just thought it was someone rabbit hunting. Stuck in my mind because that's the first time I ever seen anyone on that road."

"And all you saw was the pickup? You didn't see anyone around?"

"It's a long ways across that valley. I didn't see anyone."

Spider stood for a moment with his hands on his hips,

looking at the toe of his boot and considering. "I don't sup-pose," he said, looking up at the older man, "that you'd have time to run out there with me, show me where you were look-ing from and where you saw the pickup. It might have some-thing to do with the body I found, and it might not."

"Oh, I've got time," Mr. Wiggins said, rubbing his hands together. "I make my own schedule. As long as I get the work done, the company don't care when I do it. Get in. I'll take you out there."

Spider walked around the pickup, glancing as he did so at the toolboxes and fuel tanks lined up with military precision in the bed. A pick and two shovels, well used but clean, stood in a rack along with a push broom. Climbing in the cab, Spider said, "Looks like you come prepared."

"Have to," the older man replied. "They've stripped the mines of everything but what's too heavy to move." Driving over the cattle guard, he turned onto the gravel road and looked questioningly at Spider. "Been deputy long?" he asked.

"I guess you could say that I was still green," Spider admit-ted, not wanting to confess that this was his fifth day on the job.

"What'd you do before you turned deputy?"

"Whatever I could turn my hand to."

"Which isn't much around here."

"Not so's you'd notice, anymore," Spider agreed.

"Did you work at the mine before it closed?"

"Yeah, over at Castleton."

"What'd you do?"

"I was a millwright."

"Is that so?" The brow folded itself into wrinkles of con-centration and beady black eyes were turned on Spider. "What's your name again?"

"Latham. Spider Latham."

The wrinkles relaxed as recognition dawned. "I've heard the name."

"You've heard my name?"

"Yeah. My cousin works in the office of the Merry Widow Mine, halfway between Sparks and Reno—that's where Keystone moved their main offices to. My cousin's the one who sent out the postings on this job. She said you'd be the one to give me a run for my money in landing it. Millwright at Castleton, she said. Spider Latham. I guess I didn't need to worry. She said you never even applied."

"I didn't know about it. Was it posted?"

"Mines closed two years ago in August. They posted it that May, hired me in July."

May. May. May. Spider's mind riffled back through the springtime months two years ago. How could he have missed that posting? Easy. He had been bishop about a year. By May, it was evident that the mines were going to close, and his time had been taken up with counseling people who were facing the loss of income and no possibility of finding another job in the area. The lame leading the halt, he thought to himself, realizing how ludicrous it had been for him to be sitting there facing the same uncertainties, dealing with the same desperation, yet, because he had the mantle of bishop, he was the one who was supposed to give strength and direction. And then, Rose Markey's marriage had begun coming unraveled about that time. Spider could still see her, sitting in the bishop's office, blinking her mascaraed lashes under that curly mop, pencil poised over her notebook as Spider tried to talk to her about the principles that applied to her situation. "So what am I supposed to say to him?" she would ask. Spider was trying to show her how to choose a course that would bring her happiness, and she wanted snappy comebacks.

Indeed, there was no mystery as to why he had missed the posting. He had not neglected his work, but all his time on the job and off had been directed toward shutting down the mines.

"I never saw the posting," Spider said. "It didn't occur to me that there might be a chance to go on working."

Mr. Wiggins grinned. To Spider, it had a hint of smugness about it, and he felt a surge of antipathy.

"Oh, there were lots of people applied for the job. My cousin told me there were three hundred applications come in. Not many of them as qualified as me."

Spider shook his head. "I never saw the posting," he said again.

The brows came down, and the beady eyes were turned on Spider. "You're not saying that someone took the posting from off the bulletin board, are you?" Mr. Wiggins's voice was defensive. "Couldn't have been me. I live in Reno. That's a long way from Castleton. Couldn't have been me."

Spider stared. "I don't believe I said it was," he said mildly. Pointing ahead to the road that turned off toward the Lucy Roberts Mine, he asked, "Was it on this road that you saw the truck parked?"

"Yeah." Mr Wiggins turned on his blinker. He slowed down and made the turn, and then picked up the conversation again. "You wouldn'ta had a chance, anyway," he stated. "I grew up with Elbert H. Smith, head of personnel for Keystone Mines." He laughed, an unattractive, open-mouthed chuckle. "Heh, heh, heh. Old Smitty and I go way back. He wouldn't dare not give me the job. I know where all the bodies are buried."

Again Spider stared at the wiry little man at the wheel.

The wrinkled countenance became a mask of innocence, and there was a hint of mischief in the eyes as Mr. Wiggins said, "That's not a very smart thing to say right now, to an officer of the law, is it? I don't know about any bodies, but I do know that Smitty's been stepping out on his wife. Not that I would use that as a lever to try to keep my job, you understand. Heh, heh, heh."

They were passing the place where the body had been stashed in the old CCC dam, and Spider looked across the valley to the mine, figuring it must be a mile wide right there. The road continued for another half mile until the valley narrowed to a point, and then it crossed over and doubled back on the other side, climbing as it went until it reached the mine shaft, halfway up the hill.

"Where do you usually park?" Spider asked, happy to be able to change the subject.

"Out back of the generator shed. You can't see it from here."

"What were you doing that day?"

"Same thing I do every time I come around. I fire up the generator, turn on the pump, flush out the water pipes, check the ceilings for evidence of leaky roofs, check for rot in any of the floorboards, make sure no one's been tampering with any of the locks. Same ol', same ol'."

"And what time did you say you saw the pickup?"

"Must have been early afternoon, because I ate my lunch while the pipes were flushing. I had just finished turning off the tap in the machine shop, and when I stepped out the door, I looked out over the valley. We'd had a rain that morning, and everything looked fresh and smelled good. I was thinking about the water I'd just run out on the ground, thinking that if some rancher had access to it he could raise a nice crop of alfalfa in that little valley. That's when I seen the pickup."

Mr. Wiggins had parked the Keystone pickup in a gravel lot behind a large metal shed and opened his door. "I'll show you where I was," he said.

Spider got out and looked around. Three corrugated metal buildings huddled together on a narrow bench. One housed the generator and water pump, another the machine shop, and the third was built to enclose the mine shaft.

"I was over here," prompted Mr. Wiggins. He was waiting at the corner of the generator shed. When he saw that Spider was going to follow him, he turned and proceeded around the shed and along the brow of the bench to the next building.

"Is this the machine shop?" Spider asked, turning to survey the valley spread out before him.

"This is it," declared the older man, rubbing his hands together.

"And this is where you were standing?"

"Yessir."

"Where did you see the pickup? Can you show me?"

"It was just dead across. There, at the bottom of that little crease in the hill. That's where the pickup was. See it?"

"Yeah, I see it. Huh." It was too far to make out the pile of rocks that he and Bud had scattered when they uncovered the body. But there was no doubt that, if Mr. Wiggins had indeed seen a pickup parked there as he said he had, it had been parked at the place where the body had been hidden.

"Did you see anybody?"

"Didn't look. But if I had been looking, I don't know that I'd a seen anyone. They could have been in the pickup, or behind it. Could have been standing in a shadow. That's a long way over there to see someone you're not looking for."

"I guess. Could I get you to drive your pickup over there and park, just for a minute, Mr. Wiggins? And then would you walk up the hill a ways—about halfway up. Just walk up and come back down."

The little black eyes became suspicious. "Why would you want me to do that? You got some information about what happened that day?"

"What day?"

"The day I was here."

"The only information I've got is what you've given me. You said you saw a pickup. I'd just like to see what you saw. You've got a pickup here. I'd like for you to drive it over there and park it as near as you can figure to where that one was parked the day you were here. It may have something to do with that woman. It might not. We may never know."

"All right. I'll drive over there." Mr. Wiggins's hands were working again, rubbing against each other as he turned away from Spider and walked around the corner.

Spider shrugged, as if trying to shake off the mental imprint of that unattractive gesture. Turning away, he walked over to the concrete steps of the machinery shed and sat down. He heard the sound of an engine starting, and presently the blue pickup came into sight, retracing the route to the other side of the valley, growing tinier with distance until it became a mini-micro toy, complete with doors that really open and close. It stopped just below the crease in the hill, and the door to the cab really opened, and Mr. Wiggins, who had become an ant, got out and began his climb up the hill. Spider checked his watch, and when he looked up again, he couldn't see Mr. Wiggins. Puzzled, he raked the area with his eyes, back and forth, back and forth. Then something moved, and Spider saw that Mr. Wiggins must have been standing still with his tan shirt and tan pants acting as camouflage against the tan earth of the hillside.

"Huh!" Spider grunted, and settled back to wait for the noxious little man's return.

On the drive home Spider quizzed Mr. Wiggins again about where he was and what he was doing and what he saw on that day last May. He did it more to keep Mr. Wiggins from gloating about his job with Keystone than to glean information. As they turned off the highway onto the gravel road to his place, Spider asked, "Any way of knowing exactly what day you were up at the Lucy Roberts?"

"Yessir. I keep a daily log of what I do and where and when. I can tell you exactly what day I was there."

"Where is that log?"

"It's in my file box at my home. In Reno."

"When will you be back home?"

"Not till next week. I'm here until next Tuesday. I should be home some time Wednesday. I could call you, let you know what day I was out at the Lucy Roberts."

"I don't suppose there's anyone else who could look it up for you? Your wife, maybe?"

"I ain't married."

"Your sister, could she . . . ?"

The hands that gripped the steering wheel became tense and the wrinkles set in angry lines. "I ain't having anyone messing in my stuff. Now, do you want to know or don't you?"

"Yeah, I want to know," Spider said in neutral tones, eyeing his companion speculatively.

"All right, then. You'll have to wait."

"I'll wait."

Mr. Wiggins turned onto Spider's place. He stopped the car, but he left his motor running. "I'll need your phone number," he said. "You got a card?"

"Uh-uh."

"I'll write it on one of mine." Leaning forward, Mr. Wiggins took a nylon wallet out of his back pocket and tore the Velcro flap open. Taking two cards out, he handed one to Spider.

Trying to ignore the "Heh, heh, heh," Spider glanced at the business card while he waited for Mr. Wiggins to fish a pen out of his pocket. It was a good-looking card, with the Keystone name in handsome lettering and the logo in full color. Kurt Wiggins, it said, Director of Maintenance. Spider stuffed the card in his pocket and gave his phone number to Mr. Wiggins. Then he climbed out of the pickup and stood by the open door. "Much obliged to you for coming out to talk to me, and for taking me up to the Lucy Roberts."

"No problemo. I'll be at the Trail's End Motel in Pioche until next week if you have any questions."

"And you'll call me next Wednesday?"

"I'll call you Wednesday."

Spider stepped back and closed the blue pickup door. "Thanks again," he called through the closed window, waiting only for an acknowledging wave before turning back to his own pickup.

Catching sight of Laurie standing on the back porch, he realized that he had missed his chance for a clean getaway, so he ambled up the walk to charm his wife out of her four-quart sieve.

13

NEXT DAY WAS THE first Sunday in November. It was eight in the morning before Laurie padded down the hall in her house-coat, pausing to poke her head into the living room and blink sleepily at Spider. He was sitting in his bathrobe with his scriptures open on his knees.

"I slept in," she said. "Today's fast Sunday. I'm not eating, but I'll fix you some toast and spearmint tea."

"Thanks, but I think I need to fast today."

Laurie propped herself against the doorway. "How many times have we been through this?" she asked with exaggerated patience. "You're not required to fast if your body is not able to tolerate going without food. As long as you keep the spirit of the fast, that's acceptable."

"I've got some things I need extra help with. Maybe I need to make some extra effort to invite the Spirit to be with me."

"And will the Spirit be with you when you're spending the rest of the day in the bathroom with cramps and diarrhea?"

"Maybe I won't have that problem today."

"Maybe not," Laurie said, her voice conveying a meaning more like, *Just wait.*

"Have you read today's lesson?" Spider asked.

Laurie came clear into the room and sat down on the couch, tucking her legs up under her and drawing her robe around her feet. "For what? Gospel Doctrine class? You know I'm in with the teenagers during that time."

"Yeah, but you're supposed to keep up on the reading assignment too."

"You only say that because you're the teacher, and because you're the teacher you've read the lesson. If you were sitting in the class you'd be like everyone else and come completely unprepared."

"No, Sister Smith always comes prepared. And Sandy and Hazel."

"And not a one of them less than seventy years old."

"Yeah. Old Hazel, she has some pretty good insights. We're studying Paul now, and talking about the hoo-hah that went on between him and the brethren about the Law of Moses."

"What hoo-hah?"

"See, if you'd been reading your reading assignment, you'd know."

"I've read the New Testament. I don't remember any hoo-hah."

"Well, old Paul's out converting the gentiles, baptizing them and confirming them left and right, and the Jewish Christians are maintaining that the gentile converts have to be circumcised. They just can't let go of the Law of Moses."

"I imagine that would put a damper on the conversion rate."

"Hazel brought up in class that the same problem cropped up in the Book of Mormon. Only in reverse."

"About circumcision?"

"About keeping the Law of Moses. They had no trouble abandoning it. The problem was that some wanted to do away with it too soon. After Christ was born, some people said that it was time. But the prophet said that they had to wait until the crucifixion. Then the law was fulfilled and could be done away with."

Laurie looked at Spider with quiet amazement. "Isn't it incredible, the way it all ties together? There's so much to learn! I wish I weren't so lazy."

"I've never noticed that laziness was a particular problem. You've just never had the benefit of a crackerjack teacher like me."

"Yes, you're always so shy about sharing your opinions!" Laurie looked at her watch and stood. "We have to leave in half an hour. I'm going to go get ready."

"Be there in a minute. I just want to finish this chapter." He put his hand out and pressed hers as she slipped past his chair on her way to the hall.

Forty minutes later Spider was walking down the hall from the meetinghouse library with a map detailing Paul's journeys under his arm. When he heard someone call his name in a soft, breathless voice, he paused to remind himself that being Christian meant loving even the exasperating ones. Then he turned to greet his new home teaching assignment.

Rose Markey had a little-girl voice and a little-girl hairdo.

She had a teenager's disposition, taste in clothing, and sense of decorum. The face and body were all woman.

Spider had never been able to decide whether the brain under that mass of curly hair was simple or subtle. Nor was he sure what lay behind those soulful eyes. They were turned up to him now, and he had seen that look before.

"Bishop Stowe said I needed to talk to you," Rose breathed, "and I'm sooo glad, because I feel really comfortable telling you about my problems." She unzipped the beaded handbag she had slung over her shoulder and began rooting around among the debris inside. "I have this money . . ." She pulled out an old shopping list, a grocery store receipt, two empty envelopes, a cassette tape, a shiny rock, and folding money from three different compartments.

"Wait!" urged Spider. "Don't take out any money. Listen, I have to go put up this map in my classroom. Come in here and you can just tell me what's going on."

"I'm just trying to find the list of rules . . ." she said. But, seeing that Spider was holding the door open, Rose obligingly trotted into his classroom, stuffing the flotsam from her handbag back inside. She needed no prodding to open up, beginning a recitation of her woes while Spider was still hanging his map. Several times Spider suggested that a particular confidence was for the bishop's ears only, but she only blinked and plowed ahead. Finally, he looked at his watch and stated that they'd be late for testimony meeting if they didn't get in there. With a promise to investigate her problem, he took the proffered piece of paper, picked up his scriptures, and made for the chapel. He slipped in beside Laurie just as the opening hymn was ending.

Laurie had seen him hold the chapel door open for Rose to

come in, and she smiled at him and winked as he sang the last snatch of song. Spider made a tiny grimace in return. Then he folded his arms and bowed his head as Sister Ekhart said the opening prayer.

Bishop Stowe, who was conducting the meeting, announced the sacrament song. Spider, determined to prepare himself to receive the emblems, contemplated each verse as he joined in the singing. Then as the deacons, twelve-year-old boys in white shirts and ties they had yet to grow into, passed the bread and water, Spider dragged his scriptures out and opened them. As he turned to Philippians, his eye lit on a verse he had marked long ago: " . . . we look for the Saviour, the Lord Jesus Christ: Who shall change our vile body, that it may be fashioned like unto his glorious body, according to the working whereby he is able even to subdue all things unto himself."

I hadn't remembered that verse, Spider thought. *Now that's comfort, after finding such a vile body in a rock pile this last week.*

Scanning on through, he found another verse, marked in the same red pencil of his missionary years. "I have learned, in whatsoever state I am, therewith to be content. I know both how to be abased, and I know how to abound: every where and in all things I am instructed both to be full and to be hungry, both to abound and to suffer need. I can do all things through Christ which strengtheneth me."

Spider read through those verses once more and closed his eyes, musing upon the beauty of the words and the hope that lay in them. Laurie nudged his arm when the bread and water were offered to him. As he partook, he felt a warm glow, a tingling of assurance, and his mind began searching for words to express this. How to package this feeling into phrases that would travel spirit to spirit? So absorbed was he that he was unaware of the sacrament cloth being spread back over the trays and the meeting being turned over to the congregation for those who felt like bearing testimony.

He was brought back to the meeting by the popping of consonants through the microphone. Looking up, he saw Ricky Stowe, three-year-old son of Bishop Stowe, standing on a stool behind the pulpit and leaning into the microphone as he breathed audibly over the public address system. "I'd like to stand on my own two feet," he said, " and bear my tessimony."

Of course he was cute. Bishop Stowe beamed. His first and second counselors beamed. Sister Stowe smiled through misty tears. The deacons giggled.

"I love my mommy and daddy. I'm glad my daddy's the bishop. I love my brothers and sisters. Name of Jesus Christ, amen."

A ripple of echoed amens ran through the congregation, and everyone was smiling.

Scotty Stowe was next. He adjusted the microphone. "I'd like to stand on my own two feet," he said, "and bear my testimony. I know that President Benson is a prophet of God. I love my mom and dad. I love my brothers and sisters. Name of Jesus Christ, amen."

Again the ripple of amens. Now there was a lineup of five children, ages three to six, ready to climb up to the pulpit and declare that they were standing on their own two feet. As each adjusted the microphone before bending over to speak into it, Spider wondered if, on the face of the earth, there existed a mike-shy Mormon child.

Sister Null was next, taking to the pulpit to earnestly exhort the members to complete their seventy-two-hour kits. Spider began to squirm in his seat. As Sister Null finished, Rose

Markey's daughter, ten-year-old Becky Snow, led her shy half-sister, three-year-old Tiffany Johnson, up to the pulpit. Becky helped Tiffany up onto the stool, adjusted the mike, and whispered in her ear. Tiffany listened intently and then leaned into the mike. "I'd like to stand on my own two feet . . ." Again she listened. Whisper, whisper, whisper. " . . . and bear my testimony." Whisper, whisper, whisper. "I love my mommy and my sisters." Whisper, whisper, whisper. "I know that Abraham Lincoln is a prophet of God."

Spider's shoulders began to shake. Laurie looked warningly at him, and he cleared his throat and sat forward with his elbows on his knees and his forehead resting on his hands. But a moment later his shoulders began shaking again, and, though he stood and left the chapel coughing into his handkerchief, Laurie was not deceived.

She took him to task on the way home. "It wasn't *that* funny," she said.

"The whole thing was pretty ludicrous," he said. "First you have the little kids copying one another. Then you have Sister Null bearing testimony that the prophet has told us to get our seventy-two-hour kits done, which is utterly not true. And then you have the Fluff children putting on the final touch. During the sacrament I had some pretty powerful stirrings in my heart about the Savior. I was waiting for someone to testify about Him, to connect with the things I was feeling in my heart. Instead, I get seventy-two-hour kits and Abraham Lincoln."

Laurie didn't say anything. She was staring out the pickup window at the mountains in the distance.

Spider didn't need any response. He was fired up. He spoke in the oratorical tone he used from the pulpit. "People need to understand that testimony meeting is under the direction of the

Holy Ghost. Parents aren't to be urging their children to partici-
pate. Teachers aren't to be assigning their class members to bear
testimony. No one is to be challenged to do it by a seminary
teacher. And certainly, children are not to have people whisper
a testimony in their ears. If you have bibble babble like we had
this morning, the whole ward is impoverished! Where is the
testimony of Christ? How are the people to be fed?"

Laurie turned a solemn face to Spider. Her eyes were shiny.
"Where indeed?" she said softly. "You say that that meeting is
to be under the direction of the Spirit. All right. I think that you
were directed to testify. And why didn't you?"

"I wasn't going to be a part of that dog-and-pony show!"

"Don't be asking how the people are going to be fed if you
deny the Spirit."

"The Spirit left the meeting when Sister Null stood up!"

"Perhaps it would have returned with you. The Church isn't
perfect, Spider. We're all still learning. We serve one another by
listening to imperfect testimonies, and, yes, bibble babble, and
by teaching each other what a testimony really is. We let the
children practice, so that later on it's easy to stand and tell others what they believe."

"Or later on they can't believe anyone because they knew
they were standing and saying the words without believing
them. They just wanted to stand up and use the microphone."

"For some, yes. And I agree that a child needs to use his
own words and not someone else's. But you can't tell me there
aren't children who are touched by the Spirit. There are! There
was another time when people wanted to repress the children,
and Jesus said, 'Suffer them to come unto me.'"

They rode in silence. Laurie broke it by musing, "Christ
said that testifying of him wasn't necessarily going to be easy.

Maybe he wasn't talking about teaching unbelievers. Maybe sometimes it's harder to do in the place and time provided. I don't know. I do know that it would have helped me if you had shared what was in your heart."

"Huh!" grunted Spider.

Silence. They turned off the highway onto their gravel road, and Laurie said, "I saw Rose Markey corner you in the hall. What did she have on her mind?"

"She got a settlement from some insurance. She slipped on a wet floor in a drugstore over in Cedar and hurt her knee. They gave her twenty thousand dollars."

"Twenty thousand dollars!"

"Yeah. Crazy, isn't it? She's on welfare, and in order to keep it, the welfare, she has to spend the twenty thousand dollars in the next two months. There are rules as to what she can spend it on."

"Like what?"

"Clothes, a house, a car. Furniture. That kind of thing. I think it would be good if she could find a mobile home that she could pretty much pay for with the money, and then she wouldn't have the outgo of rent each month."

"Does she still have the entire twenty thousand?"

"She doesn't get it until day after tomorrow."

"You'd better be quick about finding a place for her to buy, or the money will be gone. It shouldn't be too hard. There're lots of places for sale."

"Yeah, but it's got to be blue."

"What's got to be blue?"

"The house. She says she reacts to oranges and yellows. In order to be happy, she has to have her house decorated in blue."

"Four walls and a roof aren't enough, huh? It's got to be blue?"

Spider drove over the cattle guard onto their own place, turned off the engine, and gathered his books. "Yeah, well, this may be a learning experience for us all." He opened his door. "Is the phone ringing?" he asked. "Yep. I'll get it." He took long, loose strides toward the back door.

"I DON'T KNOW WHY Debbie couldn't just talk to me," Spider complained.

It was Monday morning. Laurie was doing the breakfast dishes and Spider was sitting at the table with his *Law in Layman's Language* open before him, intending to study as he waited for his sister to arrive from Las Vegas. She was bringing his mother to visit for the day.

"Maybe because you dropped the phone and bolted for the bathroom."

"Yeah, but when I came back in, you were still talking to her. She always has plenty to say to you. She hardly ever visits with me anymore."

Laurie finished drying a skillet and put it in the cupboard before she spoke, choosing her words carefully. "Maybe she feels that you don't understand the situation. Maybe she feels like she's carrying this burden alone and you're being judgmental."

"What burden? Mother went to live with her when Allen died as a favor to her, to cook and clean house and tend the kids so she could go back to work. Sounds to me like there's a couple of ways of looking at the 'burden' bit."

"That was ten years ago. A lot has changed since then."

"Yes. Her youngest child is thirteen. Things should be easier for all concerned."

"Debbie thinks your mother has changed, too, Spider."

"Oh, well, she's a little forgetful. But she's seventy-five. That goes with the territory."

"She can't cook anymore."

"What do you mean?"

"Debbie says that she doesn't do any of the cooking anymore. The last pie she made was an absolute disaster. It was like something a six-year-old child would do."

"Well . . ."

"And she doesn't bathe."

"Doesn't bathe?"

"Debbie says that getting her to take a bath is a major battle. Your mother was always fastidious about her personal cleanliness. And . . ."

"And what?"

"Well, it's ridiculous, of course. But she says your mom says your dad was having an affair with another woman. No, don't look like that. Debbie doesn't believe it either."

"Just who is it that Dad was supposed to have had an affair with?"

"Someone named Grace. Who would that be?"

"Grace? I don't know anyone named Grace. What does Mom say? Dad never went anywhere without her. Great

Suffering Zot, when would he have an affair? Why would he have an affair? He loved her. What does she say?"

"She just talks about how much he loved this woman, Grace. She says he met her when he was an older man. He loved her. Even spoke of her on his deathbed."

"I don't believe it!"

"Nobody does. That's the thing, Spider. There are too many things happening, too many indicators—I don't know. Deb says your mother loses things and then accuses people of stealing from her. She throws tantrums, screaming and crying, and sometimes threatening. It's all so totally out of character for your mom. Debbie thinks something is dreadfully wrong."

"Dreadfully?"

"She thinks it's Alzheimer's."

Spider stared. He swallowed. He closed his book with a snap and pushed it away. "She thinks," he muttered. "Huh!"

"Debbie says it's affecting the children, and she's about at the end of her tether. That's why she's taken this personal leave day to visit a friend in Cedar." She glanced out the window, wiping her hands on a dish towel. "There they are."

A red sedan came across the cattle guard. Spider and Laurie went outside and stood on the back step as Debbie swung the car around and stopped with the passenger door nearest them. She didn't turn off the engine. Laurie went to open the door and help Mrs. Latham out while Spider went around to Debbie's door. She rolled down the window.

"I'm late," she said. "In Mother's purse is a list of her medications and times to give them. Also, there's a list of what she can have to eat today and when. I've got her insulin in my purse, and I'll give her a shot tonight when I pick her up. I'll be back around eight." She glanced to her right to assure herself that their mother was out, waved good-bye, and was off.

Spider gazed thoughtfully after her and then turned to welcome his mother.

Rachel Latham was small, with silvery hair, fine features, clear blue eyes behind an attractive pair of glasses, and an expressive mouth. She was dressed in powder-blue sweats, Adidas, and a blue windbreaker.

"Hello, Mom," Spider said, walking over to give her a big hug.

"Hello," she replied, returning the hug. Spider wondered if he was imagining things or whether there was a shade of hesitation.

"I've got some free time this morning, and I wondered if you'd like to go out to Jackrabbit?" he asked.

He was immediately rewarded with his mother's familiar, incandescent smile. "I'd love to!"

★   ★   ★

Half an hour later found them turning north off the gravel road onto Highway 93. Mrs. Latham settled her hands into her pockets and glanced at the dashboard with all its switches and dials. "Is this your new car?" she asked.

"It belongs to the county," Spider replied. "I'm the new deputy sheriff."

Mrs. Latham pulled her hand out of her pocket and opened it. Inside lay two quarters, a dime, and three pennies. "Look at that!" she exclaimed. "I found it in my pocket."

"Boy, howdy," Spider said, smiling. "We can go out today and be big spenders!"

"Yes," his mother agreed. "We can really have a time!" She

jingled the coins in her hand and twinkled up at her son. Then she put them back in her pocket.

As they skirted by Pioche and dropped down into the valley beyond, Spider looked at the Bristol Mountains marching along on his left and said, "I bet it's been twenty years since I was out to Jackrabbit."

"I haven't been out since before Bill died. We came out on a picnic, all the old-timers that were left in the area. We sang songs and told stories and remembered how grand it was to live there."

"Without running water or electricity?"

"Oh, we had running water, and they had a light plant, so we had electric lights. No hot water, though, or refrigerator. Bill built shelves in the old Empress Mine—it was just a few feet from our house—and it was so cool in there that it kept things as cold as a Fridgidaire. Oh, look what I found in my pocket!" Mrs. Latham was holding the sixty-three cents out for Spider's inspection.

"You are Mrs. Moneybags!" Spider said, casting a half-quizzical glance at his mother.

"Yes!" She flashed a teasing smile at Spider. "I've got a pocketful of money and a good-looking man beside me. Let's go out and paint the town!"

"Shall we paint Jackrabbit?" Spider slowed down to turn onto the dirt road that led up to tumbledown walls and empty foundations scattered over the hillside.

"Jackrabbit will do," she laughed as she jingled the change in her hand and put it away in her pocket.

Spider drove carefully over the little-used track and pulled onto the old railroad grade, where the going was easier.

"I used to walk out to that saddle there in the evening,

about quitting time," Mrs. Latham said, pointing to a gap in the hills half a mile distant, "and wait for the train coming back from the mill. Bill was the engineer, and I'd ride back with him. I'd take Spider with me, and Bill would let him toot the horn."

"Yeah, I remember." Spider parked by the old tram house and turned off the key. "I'll come let you out," he said as he opened his door, and quickly came around to do so.

Mrs. Latham emerged from the car and stood a moment looking it over. "Is this a police car?" she asked.

"It's the deputy's car. I'm the new deputy sheriff, Mom."

"Ooooh," she said, nodding. "I wondered."

"Do you want to go up and see your old house? It seems to be the most intact building out here."

"Yes, let's."

Spider held his mother's elbow, and as they picked their way across the rocky hillside, they passed the old Empress Mine shaft.

"I remember this place!" Spider exclaimed. "I remember these tram rails coming out of the mine, and I remember standing in front on a hot day and feeling the cool breeze blow over me. How old would I have been?"

"We left when you were four," Mrs. Latham said. "That's where your dad built the cooler for me—just a ways inside."

"I don't suppose it's still there," Spider mused.

"Anything your dad built was built to last."

"Wait here just a minute. I'm going to see."

Picking his way over a jumble of beams that lay like giant jackstraws on top of the tram rails in front of the mine, Spider climbed down to the entrance.

"Well, isn't that strange," Mrs. Latham called to him. "They've put a door on it!"

"They did that years ago. Don't you remember, Mom? After that kid fell down the mine shaft over at Castleton, the company closed off all the mines so people couldn't get in."

The barricade had been built out of timbers and three-by-twelves. It was a square cover on a round hole, but still no one could squeeze through the spaces left at top, bottom, and sides. Spider stuck his face in one of the vertical slits and felt the chilly breath blowing up from the black throat of the mine.

He felt a warm hand on his arm and looked to see that his mother had joined him.

"A lotta history here," he observed.

"Oh yes, indeed. It was these mines that saved the folks in the Dixie mission."

"How so?"

"Well, you know, Brigham Young had called them to St. George to raise cotton. They'd plowed all their time and money into putting in that crop and into trying to build a dam that would hold the Virgin River—and they were failing at both. In the beginning they had no market for the cotton, because there wasn't a cotton mill. Anything else they grew—well, it was too hard going north over that slick-rock country to get to a market with their produce. So there they sat, sent by the prophet to do something that was well-nigh impossible, but doing their best, and starving in the process. And then, when things were looking the blackest, silver was discovered here and at Silver Reef, and a marvelous market for their goods moved right next door. The people in the Dixie mission were able to get wonderful prices for the beef and produce they brought in to the miners. I know my great-granddaddy, Luther Cram, got fifty cents a pound for potatoes in the year 1871."

"Fifty cents a pound! That's twice what we pay now."

"Yes, isn't that marvelous?" She patted the barricade. "The Lord heard the prayers of the faithful, I'm sure, and gave them a way to save themselves." She paused a moment, staring at the wide door, set on sturdy hinges and equipped with a heavy-duty hasp that stood in the middle of the wall. "You'd think," she mused, "that if they wanted to keep people out, they'd hang a padlock on that door."

"Well, I'll be danged. There's no lock on that hasp! Let's just go see if my daddy's shelves are still there. I wish I had a flashlight."

"They're not too far in. I never brought a light when I carried stuff out here."

Spider propped the door open and stepped through into a cool, dim netherworld of smoky-colored shale.

His mother hovered at the door, blocking the light. "Don't go too far," she cautioned. "There's a vertical shaft that drops down a hundred feet or so. It's just a ways in."

"I just want to see the shelves," Spider said, conscious of his voice echoing around him. "They're right here."

"Yes, I can see them."

"They've got newspapers on them."

"I couldn't afford shelf paper."

Spider stood by the old tram tracks with his hands on his hips and examined his father's handiwork. It stood about six feet high and four feet wide. "That's a lot of storage space. What'd you put out here?"

"Oh, milk and meat and anything I didn't want to spoil. Cheese and such. And I kept my onions and cabbage, and all the winter-keeping things that I was storing. Apples and pears. It was handy, all right."

Thinking of the trip from house to mine every morning to

get milk for breakfast, Spider said dryly, "Yeah, like a pocket on a shirt."

Taking a newspaper from one of the shelves, he carried it out into the sunlight. "August 1952," he said as he unfolded it. "There's a big write-up here about them putting in the water system in Panaca. And watermelon is two cents a pound at the Panaca Emporium."

"Let's see."

Spider handed the paper to his mother, who held it up and tipped her head back to look at it through her bifocals.

"Oh, look. Here's a picture of Aunt Birdie Wentworth. She's just finished a genealogy quilt. They're going to raffle it off at the Wentworth family reunion next week."

Spider closed the door to the mine and stuck a stick through the eye of the hasp to fasten it. "Why don't we go on up to the house now, and you can read the rest of the paper on the way home," he suggested. "I need to get you back by noon so you get your lunch on time."

"I wouldn't mind having that quilt," Mrs. Latham said. "The tickets are fifty cents apiece."

"I'll get you one," Spider said, smiling as he took the paper from his mother and folded it up.

"Get two," she said over her shoulder as she started up the trail.

Spider had the feeling that she wasn't kidding.

The tiny cottage was perched on the hillside about fifty feet from the Empress Mine. It was a lonesome sight. There was no glass left in the windows, and the corrugated tin roof was a rusty, ugly red. Other than that, the house was in fairly good shape, considering it had been abandoned and left to the elements for almost forty years.

The path led to the back of the house. Spider opened a screenless screen door and pushed open the back door, shivering as the door grated a fan-shaped pattern across the dirt on the floor. He stepped back to allow his mother to enter, saying, "Don't brush up against anything. You'll get your jacket all dirty."

Mrs. Latham stepped into the tiny kitchen, smiling as her bright gaze rested on familiar planes and angles. "It's smaller than I remembered," she said after a moment. "But it was a handy kitchen to work in."

Going over to the sink, she looked out the window that gave onto the hillside in back. "The garden was on that first little rise," she said. "Remember? I planted flowers so I could see them when I did the dishes."

"I don't remember much."

"And the stove was right here. They'd bring a carload of wood and dump it over by the tram house, and we could help ourselves to it. It kept the house toasty warm in the winter."

"And in the summer?"

"Oh, it was hot, but I managed. Look here, above the wood box, where you put your fist through the wall that time when you were so upset about them calling Hose Watkins to the high council."

"That was Dad."

Mrs. Latham blinked.

"It was Dad that put his fist through the wall, Mom. I'm Spider."

There was just a fleeting moment of blankness in Mrs. Latham's eyes before clarity returned, and they crinkled at the edges as she smiled up at Spider. Patting his cheek, she said, "Of course you are!"

Spider held his fist up to the hole in the Cellotex. It went through easily. "Either Dad had a big fist, or he hit it pretty hard," he observed.

His mother closed a cupboard door and wiped her fingers on her handkerchief as she glanced again at the hole in the wall. "Both."

"So, tell me. Why was Dad mad about them calling Hose Watkins? And who is Hose Watkins? I've never heard of him."

Mrs. Latham walked to the window overlooking the old railroad grade. "He was one of the superintendents of the mine. Bill felt that some of the decisions he made as superintendent were at odds with gospel principles."

"Like what?" Spider joined her at the window.

"It's been so long ago, and I didn't know everything about it. I think there were a couple of things that happened. One fellow got disabled on the job, and there was some technicality that made it so the mine didn't have to pay anything for the limb he lost. Then they fired him. Bill didn't think that was right. Then there was Otto Payton. He was killed on the job, left a wife and eight little children. The settlement that the company gave Marge Payton didn't hardly cover the cost of moving the family back to Logan to be near her folks. Hose Watkins was the one who made those decisions."

"I see."

Mrs. Latham wandered through an archway. "This was the front room. I remember this linoleum. We saved up and bought it just before Spider was born, remember? We didn't want our baby walking on that bare wood floor."

The linoleum was a floral pattern, overblown pink roses and trailing ribbons on a blue-green background. The walls of the tiny room had been painted a soft aqua that had turned dusky with time.

"We lived in this house for ten years," she went on. "It was hard to see other fellows who weren't half as capable as Bill getting promoted and moving on to better jobs and better houses. He was put up for promotion every year by his supervisors, but until Hose left, it never went through."

"Huh!" Spider grunted. "That's a hard one."

"I think it was harder for me than Bill. We had everything we needed, and we were so happy here. Especially after Spider and Debbie came along. We had to wait a lot of years for children, you know."

"Yeah, I know."

"Bill was funny. He'd go toe-to-toe with anyone over someone else's problems—things he saw as unfair. He'd gone a round or two with Hose Watkins. But he wouldn't spend five minutes on his own affairs. 'I don't want anything my neighbor can't have,' he'd say. And he didn't. He was the most unworldly man I've ever known."

"Want to see the bedroom?"

She shook her head. "I don't want to see it all faded and bare. Let's go sit on the front porch."

After the closed-in feeling of the tiny sitting room, the vista that spread out before them was breathtaking. It was twenty miles across the valley floor to the rugged majesty of the Winslow Range. Highway 93 rolled out below them like a blue grosgrain ribbon set out to measure the mountains. In the near distance a herd of wild mustangs kicked up a cloud of dust that lay like a smoky smudge against the darker terrain.

The weather-beaten wood porch had probably never seen a coat of paint. The grain was raised and ridged, and it had turned the color of native sand. It had hardened with age, too, and had seized up around the nails, so that it was sturdy and sound. Rachel Latham sat down on the top step of the porch.

"I don't know how clean that is, Mom," Spider cautioned.

"I've had worse things happen to me than a dusty backside. Come and sit by me for a minute."

Spider sat. The day was becoming warm, with a crisp little breeze flitting by every now and then, lest anyone forget it was November.

"We used to sit out here of an evening, remember?" Mrs. Latham asked, and her voice was soft and wistful. "I'd bring out my knitting and you would sing to me. 'When your hair has burned to silver, I will love you as today,'" Mrs. Latham sang in a trembly soprano. "Remember?"

"That was a long time ago."

"Yes it was. My hair has turned to silver." The blue eyes that she turned to Spider were moist, and the smile was brave enough to break his heart.

"And I love you," Spider said, putting his arm around her and kissing the silvery hair. Then he leaned back on his elbows and stretched one long leg out in front of him, considering the carefully polished toe of one worn cowboy boot.

"I like hearing about Dad," he said after a while. "I miss him. I could use some fatherly advice right now. Do you think . . ." Spider paused to think of a way to phrase his question. "Dad was sixty when he died. Do you think that he would have punched out the wall at sixty because Hose Watkins was called to the high council?"

"Not with his arthritis, he wouldn't," Mrs. Latham said, chuckling. "No, I know what you mean. Let me think." Her brow wrinkled, and she looked slantwise at something within, some memory. "I think . . . I think that he would have understood that the stake president was doing the best he could with what he had to work with. And, maybe, so was Hose. Maybe it was an imperfect decision, but Dad grew to feel that an imperfect decision made by someone who was really trying would be acceptable. He often said that God wasn't going to take away our agency by giving us continuous revelation about every little thing. He was very clear about that, and grew impatient with anyone who felt that God was guiding every decision from wallpaper to Sunday School chorister. 'God gave us reason,' he'd say. 'He expects us to use it.' 'Agency's a burden we all have to bear,' he would say, 'and most of us are making a hash of it.'"

"Boy, isn't that the truth!" Spider gazed at the snowy mountaintops glistening across the way in the noonday sun and smiled at the memory of his dad. "Thanks, Mom, for telling me that." He glanced at his watch. "Now we need to hustle if I'm going to get you home in time for lunch."

Standing, he offered a hand to help his mother up, and then they walked arm in arm down the path to the county car.

When Spider opened the passenger door, Mrs. Latham looked at the lights on top and asked, "Is this a police car?"

"It's the deputy's car, Mom. I'm the new deputy sheriff."

Closing her door, he went around to get in, and as he started the car, Mrs. Latham pulled the sixty-three cents from her pocket once again.

"Look at what I found!" she said, displaying the coins.

Spider smiled down at her. "Well, since you've got money, you can pay for lunch."

SPIDER AND HIS MOTHER drove across the cattle guard just as
Murray Sapp dumped a load of pit-run gravel in the middle of
the driveway. Spider drove slowly around it and parked in front of
the house. He stared into the rearview mirror a moment and then
got out and went around to open the door for his mother.

"Who's that?" she asked, tentatively answering the wave
sent her from the yellow truck.

Spider was watching the dump bed grumble back down to
rest.

"What? Oh, that's Mur."

"Mur? Mur who?"

"Murray Sapp, Mom. Aunt Dolly and Uncle Elmo's boy.
He's my second cousin. Remember?"

"Well, of course I remember! What's he doing?"

"I haven't the slightest idea."

Spider closed the car door and leaned against the cruiser

with his arms folded as he watched Murray cut the engine and climb down.

"Hello, Aunt Rachel!" Murray's face crinkled into the old familiar smile as he strode across the driveway. He dragged off his battered Stetson, and sandy curls fell over his brow as he enveloped her in a bear hug that swept her off her feet. Twirling her around with her shoulder bag flying out behind, he kissed her soundly on the cheek.

Mrs. Latham whooped, and her cheeks grew pink as she hung on. When she finally regained her footing, she stood for a moment with her hands on Murray's shoulders looking up at his weathered countenance. "Well, my!" she said, a little breathless. "You're all grown up."

Murray threw back his head and laughed. "Well, yes. I guess I am, Aunt Rachel."

"How are your folks? Are they coming over?"

Murray's puzzled glance flicked to Spider and back. "No, Aunt Rachel. They're dead."

Mrs. Latham turned away, groping for her purse. Clutching it in front of her, she closed her eyes and shook her head. "I don't know why I asked that. I know your folks are gone."

Spider put his arm around her and gave her a squeeze. "That's all right, Mom. We all forget every now and then. Do you want to go in and let Laurie know we're back? I just need to find out whose gravel Murray dumped here by mistake, and then I'll be in. She's in there in the kitchen. I can see her through the window. See? Yeah, tell her I'll be in in a minute. Tell her we're ready for lunch."

Both men watched the small figure in powder-blue sweats until the back door closed. Neither said a word.

Murray concentrated on the crease of his Stetson, running

it between his thumb and forefinger. Finally, he swept back his unruly hair and put his hat back on. Indicating the dump truck with his thumb, he said, "That ain't no mistake."

"Well, I certainly didn't order any gravel."

"Bud sent it over."

"Bud?"

"Yeah. He said he saw you down in the wash Saturday, shoveling gravel."

Silence. "He say anything else?"

"Nope. Figured to save you some time, I guess. Or maybe it's because the wash is on Hughes land. Maybe he's sending you a message."

"Bud's never been shy about speaking his mind."

Murray shrugged and looked around. "Your drive don't look too bad. What you shoveling gravel for?"

Spider glanced at his watch. "I was working on a project. Say, Mur, I've got to go out to Delmar to serve a paper. What you got going this afternoon?"

"You mean besides my meeting with the governor and my luncheon with Princess Di? I was going to get the grader and spread this gravel."

"Want to have a bite to eat and then come with me?"

"Well, I tell ya, Spider. I don't care about the governor. But you know, that'll about finish it with Princess Di and me if I stand her up to go off to Delmar with you."

"I'll bet Laurie's got bread just coming out of the oven."

"I'll be right in."

★   ★   ★

An hour later, Spider drove back out over the cattle guard. Murray was riding shotgun. Spider's badge was on his shirt, and an official summons was stuck in the visor above his head. Instead of turning right toward the highway, he turned left. The graded gravel road would dwindle in ten miles to a graded dirt road. Five miles beyond that, the dirt road would become a track. Two more miles, and the track would dead end at the ghost town of Delmar.

Spider glanced in his rearview mirror at the plume of dust rising behind them. "One thing about having just you and me and a ghost town sharing a road, there's not much traffic."

"Nope. You can pretty much figure, anyone who's on this road is coming to see you or me."

"Or this fellow in Delmar."

"Yeah. Or Bud, if he has cattle out here."

"No, sir. Not much traffic."

"Nope."

Silence.

"Your mom," Murray said, finally broaching the subject. "Is she all right?"

"She's getting a little forgetful."

Murray nodded and fished inside his shirt pocket for a mint-flavored toothpick in a white paper wrapper. He peeled off the paper and held up the toothpick. "I'm trying to quit smoking."

Spider nodded.

Murray put the toothpick in his mouth and chewed thoughtfully.

"What you doing for Thanksgiving?" Spider asked.

Murray shrugged. The toothpick bobbed.

"Want to come to our house?"

"I wouldn't be putting you out?"

"Naw. Neither of the boys are coming home."

"How about your mom?"

"I imagine she'll stay at Deb's. But it wouldn't matter who came. You'd be welcome."

Murray nodded. The toothpick moved to the other side of his mouth.

Spider didn't take his eyes off the road. "Any chance that Missy will show up this year?"

The toothpick froze. Murray glanced sideways at Spider. "Why?"

"Well, last Thanksgiving was kind of hard on me. Here I had invited a fellow, a good friend of mine, to come have Thanksgiving with us. He's a hard worker, has his own business. Maybe he's a bit down on his luck, but so'm I. He's had a bigger day than I, 'cause he's been a champion roper. Anyway, I think I'm doing pretty good to have this good friend to my home for Thanksgiving. Then Missy turns up and tells me that he's nothing more than a broken-down, has-been worm."

Murray was silent. The toothpick was still.

"I don't want to hear her call you a worm again this year," Spider said quietly.

Murray rolled down the window. "Missy won't be coming." He spat out the toothpick.

Spider nodded. Murray rolled the window back up, and they rode without speaking.

There wasn't a cloud anywhere. The air was so clear that the dun-colored mountains in the distance were crisp, spiky cutouts against a brilliant blue background. The afternoon sun etched a small shadow under each sage bush, setting it in relief, distinguishing it from the like-colored soil. Spider breathed a big sigh. Right at this moment everything was defined. Right now there were no subtleties. Even though they were on the part of the road that wasn't maintained, the tracks were visible, and the little gullies, carved by the last rainfall, were sharply outlined and easy to see.

Spider bumped slowly over an eroded spot and then pointed. "Delmar ahead," he said. "See, on that little rise?"

"We're still a ways away."

Spider glanced at his odometer. "Another couple miles, I think. It's longer this way than cutting across like we did that time."

"I was just thinking about that. I haven't been to Delmar since then. How old were we, thirteen? Fourteen?"

"Musta been. We had just graduated from eighth grade."

"Yeah. We were pretty hot stuff."

"Old enough to take a pack horse and ride out camping for four days by ourselves."

"But young enough to play good guys and bad guys in the street."

"Well, what's a fellow to do?" Spider said. "We rode in and it looked just like *High Noon.*"

"What was that guy's name that went with us? Tommy? Tony?"

"Toby. Toby Bradshaw."

"Yeah," Murray mused. "He moved away the next year."

"Toby Bradshaw. I haven't thought about him in years. Now that I think about it, I'm still mad about how he never would die when we'd yell, 'Got ya.'"

"Nope, he was pretty much immortal. You couldn't kill him."

"But he fancied he was a crack shot. You could be behind something that was absolutely bulletproof with your head down, and he'd think he'd killed you. I mean, there wasn't a chance."

"Yeah, old Toby," agreed Murray. "I never much liked him after that."

"Well, a person needs to die when they're shot."

They were close enough now that the rusted tin roofs and weathered-gray walls of the ghost town could be made out distinctly. There were perhaps a dozen buildings, facing each other across a main street.

"Will you look at that," breathed Murray. "It don't look a bit different than last time we was here. How long ago was that?"

"About thirty, thirty-two years. Still looks like Gary Cooper's gonna come walking up through that main street."

"Yeah, he's gunning for Toby Bradshaw, I guess."

Spider pulled up at the end of the street and parked the cruiser beside the last building on the north side. "Sure looks lonesome."

As if on cue, the wind whined through a crack where Murray hadn't rolled up the window tightly, and a tumbleweed rolled across in front of them.

"You sure anyone lives here, Spider? Who'd want to live here? I'll bet no one's lived here since the mines closed back in the thirties."

Spider pulled the summons from behind the visor. "Addison Haverman III lives here. At least that's what it says on this summons."

"Who's the summons from?"

"Las Vegas Municipal Court. Law offices of Jonas R. Vantage are after him about something."

"So it's not somebody that's on the dodge? It's not the law that's after him? He's not a criminal?"

"Not that I know. I think it's a civil matter. I just serve the summons. All I have to do is hand it to him."

"Well, I tell ya, Spider. This is a mighty lonesome place to be walkin' down the street, all exposed, lookin' for some guy."

"Just call me Coop."

"I'm coming with you."

"Naw. I'm fine."

Spider got out of the cruiser, and Murray got out too. They both instinctively closed their doors quietly and spoke softly.

"I'm gonna poke around in one or two of these old buildings," said Murray. "Call me if you need me."

Spider nodded and walked to the middle of the dusty street. The buildings on both sides were single story and frame. Wind-blown sand had erased all identities. The glassless windows looked like vacant, staring eyes. *Like Alzheimer's,* thought Spider. A grating squeal behind made Spider whirl, but it was only Murray forcing a door on rusty hinges. He spread his hands and hunched his shoulders in apology, and Spider waved "no matter." He looked for the cruiser, but it was hidden behind the building.

Willing away the prickly feeling at the back of his neck, Spider let his gaze wander slowly down Murray's side of the street. At the end, a wispy shred of curtain hung limply at a window and was stirred by a breeze passing through from the dim interior. There was no other movement. No sign of life.

Whistling tunelessly through his teeth, Spider strolled on. On examination, the other side of the street seemed just as lifeless as the first. Vacant windows. Doors hanging awry on broken hinges. Stillness.

Right in the middle of the street, though, was a tiny shop with windows intact. Ralph W. Meyer, it said on the window. Assayer.

As Spider headed toward Mr. Meyer's establishment, a figure stepped close to the window and stared out.

Neck prickles returned.

The figure at the window was a man. He had a dark halo of long, curly hair. And he was holding a shotgun.

"Addison Haverman III, I presume," Spider muttered as he stepped up on the boardwalk. He glanced around but saw no sign of Murray. The man at the window had disappeared.

Spider knocked at the door. Immediately it swung open and Spider found himself staring into a pair of brilliant blue eyes. The eyes belonged to a young man of about thirty years. He was dressed in jeans and a tan canvas shirt. At his waist was a heavy, turquoise-encrusted, silver belt buckle. His watchband was an ornate turquoise-and-silver bracelet. That, and the shotgun, cocked and cradled in his right elbow, were at variance with his fine-chiseled features. The brow, the cheekbones, the jaw—even the long mass of curly hair—reminded Spider of pictures in his mother's Bible.

"Uh, good afternoon." Spider tried for a brisk, professional approach. "I'm Deputy Sheriff Spider Latham. Are you Addison Haverman the third?"

The eyes remained fixed on Spider's, and a smile of calm sweetness curved the mouth. Spider tried to relax, realizing that his breathing was shallow. He took a deep breath. "Mr. Haverman?" he asked again.

"Yes. I'm Addison Haverman." The voice was soft and uninflected.

"I have something for you." Spider held out the summons.

The burning blue eyes stayed locked on Spider's face. The sweet smile still softened the mouth. Addison Haverman stood as still and unmoving as the ghost buildings around him.

Spider began to feel uncomfortable under the relentless light of those eyes. He glanced over his shoulder. No Murray.

"Um. I'm here to serve you with this paper." He held it up, hoping to snare Mr. Haverman's attention away from his face.

The eyes were still locked onto his own. The smile and voice were still calm and pleasant. Addison Haverman made no move to take the summons. "There is a higher law than Jonas R. Vantage's law," he said.

"We all operate under Nevada state law. I'm here to give you this paper."

Silence. Stillness. Nobody moved.

Spider dropped the crisp white document. The noise it made as it hit the dusty gray boardwalk cracked through the air. "You've been served."

Spider turned and walked to the edge of the boardwalk, wondering where Murray was. Just as he stepped down into the street, a shotgun blasted behind him. Diving for the dirt, Spider rolled to the boardwalk for protection, swearing at himself because his gun was locked in the glove compartment of his car, a hundred feet away.

But he had no need for either a gun or cover. Peeking up over the boardwalk, Spider saw Addison Haverman III standing as before with the shotgun in the crook of his arm and a half-smile on his lips.

Slowly Spider stood. He dusted himself off. The summons had disappeared, along with the part of the boardwalk where it had lain.

"Who said that matter can neither be created nor destroyed?" the younger man asked conversationally.

"I don't have the faintest idea," Spider answered tersely, keeping his eyes on the gun.

"He was wrong."

Spider glanced down at the hole in the weather-beaten decking at the young man's feet. He looked up the street, at the abandoned buildings with vacant windows and sagging doors, and down, at the tumbleweeds piled eight feet high at the end of the street. Finally he met those intense blue eyes. "You know, Addison, you can't do that," he said.

"I did it, though."

"Yeah, well, I could charge you with—" here Spider vowed to spend more time in his Triple L notebook—"reckless, uh . . . reckless endangerment. I'm not going to. The papers have been served. What you choose to do about it is up to you."

"What papers?" Addison asked innocently. "I don't see any papers."

At that moment, the cruiser came roaring around the corner of the building with Murray at the wheel. Skidding to a stop, he popped the passenger door open. Spider, trying to maintain a hasty dignity, got in. As Murray sped away, Spider watched in the passenger side mirror. The figure in the doorway was as still as a painting.

They reached the end of the street, and Murray did a full power drift, turning back toward the road home. With both hands on the wheel, he stared grimly ahead as they bounced over the dirt track. "Is he following?"

"Naw, I don't think so. What's he got to follow us in?"

"There was a pickup parked out back. I saw it through the window of one of the other buildings."

"Huh." Spider turned around and watched for a moment. "Naw. I don't think he's coming after us. He wasn't shooting at me, anyway."

"I didn't see him fire the shot. I was in the store right across from you when he opened the door. As soon as I got a load of that shotgun, I went out the back and around to the car. I thought maybe you'd have a rifle or something in here."

"There's a pistol locked in the glove compartment."

"Handy."

Murray stopped the car, and he and Spider changed places. Both of them looked at Delmar more than once as they walked around the car.

"Thanks, Mur," said Spider, as they continued at a less punishing pace.

"Well, I didn't do anything."

"Oh, I don't know. I see you washed the windows."

"Oh, yeah. I grabbed that lever. I thought it was the gearshift. I'm used to it being on the steering column."

"I always say there's nothing like a hero who has presence of mind to wash the windows in a crisis."

"Yeah. Well, you know me. I'll bet old Toby wouldn't have remembered to do that, if he'd been here."

"I was sure wishing for some of Toby's immortality, back there."

"Yeah. Immortality's good."

"Old Toby. I never liked him much after that. But he sure had the right idea."

16

THE NEXT MORNING, TUESDAY, Spider woke early, jerked suddenly from a dream where he was all alone in a deserted city. He blinked twice, grateful to find himself in familiar surroundings, and lay cocooned in blankets up to his ears until the feelings of despair and abandonment ebbed away. Laurie lay beside him. He couldn't see her, turned away as he was, but he heard her rhythmic breathing and felt the comfort of her presence. Unwilling to disturb her, he lay still, watching through half-opened eyes as the sun painted the west wall of the bedroom a cheery golden color.

"Spider?" It was Laurie, speaking his name in a sleepy voice. "You're awake. I can tell."

"Yeah, I'm awake."

She moved over and curled against him, putting an arm around his waist and tucking her hand under him. He felt her cheek against his back. "Good morning," she whispered.

"Good morning, Darlin'."

"Did you sleep all right?"

"Yeah. You?"

"Like a rock. I just now woke up."

Silence. Then, "Spider?"

"Yeah?"

"You haven't mentioned your visit with your mother. I've been waiting for you to say something about it. What did you think?"

"What did *you* think?" he countered.

"Well, I don't know." She sighed, and Spider felt the tickle of her breath across his back. "Sometimes she seemed like nothing was different. And others . . . I don't know. She must have asked me where Bobby was fourteen times. She had it in her mind that he was at Scout camp. 'So, is Bobby at Scout camp?' she'd say. And she'd ask about Dad. I felt funny telling her over and over that he was dead. I finally just started saying he was fine. Then every now and then, she'd remember that she had asked that question before, and she'd get embarrassed. I felt so sorry for her."

"Yeah, it was a different day. Sometimes I felt like we were in the Twilight Zone."

"What do you mean?"

"It was like we were slipping back and forth through time. At least she was—like she had stepped through into another dimension where time flowed back and forth like a tide. One minute she'd be talking to me like it was now, and the next minute it was like I was my father and it was forty years ago. Here she'd be telling me the history of the Dixie mission or quoting scripture, and yet she couldn't remember that I was deputy sheriff. It was weird."

127

"I know. And she never called me by name. She spoke to me, and remembered things we had done. But she never said my name."

Spider rolled over on his back and spread his arm so Laurie could come lie against him with her head on his shoulder. The familiar scent of her hair and the fit of her body comforted him, and he drew her in close. "She said my name," he said with a bleak little laugh. "She told me things that she had done with Spider when he was a little boy."

"How did that make you feel?"

Something in Laurie's voice made him pull away so he could look at her. She turned her face up to him, and he saw that her eyes were moist. He sank back against the pillow and tightened his arm around her, and after a moment he replied, "I felt kind of . . . displaced."

They both lay lost in their own thoughts, and it was Laurie who finally broke the silence. "Well, you can see a little of what Debbie is talking about."

"Yeah."

"That's not a very positive 'yeah,'" she said. "Where are you going?"

"I've got to get up. I've got lots to do today."

Laurie pulled the covers that Spider had thrown off back around her shoulders and regarded her husband from her pillow. "So you're just going to abandon me? No more cuddle time?"

"Nope."

"And you're not going to answer me?"

"Answer you what?" Spider had his pants on and was tucking in his shirttail.

"I said, you can see what Debbie is talking about, can't you?"

Spider sat down on the edge of the bed to pull on his boots. "I can't see why she's so angry," he said. "Yesterday with Mom was a tremendous experience for me. She told me things I had no idea of. Things about Dad. Things about the gospel. I've spent hours thinking about the things she said to me." He stood up to stomp his second boot on and went to the dresser to get his wallet and change and put his watch on his wrist. "What is there to make Debbie so angry? When she came by to pick Mom up she could hardly even look at her. She orders her around and treats her like a disobedient child."

"Maybe she acts like a disobedient child sometimes. You forgot your badge."

"I'll wear it if I go out. I'm just going to be digging out in the wash today."

"You need to remember that you had your mother for one day, Spider. In fact, you only spent half the day with her. I had her the other half. You can't judge Deb until you've walked a mile in her shoes."

"Technically," Spider said, stepping into the bathroom and closing the door.

"No 'technically' about it," Laurie called to the closed door.

When Spider emerged from the bathroom, Laurie was dressed in jeans, a long-sleeved flannel shirt, and running shoes. She was just finishing making the bed. "No 'technically' about it," she said again as she tucked the bedspread under the pillows.

"What?"

"I said you can't judge Debbie, and you said 'technically.'"

And I'm just saying there's no 'technically' about it. Period. You can't, Spider."

"Yeah, well . . ." Spider headed down the hall.

Laurie followed him to the kitchen. "I think we need to talk about it some more."

"About what?" He went onto the service porch.

"About your mother, and the whole situation. Maybe we need to think about having her come here and stay with us. If it is Alzheimer's, the time will come when she won't be able to be home alone."

"But that would be making her your responsibility. She's Deb's and mine."

Laurie walked to the door of the service porch. Spider had his jacket on and was just taking his hat from the peg by the door. "Don't you want breakfast?" she asked.

"I'm not hungry."

"You will be. Wait here." She was gone just a moment, coming back with some leftover rolls from dinner the night before. Handing them to him she said, "Deb has to work and support her family. Listen, Spider, you need to think about this."

Spider took the bag of rolls and then put on his hat. "I don't know if I can bear to think about my mother having Alzheimer's," he said. "I'm going out to the wash. I'll be in for lunch."

Laurie had such a troubled look on her face that he paused to touch her cheek. "We'll work it out," he said gently.

Then he was out the door and down the steps, thinking that his life had become a set of Chinese puzzles. "And I never much cared for puzzles," he muttered. "What a deal."

17

AT MIDDAY SPIDER RETURNED, bear hungry. The aroma of corn bread and beans greeted him. "Smells good," he called as he hung up his jacket.

"It's ready."

Spider washed his hands at the sink and glanced at the pile of papers surrounding Laurie at the table. "What're you doing?"

"I'm filling out the Publisher's Clearinghouse Sweepstakes. If you don't order anything, you have to do something different each time when you enter. I've got to find the stamp that has the gold ring on it and paste it here on this card. Then I have to send it to a different address."

"That's gambling, you know."

"It's not. It's just filling in forms and sending them in."

"It's hoping for something for nothing. You're the one who wouldn't play a slot machine if her life depended on it."

Laurie moved the jumble of perforated pages to the counter and began to dish up the beans. "Well, I figure they're going to give the money to someone, and my name might as well be in the pot."

"No one ever wins any money."

"Oh yes, they do. My cousin's friend in a ward down in Phoenix knew a family who won."

"Yeah, it's always a cousin's friend's brother's acquaintance that those kinds of things happen to. What's this? Pepsis? I thought you weren't going to get any Pepsis until I got paid."

"I saw Bud in town this morning, and he paid me for that help I gave him last week with his calves. You want to pray?" She sat opposite Spider at the table and bowed her head while he asked a blessing on the food. Then she continued, "You've been having a hard time of it. I thought it would brighten your week."

"Thanks. It does. Did you tell Bud you didn't expect to be paid?"

"Sure I did. Especially since he's said I can put the heifers in with his bull. But he says he's short a hand and appreciated the help. And," she smiled, "he says I'm worth any two cowhands when it comes to vaccinating. So he figures he got a bargain."

"Dang right he did! You're worth any two when it comes to just about anything to do with cattle."

"It's in the genes, I guess. My daddy was just about the best there was. Corn bread?"

"Thanks. Well, the cattle genes didn't seem to come out in the kids. There's Bobby working in some high-rise office, and Kevin's out in the jungle looking for buried treasure. You got any jam?"

"He's an archeologist," Laurie corrected, sitting down with the jam jar and pushing it over to Spider, "more likely to find potsherds than treasure. And watching you this last few days makes me wonder what you've passed on to him, genetically. Seems to me you've been doing some of the same kinds of things down in the wash that he's doing in Chiapas."

"I read his textbooks." Spider smiled in spite of a mouthful. "And I listened when he talked about it. I may be dumb, but I'm not stupid. I can learn."

They ate for a while in silence, and then Laurie said, "Bud mentioned he saw you down in the wash again this morning. He asked me what you were doing down there."

"Did he say how he came to see me?" Spider was suddenly serious.

"He was on his way out to see Murray about having him build a reservoir, and he happened to be at that one spot on the bridge where you can see down the wash, and he happened to be looking, and you happened to be there. The three-wheeler is red. Maybe it caught his eye. It was a coincidence. Had to be."

"What did you tell him?"

"I said I didn't have any idea what you were doing, which has a grain of truth to it, because I've tried to stay out of your way."

"Only occasionally offering suggestions."

"And there's another grain of truth."

"So, what else did Bud say? That's the second time he's seen me down there. He seems to go out of his way to let me know it."

"His interest is natural. After all, it's Hughes land."

"Yeah. But I'd just as soon nobody knew I was down there

till I know just a little bit more what I'm dealing with. I imagine he told Murray. No telling who else he mentioned it to. It'll probably be all over the county. You want a glass of milk? No, don't get up. I'll get it."

Laurie regarded Spider. "So, what do you think about what we talked about this morning?"

Spider was at the refrigerator pouring milk from a plastic pitcher. "If we can afford a Pepsi every now and then, does that mean we're going to be able to buy real milk soon?"

"We're going to have to. I've only got one more can of powdered milk in our food storage. In fact, I'm about out of everything. It lasted just long enough."

"And you think if we'd had a little less food storage, maybe I'd have gone back to work sooner?" Spider sat down with his milk.

"You can joke about it if you want, but it's serious business for me. I feel uncomfortable that we've let it get down so low."

"Well, honey, of course it's down low. We've been living on it for over a year."

"You're not answering me."

"What was the question again?"

"I was asking about your mother. What we talked about this morning. What do you think?" She gathered dishes from the table and put them in the dishwater.

"I'd like to hear what you've been thinking," he said. "You got something on your mind?"

"Well, I think it'd be hard for your mother to leave the kids," she said. "That's all she talked about all afternoon. She must have told me fifteen times that Patty got the lead in the school play. And ten times each she said Patty was a hard worker, she was really growing up, and she was such a love." Laurie counted them off on her sudsy fingers.

"And?"

"And what?"

"You sound put out at Mom. This morning you were saying she should come here to live. Now you act like you have a problem with her repeating herself." Spider smiled to soften the accusation, but Laurie had her back turned.

"Did I sound put out?" She let out the water and turned around. "It wasn't that. I think it was . . ."

"What?"

"Well, I think it was that she didn't even ask about Kevin. I showed her pictures of him at his dig and told her how much he loved it. She said, 'That's nice,' like I was talking about a stranger." Laurie shook her head.

"Yeah, yesterday was quite the day."

"It was an unsettling day."

"Yeah, but . . ." Spider paused.

"But what? What? Tell me. You've got that self-satisfied look on your face. What?"

"Well, sit down."

"Why?"

"Sit down. I can't talk about this with you hovering over me with a dish towel draped over your shoulder."

Laurie didn't remove the dish towel, but she sat expectantly across the table from Spider, hands folded. The crinkles at the corners of his eyes told her how much he was enjoying her suspense. "Spider . . . " she said warningly.

"All right," he said. "It's about Grace."

"Oh, Spider!" she breathed. "Did you talk to your mom about her?"

"Yes, I did."

"And?"

The grin that Spider had been trying to restrain finally broke through. "It's not a woman. Mom has been talking about the grace of God, and how much Dad loved the principle."

"No!" Laurie sat back for a moment, trying to remember all that had been said about the subject. "Debbie said he loved Grace. Grace gave meaning to his last years. He spoke of Grace on his deathbed. Oh, Spider!" She laughed outright. "What a mix-up! Really? Are you sure?"

"Yeah. And I've been doing a lot of thinking about it," he indicated the direction of the wash with his thumb, "while I've been out there digging. Tell me what you know about grace."

"What I know about grace? Let's see." Laurie put her elbows on the table and propped her chin on the heel of her hands. She stared out the window at her heifers, walking single file in to water. "Well . . ."

The telephone rang.

Spider tipped his chair back and snared the receiver off the hook in a long-armed reach. "Hello. . . . Oh, hello, Ethan. Yeah, I'm the new deputy. What can I do for you?"

The chair came back down foursquare, and Spider listened intently, rubbing the palm of his hand along his jaw line. "And what's she doing now?"

Spider frowned. Finally he said, "All right, Ethan. I'll come right now. See you in ten minutes."

He stood to replace the receiver and stayed so long like a statue with his hand still grasping the instrument that Laurie asked, "What's the matter?"

"What? Oh, Uncle Oliver is drunk again and Aunt Lola is

upset. She's chasing him around the place threatening to break his legs so he can't go out to The Junction anymore."

"My goodness! Could she do that? Would she do that?"

"Well, when you think that she outweighs him by about a hundred pounds, maybe she could. Ethan says she's got a two-by-four, and that last time they had a set-to she gave Uncle Ollie a concussion. I'd better go."

"Yes, you'd better. Don't be standing around talking. That poor man!"

Before he left, Spider took time to go to the bedroom and get something out of his top dresser drawer. He stashed it in his shirt pocket, buttoning the flap as he strode out to the cruiser. Grateful that Murray had graded the gravel road, he clipped along, slowing only to check for traffic at the highway. He didn't stop, but turned toward Panaca and pushed the accelerator to the floor. Spider wondered if he should turn on the siren. He decided not.

Just outside the town limits, where the highway from Utah tees into Highway 93, there is a gas station and tavern. Liquor is not allowed in the town of Panaca, nor is gambling. Both can be found a mile away at the ramshackle, thirties-vintage den of iniquity called The Junction.

Spider slowed at the intersection, turned, and drove into Panaca at a pace that would not excite attention. Two blocks down the first street to the left was Ethan Walters' place, a small frame house gone slightly to seed and set in a yard that knew not the pruner's shears. As soon as Spider pulled up, the front door opened and Jessie Walters came down the walk. Fortyish, she was tall and willowy, with ginger hair curling halfway down her back. She wore a long skirt of flowing, autumn-colored fabric that rustled in the leaves scattering the walkway. Her top was a turquoise T-shirt with raw edges showing on the scoop neck that she had cut. A heavy silver pendant matched dangling silver earrings.

"Hello, Spider. Welcome to Family Circus."

"Ethan called me. Said there was a domestic squabble. Is it still going on?"

"Yes, listen." She pointed to the back and led Spider along an overgrown flagstone path.

He could hear the shouting, but could see nothing because Ethan's studio blocked his view. Ethan himself stepped through the doorway as Spider approached.

"Thanks for coming, Spider. I didn't want to get mixed up in the fracas. Last time I tried to intervene, she took after me." He led the way around a leggy rosebush to the back of his lot.

Spider had a ringside view through the hog-wire fence that separated the Walters and the Wentworth properties. In the neighboring backyard, a bald-headed, bandy-legged, skinny bit of an old man was cornered by gray-haired Two-Ton Tessie in a pink print housedress. She had a six-foot two-by-four in her hands. For the moment, she was wielding only her tongue, cataloging for the neighborhood the sorrows that forty-five years of marriage to a hopeless drunk had brought her.

"So, how would Tharon handle this?" Spider asked softly. "Would he haul her in?"

"No. He usually just gave them a lecture. This doesn't happen often. They live on Social Security. There's not a lot left over to spend at The Junction."

Just at that moment, Oliver turned and scrambled over the fence. He was spry and quick, and once over, he stood at the far end of the Walters' backyard and grinned foolishly at his mate.

"Don't you smirk at me, you drunken old spendthrift!" she hollered. "That was my new Sunday dress you drank up at The Junction." She tossed her two-by-four over the fence and began to haul herself up. The squares of hog wire bent into diamonds with her weight.

"My fence," Ethan groaned.

Oliver still remained, grinning crookedly, impervious to the lashing tongue.

Lola put one leg over the fence and found a foothold on the other side. Her pink flowered skirt hiked up, revealing a fat thigh.

"My goodness!" breathed Jessie.

As Lola descended, still scolding, the fabric of her skirt hung up on a nail, and the hem rose to her waist, pinning her to the fence. She bent over to unhook it. White underwear, stretched tight across her broad beam, reflected the sun as she continued her tirade, bottomside up.

Jessie, Ethan, and Spider stood transfixed by the sight, but Oliver was galvanized into action. Picking up the two-by-four, he swung it in a mighty arc and whacked his dearly beloved across the target she presented. She straightened up and howled. Oliver threw the two-by-four in the air in a joyous, abandoned gesture of triumph. Then he began a hasty, prancing exit. Knees high, arms pumping, he looked like a jubilant, geriatric drum major as he double-timed through the back corner of the Walters' lot to the vacant field beyond.

Lola stood by the fence, finally silent. Her face was red, but she had ripped her skirt off the snag, and her hem was in its proper place. The two-by-four lay where it had landed, back in her own yard.

"I believe that's your cue," murmured Ethan. He ducked back into his studio, followed by his wife.

"Great Suffering Zot," muttered Spider. "I don't want to do this." He put his hands in his pockets and strolled across the lawn, scuffing through a patch of crunchy yellow elm leaves. "Afternoon, Aunt Lola. Um . . . can I help?"

She was weeping. Shoulders sagging, arms hanging down, her hurt was as quiet and still as her anger had been dynamic.

Spider put an arm around her shoulders and held her. He leaned his cheek against her wiry gray hair and said nothing. After a moment, he fished his handkerchief out of a back pocket and offered it. Lola took it and wiped her eyes and blew her nose. "That old fool," she whispered.

"Are you all right?"

He felt her head move against his shoulder as she nodded.

"Do you want me to go get him, haul him in for assault?"

"He didn't hurt me. I'd a hurt him worse if I'd a got ahold of him. Much to my shame."

"Here. Let me help you to your house. Let's go make sure you're all right."

Aunt Lola drew away from him. "I'm plenty all right, Spider Latham. Just you mind your own business. I'm going to go in now and scrub my floor and start dinner. When that old coot comes home, he'll be hungry." She thrust the wadded-up handkerchief back at Spider. Then she turned and stalked off along the fence line.

Spider watched Aunt Lola's sturdy bulk until she disappeared around an ornamental pine tree at the edge of her lot. He shrugged. Then he stuffed his handkerchief back in his pocket and strolled back to the Walters' studio.

Jessie and Ethan were silversmiths. They worked in an old

double-walled adobe food storage building—locally called a cellar, even though it stood above ground. They had finished the interior in board and bat scavenged from a derelict barn. Skylights and a French door opened up the windowless building to winter sunshine or the summer greenery of a giant, sheltering elm. In the corner sat a nickel-plated wood stove that had come off an old caboose. Summer or winter, the room was a pleasant retreat.

Both Jessie and Ethan still trailed the aura of the hippies they had been during the early seventies. He wore Levi's and a blue denim shirt, cowboy boots and a silver pendant on a rawhide strip. His salt-and-pepper hair was clubbed back in a ponytail that reached past his shoulders. He had a cookie-duster mustache and a small silver hoop in his left ear. A serious scholar, he had one degree in archeology and another in anthropology from the University of California at Berkeley.

Ethan's return to his Mormon roots came through a dedicated home teacher who had turned up on Ethan's doorstep each month for the ten Berkeley years. Brother Clayton was middle-aged and ex-Navy enlisted. He had nothing in common with the free spirits who occupied the tumbledown cottage in the Berkeley hills. But he visited faithfully and prayed for them. He fixed their leaky pipes and rewired their kitchen. He blessed their babies and stood up with them as the bishop of the Berkeley Tenth Ward married them in their backyard. He ordained Ethan an elder and stood as witness as Ethan baptized Jessie. And finally, he helped them pack their belongings in their aging VW bus and waved good-bye at five in the morning as they headed back to Utah.

That was ten years ago. They made it as far as Panaca before the bus broke down. The bus got fixed, but somehow they never left Panaca.

Spider stepped into the sunny studio. Jessie looked up from the wax she was carving, and Ethan turned off his propane torch. "How's it going?" he asked.

Spider took off his hat and set it on the corner of the workbench. "Aunt Lola's gone to fix dinner. Said Uncle Ollie would be hungry when he got back."

"She's a good soul." Jessie put down her project and started shelving her tools.

"Well, so is Ollie," said Ethan. "I don't think we could have a better neighbor."

Jessie sighed. "She just grieves, I know, because his drinking keeps him out of the temple."

"Well, he was drinking when she married him," Spider said, unbuttoning his shirt pocket. "I don't think she can hold it against him that he wouldn't change."

"Whatcha got there?" Ethan took the ring that Spider fished out of his pocket and held out to him.

"I wonder about that ring, Ethan. Anything you can tell me about it?"

"Like what?"

"Oh, where it was made, maybe? Who made it? I don't know. Just thought I'd take an outside chance."

Ethan turned on a bright swing-arm lamp and adjusted it. He put on magnifying goggles and peered intently at the ring. Jessie hovered over his shoulder. When he was finished, he handed it to her and slipped from the stool so she could sit and use the light.

"It's really a very nice piece," Ethan said. "Probably Navajo, though there are lots of smiths who do work in the Navajo tradition. I've even tried a piece or two. What makes me think it *is* Navajo is the mark on the inside. Looks like it's been left as pawn at a trading post. Navajos do two kinds of work: fabricated and sand cast. This is fabricated. It's finer than the sand cast. Lighter, finer finish. Rings aren't usually sand cast."

"What does the sand cast silver work look like?"

"Well, as I said, it's not so fine. The turquoise is larger, more lumpy looking. You've seen Bud Hefernan's watchband. That's a good example of Navajo sand cast. Has the big, lumpy turquoise."

"I haven't seen Bud's watchband. He has a turquoise watchband?"

"Yeah. He brought it to me to repair. When was it, Jessie? Sometime last spring, I guess."

"Where did he get it?" Spider asked.

"Said he'd had it for a while. Didn't wear it because it was broken. He had a Navajo cowboy work for him, and he bought it from him, I think. Though somehow I can't see Bud investing in jewelry for himself."

"Oh, I think he said it was a gift from the cowboy, wasn't it?" Jessie offered. "Something about taking the cowboy's son to the hospital and making sure he got proper care—I don't know. Bud isn't one to boast of his good deeds."

"I must not have been there when he said that. I was working on the watchband. I fixed it right then, and he took it with him."

"I don't suppose you could draw for me what it looked like. I'd like to get an idea of what the sand cast silver looks like."

"I'll do better than that. I've got a picture of it."

"Of the watchband?"

"Yeah. It was a tricky piece of work, fixing it. There was

some inlay work close to the clasp, and the whole clasp had been ripped off. There's always a danger, when you solder close to inlay, that the metal will expand and you will lose the stone, have to re-inlay the whole thing. I felt good about what I had done, and I took a picture."

"Can I see it?"

Ethan turned to look at Jessie, who sat with goggles pushed up on her forehead. She wrinkled her brow. "What do you think?" she asked, looking at Ethan. "Hefernan?"

"Watchband? Turquoise? Broken Clasp? What would we have filed it under?" Ethan opened the top drawer of a battered filing cabinet.

"Maybe *M* for Miracle. I really didn't think you were going to be able to save the inlay. If it's not under *H* for Hefernan, try *I* for Inlay."

"Give the lady a prize. *I* for Inlay." Ethan laid a glossy close-up photo on the table.

Spider examined the picture. "Huh. Tell me this, Ethan. Do you see much stuff like this around here—I mean lumpy watchbands and belt buckles?"

"Around Lincoln County?"

"Yeah."

"Uh-uh. You might see some in Vegas. The place you're going to see lots of them is in Scottsdale or Sedona, down in Arizona. Someplace where there's lots of money and where the Navajo presence is stronger. Good stuff like this doesn't come cheap."

"Well, I don't know that I've ever seen a single watchband, and here, two days running, I've seen two. That sound like a coincidence to you?"

"Not if you're talking to a silversmith and asking about Navajo jewelry."

Spider picked up the picture and examined it closely. "You say the clasp was broken off? What happened?"

"Bud didn't say. It would have taken quite a bit of force to have ripped it apart like it was. It was torn from here to here. You can barely make out how I've put it back together. See that faint line there? The slight discoloration?"

"Huh." Spider picked up the ring. "Any similarity between that work and this ring?"

"They're both Navajo. From the same smith? I don't think so. Because of the pawn marking, I'd say the ring is older. It's only lately that you find inlay in Navajo work. But I think the turquoise is from the same mine. I would say it's Morenci turquoise. They're both very nice pieces of jewelry. Where did you get the ring?"

"It's, ah, sheriff department stuff. Department wanted me to find out more about it. I figured since I was here anyway, I'd ask you about it. Since I'm here on, ah, sheriff department stuff, anyway."

"Well, mine is certainly not an expert opinion. If you want me to give you the name of someone who can give you one, I will."

"Naw. I appreciate your taking the time to look at it." Spider put the ring back in his shirt pocket and picked up his hat.

"Thanks for coming so quickly when we called." Ethan held open the door for Spider and then followed him out. "How's your case of the lady in the desert coming? Find out who she was?"

"Haven't a clue."

"Sheriff still out of the county?"

"Yeah."

"Is that good or bad?"

Spider laughed and shook his head, but he didn't answer.

They paused at the front-yard gate. "How's seminary going?" Spider asked Ethan.

"I've got a good class this year. A good bunch of kids. We're studying New Testament." Ethan put his arm around Jessie, who had drifted up beside him.

"Let me ask you a question about doctrine." Spider studied the toe of his boot and then looked up at Ethan. "What do you think about grace?"

Ethan didn't answer. He stood staring back at Spider while tears filled his eyes, spilled over, and ran down his cheeks.

Spider glanced askance at Jessie, but she was watching Ethan, and she was misty-eyed too.

"Ah," Spider began. "I didn't mean to . . ."

"No, that's all right. I'm still a little tender about this." Ethan pulled out his handkerchief and blew his nose. "Funny you should ask that question. I got a phone call last night . . ." He looked down at Jessie, and she nodded reassuringly.

"I was in a relationship before I met Jessie—I mean, we broke up before I met Jessie. But when we broke up, the girl was pregnant. She left town, and for twenty years I haven't been able to find a trace of her. And then, last night I got a phone call from my daughter. I have a daughter, Spider, one I've never seen. She found me, and I have been able to tell her that I tried to find her. I have a chance to build some kind of a relationship with her. To me, that's grace. The consequences of what I did are still there—this girl grew up without a father. But I get this beautiful second chance. I get to rock my grandbabies and teach them to sing 'I Am a Child of God.' That's the grace of God in my life." Ethan blew his nose again.

"I didn't mean to pry, Ethan. I had no idea."

"Oh, I'm making no secret of this. It's a cause for celebration. I'm going to tell my seminary class as soon as I can do it without weeping. I want them to know the pain and suffering that come from disregarding the commandments. That's justice. But I also want them to know about mercy."

Spider offered his hand to Ethan. "I appreciate your telling me. I'll celebrate with you." He patted his pocket. "Thanks for the other help, too. 'Bye, Jessie."

Spider closed the gate behind himself and had just gotten to the bridge over the irrigation ditch when a blue 1975 Oldsmobile drove slowly by. A fragile-looking, silver-haired lady waved from the passenger seat, but the driver stared blankly at Spider.

"Oh, shoot! I forgot about Nephi Wentworth," Spider exclaimed.

"What about him?" Jessie waved to her neighbors as they cautiously rolled over the irrigation culvert and into their drive.

"He can't be driving. He's legally blind."

"Well, it depends on what your definition of *blind* is."

"No, it depends on what the state's definition of *blind* is. He failed his eye test and they yanked his license."

"That's because they kept telling him to put his forehead against the vision tester and look straight into the lenses. If they'd let him turn his head, he might have passed. His peripheral vision is amazing," said Ethan.

"Yes," Jessie added, "and he only drives to take his mother to church and to the store. It's too far for her to walk. He only goes on the back roads. He drives slowly, and his mother warns him of unexpected things."

"And the whole town knows to get out of his way," Ethan summarized.

Spider grimaced. "Yeah. I used to say the same thing. Now I gotta go tell him he can't drive."

"Tharon used to do that, too," said Jessie.

"I'm glad to hear it. Thanks again for your help. I'll see you later."

Spider walked down the path alongside the ditchbank to Nephi Wentworth's place. He opened the gate and strolled up the narrow, aging sidewalk that bisected a well-tended yard. The house was small and freshly painted, with a screened-in front porch sheltering two rattan rocking chairs. Spider opened the screen door on the porch just as Nephi Wentworth opened the front door.

"Afternoon, Spider."

"Afternoon, Brother Wentworth. Can I talk to you for a minute?"

"Sure, sure. Have a seat."

Nephi's eyes were focused on the Walters' gate, but Spider could feel them reading his intentions. He sat and tried to think of a way to say what he was going to say.

Nephi said it for him. "Heard you took Tharon Tate's place. I guess you've come to tell me I can't drive anymore."

"Well, yeah. That's what I've come for."

Nephi turned to face Spider. He was a good-looking man, of medium height and build. At sixty-five his hair was ungrayed, and he had the distinctive bushy black brows and dark eyes of the Wentworth clan. "We go back a ways, don't we, Spider? I remember when you used to drive the tractor when Dad and I were putting up hay out in Plumlee Canyon. How old were you?"

"Probably about eight, I guess."

"And later on, I taught you in high school."

"Yeah. History and English."

The brown eyes were turned back to the Walters' gate. "And I was your bishop when you were a young father. I interviewed both your boys before baptism."

"Yeah. I remember. You asked Bobby if he knew what repentance was. He said it was when you took the bad sins out and put good ones in."

Nephi chuckled. "I had forgotten about that. How is Bobby?"

"He's fine. He's working in Seattle. Computers."

"He's out on his own. That's what happens. Time marches on. You were my bishop when time marched my Julie away from me. Remember?"

"I remember. It was my first funeral. My first . . ." Spider searched for a name to pin on the night he spent with his old teacher watching the vibrant life forces that had driven Julie Wentworth shut down one by one.

"You did fine. And you were there for me when this—" Nephi pointed to his eyes. "When I had my macular occlusions. That was a rough year. I remember you telling me that I had to get on with my life, that I had to figure out a way to cope and live a full life."

"Did I say that?"

"Yes, you did. And it was the kick in the pants that I needed. It was because of what you said to me that I made a deal with my mother. I came back to live with her, and she is the high-definition part of my eyes that I lost. Reading is laborious—I can read very large type if I magnify it, but it's faster if she can read for me. In return, I keep up the house and yard and take her places. It's little enough that I do in return for being able to continue my scholarly activities. Now, Spider, I don't drive for myself. And I don't drive anywhere except to take her to the store or the church or her senior family home evening group. If I didn't do this for her, she wouldn't go, because she's determined she's going to make her own way. You needn't worry. Between the two of us, we can see just fine to drive."

"How old is your mother, Brother Wentworth?"

"She's ninety next month."

"And her eyes are good enough to—"

"Her eyes are good enough to notice half a block away that the word *sheriff* is misspelled on your car."

"Ah, I see. Well, as deputy sheriff, I've got to ask you to stop driving. And then, I've got one more thing to ask you."

"All right."

"Tell me what you understand about the doctrine of grace."

C H A P T E R

18

SPIDER SPENT HALF AN HOUR in Nephi Wentworth's rocking chair. Then he drove home, thinking all the way about the perspective that his old teacher had given him. As he drove by Murray's place, he saw his cousin standing on the bumper of his dump truck, bent over under the opened hood. On impulse, he turned into the drive.

Murray looked up as Spider parked by the truck, but he didn't stop what he was doing. One arm was extended into the bowels of the engine compartment, and the strafing click of a ratchet drifted out.

Spider got out and sauntered over. He leaned against the truck, crossing his arms on the yellow fender and resting his chin on a wrist. He waited for the sound of the ratchet to cease. "Got a problem?"

"Had to replace the starter. Luckily, I was able to get one in

Pioche. I'd a been in the soup if I had to order one. I need the truck tomorrow."

"Oh?"

"Bud wants a tank built on the north part of the range there on the Lazy H. I'm supposed to start in the morning."

"Say, Mur. Have you ever seen Bud wear a turquoise and silver watchband?"

"Bud? I've never even seen him with a wristwatch. He carries a pocket watch."

"Huh. Come to think of it, I guess he does. Well, listen. I want to ask you something else. You remember yesterday when we were out at Delmar?"

Murray climbed down from the bumper and tossed his ratchet into an open toolbox. "Yeah?"

"Do you remember what color that pickup was that you saw?"

"It was a dark color."

"Dark blue? Dark green? Black? Gray?"

"Shoot, I don't know, Spider. I'm color blind."

"You're color blind? I never knew that."

"Neither did I, until a few years ago. It was one of those things I learned about myself after I married Missy."

"Huh. But you know it was a dark color. New or older?"

"I only got a glimpse. I would say not too old—three, maybe four years. Why?"

"Just curious. Wondering about the guy—why he was there, how long he's been there."

"So, what's the color of the pickup got to do with that?"

"Ah, I don't know. I was just curious. I'll tell you another thing I'm curious about: Navajo cowboys. You ever meet any Navajo cowboys?"

"Sure. I met some on the rodeo circuit."

"You ever heard Bud mention a Navajo cowboy who worked for him?"

"Spider, why are you asking all these questions? I don't know the answer to any of them. If you want to know, go ask Bud. He drove by just a while ago. He's either at his range there by your place, or he's parked in your driveway."

"Is that right? Thanks, Mur. I will." Spider slapped the fender of the truck and waved to his friend. Then he got in his cruiser and headed down the gravel road, checking at each gate to see if Bud's pickup had driven off the road onto Hughes rangeland. There were no tracks in the soft desert soil. Bud must be there at his own house. Spider began to wonder how he was going to frame the questions he needed to ask the older rancher.

The only vehicle in Spider's drive was his own pickup. He slowed, considering, but he didn't turn in. He drove half a mile farther to a place where the road topped out on a rise. Hughes rangeland stopped right here. The gravel road fell away, straight and empty, for miles. Then it curved and dropped out of sight on its winding way to Delmar. Spider turned around and drove back to his house.

Laurie was working in the barn when he drove up. She set her tools down and came over to meet him as he got out of the cruiser. "You were gone so long, I began to think Aunt Lola had hurt Uncle Ollie pretty bad."

"No. He smacked her a good one across the backside, but that was the upshot of it."

"He didn't! So what did you do?"

"Wasn't much I could do. She wanted to forget the whole thing. Went to make him dinner. What're you doing out here?"

"Bud brought one of his saddles by for me to repair."

"I stopped at Murray's. He said Bud had come this way, but hadn't gone back."

"No. He went on out toward Delmar. There's some BLM land out there that is going to be available for lease, and he went to check it out." She paused to listen to a ruckus from her chicken pen. "Sounds like I need to feed my hens. They're getting testy."

Spider opened the back door for her and followed her in to the kitchen. "I had an interesting talk with old Nephi Wentworth."

"So that's what took so long! What were you talking about?"

"I asked him what I asked you—asked him about grace. Did you know that grace and works was why old Martin Luther nailed those papers to the church house door?"

Laurie opened the cupboard under the sink and took out her bucket of chicken scraps. "I thought he was protesting the sale of indulgences."

"Well, he was, partly. But it was also because the Catholic Church taught salvation by works, and he believed men were saved by grace alone. Tell me what you know about grace."

"Well, grace is the gift of God to us. It's the Atonement."

"And so it's a gift? It's given without discrimination to all men?"

"And all women? Uh-uh." Laurie shook her head. "Resurrection is. Resurrection comes free to all. But grace is a gift that I think you have to merit in some way. It's like the Publisher's Clearinghouse Sweepstakes—you have to send in the reply and paste on the little stickers where they tell you to in order to be eligible."

"You're saying grace is like a sweepstakes?"

Laurie smiled. "Yeah. But in this one, everyone who pastes on the stickers and mails in the card wins. Wins big."

"But what does he win?"

"She wins," Laurie winked at Spider, "an advocate, someone who will say, 'Heavenly Father, here's Laurie Latham. She tried hard, and was truly sorry for the things she did wrong and for the things she didn't do. She wasn't perfect. But she took my name and truly tried to live up to it. Even though I know that no one can live with you who isn't perfect, let her come and dwell in your kingdom. I'll make up for all that she's lacking.'"

"So, you're saying that we're saved by grace?"

"Yes, of course."

"Well, I'll be!"

"What?"

"So, where did you get that idea?"

"I've always believed it."

"Even though it was never taught in Sunday School and Primary?"

"But it was taught."

"That we're saved by grace?"

"Not in so many words. It wasn't always called grace, but it was the same thing. Why are you smiling like that?"

"I'm just thinking of all the time I spent on my mission, teaching all those folks in Mexico that we're saved by works."

"Oh, but we are!"

"You just said that we're saved by grace."

"Yes, but only after we've pasted on the stamps and sent in the card."

"We weren't allowed to mention the word *grace* on my

mission. I don't ever remember being taught about grace, in all my years in the Church."

Laurie stared out the window. "I think . . ."

"What?"

Laurie set the scrap pail on the counter. "Well, I was trying to remember what my grandma used to say. She was real bent out of shape when my mother joined the Church. And she used to talk to me about Jesus. I don't remember just how it went, but it was something like, grace was given if you accepted Christ as your savior. Then, it was just sort of locked in, and out of your control. It didn't matter what you did after that, you were saved. I asked what would happen if you committed some awful sin. She said that, technically, it didn't matter, though if you had accepted Christ you would just naturally live the very best you could."

"Huh!"

"She and Mom used to go round and round. Mom would say, 'Faith without works is dead,' and Grandma would say, 'For by grace are ye saved through faith; and that not of yourselves: it is the gift of God.' I wonder if the reason we didn't hear grace taught in the Church while we were growing up was because most Protestants believed it, only maybe weighted more on the gift part. So the Brethren and all the missionaries were teaching people who believed in grace alone that works were necessary. And then, when you got a generation or two of just Mormons being taught, all you heard was works."

"Yeah, we're told that we've got to be perfect, and we get to thinking that we can do it ourselves. You know . . ."

"What?"

"Well, I spent the morning shoveling and thinking—"

Spider looked at his watch, "—and I've got to get back to that, but I want to tell you what I've been thinking."

Laurie's eyes crinkled. "Remember, my chickens are waiting."

"You need to teach your chickens that they can't live by bread alone."

"Maybe we should go out to the chicken pen, and you can tell us all what you've been thinking."

"Or, you could invite them in."

"So, tell me what you've been thinking."

"Well, I've been thinking about President Benson preaching that we need to read the Book of Mormon. He's telling us how important it is, saying if we don't do it, we're under condemnation. So, I'm reading the Book of Mormon, and all of a sudden I realize that every time I turn around, here's someone preaching the gospel, and they're going back to Adam."

"What do you mean?"

"Well, think about it. Lehi calls his sons to him, blesses them, and teaches Jacob about the fall of Adam. Then you get Ammon teaching King Lamoni, and where does he start? With the fall of Adam. And Alma and Amulek? Where did they start?"

"With Adam?"

"Bingo. And why?"

"I don't know. But I think I'm about to find out."

"Yes, you are. The fall of Adam—what did it do?"

"Well, it brought death into the world."

"But, what kind of death?"

"Death death. Like the lady in the barn. Death."

"Yes. But it brought spiritual death, too. And what is spiritual death?"

"Is this the crackerjack teacher in operation? I should have invited the chickens in; they would really enjoy this. Spiritual death, she said like a good little student, is separation from God."

"Right! And don't you see? Our condemnation is that we've been going along thinking to ourselves that we can overcome that separation by ourselves, by doing all the things we've been taught—home teaching and attending meetings and going to the temple and keeping our journals and magnifying our callings and going on missions and not speaking evil of the Lord's anointed—"

"And taking care of the poor. It's all important, Spider."

"Yes, it is. But don't you see? The condemnation comes from not knowing that we can't do it alone. The gulf between God and man is too wide for us to build a bridge alone."

"But Spider, that's what we've always believed."

"I'm not explaining this very well. Yes, we've always believed it. But what we've believed was that it was like, we only had to stretch up our hand, because we had climbed up this tremendous mountain that reached almost to heaven, all by ourselves. When, really, we're lucky to stay pointed in the right direction toward the mountain and put one foot in front of another in the journey to get there. The best of us haven't even reached the foothills. The best of us is still on the plain, with just a glimpse of the foothills in sight."

Spider paused, frowning at himself. "Dang. I've never had this kind of trouble getting an idea across. I think . . . I think our condemnation is that we have become too proud of our own abilities. We have equated our efforts as almost equal to those of the Savior's. Boy, does this ever put the Tower of Babel in a new light. I understand now why the Lord was so angry with them."

"You're digressing."

"Since you're not willing to digress with me . . ."

"My chickens, you see. So, with all this thinking you were doing this morning, did you get any work done? Were you thinking and shoveling, or were you leaning on the shovel while you ruminated on all these things?"

"Oh, I got a fair amount of dirt moved."

Laurie picked up the scrap pail again and walked to the doorway of the service porch. Pausing there, she began, "I wonder . . ."

Spider followed her and picked up his gloves from a shelf on the porch. "What do you wonder?"

"Oh, whether you would have discovered this if you hadn't lost your job and been released as bishop so soon?"

Spider paused with one sleeve of his jacket on and regarded his wife. "Huh!" he said, and pulled the other sleeve on. He took time to put on a yellow Caterpillar baseball cap and pull down the brim before he answered. "Maybe not." He grinned. "'*Because ye were compelled to be humble ye were blessed, [but] . . . they are more blessed who truly humble themselves. . . .*' That's me. Compelled to be humble. I'll see you later. If you don't need the truck, I'll take it. I think I'll probably finish the job today. I'll stay with it till I'm done."

Just as Spider stepped out the back door, Bud Hefernan drove by and tooted, on his way back from wherever he had been out toward Delmar.

LAURIE FOUND SPIDER DOWN in the wash at dusk when she rode out to see why he hadn't come in for supper. He was sitting in the pickup, the beam of his flashlight trained on a piece of paper he held in his hand. He looked up as she tapped on his window, and rolled it down so he could talk to her.

"Did you find out who it belongs to?"

"It's registered in the name of Mary Margaret Barnett."

"Mary Margaret Barnett?"

"Yeah."

"Do you know anyone by that name?"

"Uh-uh. Do you?"

"I think so. I don't know. The name is familiar. I've heard it before. I can't put a face to it, though."

"That's because there isn't one."

"Isn't one what?"

"Face." Spider grimaced. "Not anymore, anyway. Mary Margaret Barnett, or whoever was driving her car, is our lodger."

Laurie's eyes grew wide. "Really, Spider? How can you tell?"

"I screened all the dirt that came out of the car and found, among other things, a couple of teeth."

"Teeth?"

"Our lodger is missing her two front teeth. She has other injuries that could mean she was in an accident when she died. And when we found her, she only had on one shoe. I found the mate to it under the seat of the car." Spider held up a mashed and muddy pump.

Laurie held on to the windowsill with white-knuckled hands and regarded her husband. "But Spider . . ."

"Yeah?"

"If she had the accident here, how come she ended up under a pile of rocks five miles away?"

"I don't know."

Laurie looked over her shoulder at the gray Chevette, barely discernible in the darkness. She shivered. "It gives me the creeps," she said. "I'm locking the doors tonight!"

Spider chuckled. "Here, let me get out. I want to show you something."

Laurie stepped away so he could open the door, and as soon as he was out, she moved close to him. He took her hand and led her over to the little crumpled car.

"You see here," he said, shining the light on the front of the car, "It looks like the driver's side took the brunt of the impact, like it hit something pretty hard on the way down. The passenger side took a pretty good hit, too, closer to the door."

"So?"

"Couple of things. First, if I can find what she hit on the

way down—and there's some pretty good rocks on either side of the wash—I can tell what direction she was traveling when she lost it."

"Is that important?"

"Might be."

"But why? If she's on this road, she's coming to see either us or Murray," Laurie said.

"Maybe so. Maybe so. Or someone out at Delmar. Now, come look at this." Spider walked to the back of the car and shone his light on the rear fender, driver's side.

"Look at what?"

"This dent. You see, the front is crumpled up like an accordion, but the back is untouched, except for this."

"So?"

"What made this dent?"

"A rock?"

"I doubt it. If it had been a rock, there would be scratch marks all along the side. This dent is too well defined. It's like someone hit it with a huge square hammer, wham! See? It's a direct blow, not a glancing one. See how well-defined and straight these edges are where it caves in?"

"Maybe she bounced sideways into a rock."

"You'd never get a rock that would make a dent with those sharp, straight edges. Besides, there would have been scratch marks from getting off of the rock."

"So what are you saying?"

Spider traced the impression with his fingers. "I'm not saying, I'm asking. What made this dent?"

"Maybe it's one that was there before. It's not terribly deep. Barely dented at all. Maybe she got it in a supermarket parking lot. Looks like someone caught her with their bumper."

"I don't know. That's a pretty big bumper to make that dent. But, could be. Do you want to drive the pickup in and I'll take the cycle? It's getting pretty cold."

"Yeah, thanks."

They walked to the pickup, and Spider opened the door for Laurie. She climbed in, started the engine, and turned on the lights, but Spider stood with the door in his hand, hesitating.

"What?" Laurie prompted.

"Do you remember last spring when some lady was out from back east talking to the ranchers about letting the rangelands go back to the elk?"

"Yes. Myrna said she's never seen Bud so angry. Why?"

"Do you remember the lady's name?"

"Spider! What are you saying?"

"You said you had heard the name before. Could that be where you heard it?"

Laurie stared at her husband, trying to read his expression by the meager light of the dash. Finally she shook her head. "I don't know. I don't think so. But, I don't know."

"That's all right." Spider shut the door. "I'll follow you home."

The moon was coming up, hanging low over the horizon as two sets of headlights climbed out of the wash, leaving behind the crumpled Chevette, a ghostly gray smudge against the gray riverbank that had lately been its grave.

★   ★   ★

After eating his warmed-over dinner, Spider sat at the kitchen table and read his handbook of procedures. When Laurie came to say she was going to bed, he followed her. He asked her to be voice for family prayer, and afterward was silent

163

and abstracted, sitting on the edge of the bed with one sock in his hand for so long that Laurie finally asked him if anything was the matter.

"No, I'm just thinking." He finished undressing and got in bed. After he turned out his lamp, Spider finally asked the question that had been on his mind. "Laurie? Are you awake?"

"Uh-huh."

"Do you remember what Missy's name was when she came to work at Keystone?"

"Before she married Murray?"

"Yeah."

Silence. Then, "I think it was Martin. I know it went together. Missy Martin. No, that's not right. It was Marlow. Missy Marlow."

"You're sure?"

"Yes."

"What was her real name?"

"What do you mean?"

"Missy wasn't her given name, was it? What was her real name?"

"I don't know. She always introduced herself as Missy. She even signed her checks that way. I always thought it was her real name. Why don't you ask Murray?"

"Maybe I will. Well, good night." Spider turned over and pulled the covers up over his shoulder. He felt Laurie snuggle up behind him, and he pressed the arm that she encircled him with. But long after her rhythmic breathing told Spider she was asleep, he lay staring into the darkness.

SPIDER WAS IN THE bathroom shaving when the phone rang early the next morning. Laurie answered it and called down the hall, "Spider, it's for you. It's Liddy Snow."

Liddy Snow. Liddy Snow. Spider walked, still half lathered, to the kitchen. Who was—oh yes. It was Rose Markey's oldest daughter, a child from the first of her three marriages. Spider remembered doing a bishop's interview when Liddy turned thirteen. That was two years ago. She had sat in his office with her ankles crossed and her clasped hands between her knees, turning an earnest face to him and confiding that, if they all worked together and acted like this marriage would last, then maybe it would.

Laurie's hand was over the mouthpiece. "What do you suppose she wants?" she asked. "A ride to seminary?"

Spider looked at his watch. It was 6:45; the early-morning class had started fifteen minutes ago. "She lives close enough to walk," he said, taking the proffered receiver. "Hello, Liddy. This is Brother Latham."

"Oh, Brother Latham!" The voice began strongly, but was squeezed off into a tight little squeak.

"What's the matter, Liddy?"

Liddy didn't reply right away. Spider knew she was still there because he heard her labored breathing. "I'm scared," she finally managed in a tiny voice.

"Is someone there? Is someone threatening you?" Spider asked, instantly alert.

"No." It was just a whisper.

"Is someone threatening your mother?"

"I don't know."

Trying to modulate his voice so the inching exasperation didn't show, Spider tried again for the right question. "Is your mother there?" Spider hoped that the answer was yes. If not, it would mean she'd been out all night and there was a man involved. Boundaries would have been stretched and more mixed messages semaphored to the children. Well, at least he wasn't the bishop. He wouldn't have to deal with it.

"No," Liddy answered. Rose wasn't there.

Oh dear, Spider thought. "Did she come home last night?"

"I don't know. I don't think so."

"Well, is the bed unmade? Does it look like she slept in it?"

"It's unmade. But Mom never makes her bed, so I don't know. She wasn't home last night when I went to bed."

"And you missed her when she didn't get you up this morning?"

"Oh, Mom never gets me up. She usually sleeps until nine or ten o'clock. No, I was sneaking into her room to borrow one of her blouses, and I noticed she wasn't there."

"Is your car there?"

"We don't have a car. Mom is going to buy one with the insurance money."

"Yeah. I remember now. I tell you what, Liddy. I'll be over in about a half an hour. Are any of the other kids up?"

"They usually get up at seven."

"Then just act like it's a normal day. Don't let them see that you're worried."

"But if it was a normal day, I'd be at seminary."

"Yeah, but your home teacher is coming by—that's me—and wants to talk to you. Don't worry. There's a logical explanation for this, and we'll get it figured out."

Spider listened to her reassured good-bye and hung up. "The logical explanation doesn't take much figuring," he said to himself. "Oh dear, dear, dear, dear, dear."

"What's the matter?" Laurie asked.

"I've been fluffed on again. Is breakfast ready? I need to go right on over there."

"Are you going to finish shaving first?"

Reaching up to feel the lather, Spider said, "Yeah, figured I might," and headed back to the bathroom.

A half hour later found him driving through the Addition, an ambitious housing development built five years before the mines closed. A few of the houses were boarded up, with summer's bumper crop of weeds brown and rattling in the morning breeze. Most houses had been moved out, leaving curving driveways and sidewalks leading up to vacant concrete slabs. Spider always had a vaguely unsettled feeling as he drove through here. It was like hanging around a family party where the invited guests had gone home soon after it started.

Liddy came out on the doorstep as he pulled into the drive

of their bungalow. It was a modest-sized, three-bedroom house. In Vegas or Cedar City the rent would have been triple what Rose paid for this one. He noticed that the house was painted blue and wondered which consideration—color or value—had carried more weight in Rose's decision to live here.

"Morning, Liddy," Spider greeted.

"Good morning, Brother Latham. Is it all right if we talk out here?" She sat down on the top step and patted the place beside her.

From inside came the sounds of children getting ready for school, and it was apparent that they had developed a system of older girls helping younger ones: "Here, Polly, let me brush your hair." "You can't wear that shirt. It's dirty. Here, let me find you a clean one."

Spider looked down at the young lady sitting beside him. She had on too much makeup, and the earrings that dangled from her earlobes would have been more appropriate at a cocktail party. There were seven additional rhinestone studs trailing around the edge of one ear. She sat huddled in a purple windbreaker, with black-stockinged leg and thigh inadequately covered by a blue miniskirt.

"You want to go sit in my car?" he asked. "It's a little chilly out here, don't you think? We can be private there."

"Thanks, but I'd rather stay here. I can keep an eye on the kids. School starts at eight, and sometimes they don't get out of the house in time."

Spider sat. "How do you know, if you're at seminary?"

"Oh, I come home between seminary and school. I have to make sure that Tiffy's fed and dressed too. She watches cartoons until Mom gets up."

"Huh," Spider grunted. "Let's talk about your mom. When did you last see her?"

"At supper time. She wasn't here when I got home from school. But pretty soon she came. Brother Lentz over at the Panaca Emporium brought her in his pickup and delivered a whole lot of groceries she had bought. Boxes and boxes. She bought things that we've never had at our house."

"Things like what?"

"Oh, stuffed olives and artichoke hearts. Grandma has those things at her house sometimes, but we never do."

"Okay. So she shows up with all those groceries, and then what happens?"

"Well, we put the groceries away, and then we fixed supper."

"And how was your mother? Was she happy, or was she sad?"

"She was happy. She was excited."

"What was she excited about?"

"Well, because she got the money from the insurance company."

"She got it already?"

"Day before yesterday. But she said that that wasn't as important as being able to make a living. She was going to go to work. She found a job."

"Where?"

"Well, I don't know for sure." Liddy smoothed out her skirt and vainly tugged it closer to her knees. She leaned down and wiped at a smudge on her shoe with her thumb. "She met someone at the grocery store. A lady. Mom said she was real nice. She had a funny name. It sounded like Twilight."

"Twila," supplied Spider.

"Yes, that's it!" Liddy glanced up from her shoe to flash a

smile of relief that Brother Latham knew this lady. But she couldn't meet his eyes as she continued. "Mom said she met this lady, Twila, and she told Mom that she made $300 a night as a cocktail waitress." Now the eyes were turned to Spider, entreating his understanding and approval. "Mom said it seemed to her that her first obligation was to her family, and as long as she didn't drink herself, there shouldn't be anything wrong with her serving drinks. She said that Brother Lentz sells coffee and cigarettes at his store, and what's the difference?"

Seeing that Rose had already been working on snappy comebacks, Spider asked neutrally, "And so, what did she do?"

"Oh, around seven or so she got dressed up and said she was going to go up to Pioche and look for a job."

"How was she going to get to Pioche?"

"Twila came and got her. They were going to go up together, and Twila was going to put in a good word for Mom. She knows all the owners."

"I'll just bet she does," Spider said dryly. "Well, ten to one says your mom spent the night at Twila's. I bet she intended to be home before you had to leave for school, but she didn't make it up."

Liddy giggled. "She's done that before!" she said.

"Let's wait a while before we start worrying. Why don't you go on to school with your sisters, and I can take Tiffy with me. Laurie'll watch her today until school gets out, and I'll drop her back by."

"Thanks, Brother Latham, but . . ."

"But what?"

"I don't like leaving her with strangers. Oh, don't get me wrong. You're our home teacher, and you were my bishop. I trust you. It's just that Tiffy doesn't know you, and it might be scary for her to be in a strange place. I'll stay home with her."

"What about school?"

"Oh, I do this all the time."

"Yeah, but what about school?"

"Well, I don't do so well at school." Again the eyes were asking for understanding. "But I'm real good here at home."

As if in support of that statement, the door opened and six-year-old Julie marched out with a brush in her hand. "Liddy, I want you to do my hair," she declared. "Kim doesn't do as good a job as you do."

"She hasn't had as much practice. Sit down here, on the step below me, and I'll do it. We have to hurry, because it's almost time to go to school."

Spider stood to let the little girl walk by. Then he propped a shoulder against the wall of the house and watched in admiration as Liddy deftly brushed out Julie's long blond hair and began to French braid it. In minutes the hair was as neat and tidy as the rest of her, and she jumped up, saying, "Oh, thank you, Liddy. You don't keep telling me to sit still like Kim does."

"That's fine. Now go tell everyone to be sure beds are made and the table is cleaned off. I'll be in to check in just a minute."

Liddy waited until Julie had gone back in the house and closed the door before she stood. "So I'll stay home . . ." she said, leaving an inflection that invited Spider to tell what he was going to do.

Dang, she's good, he thought. *She's got me whipped into line too.* Aloud he said, " . . . and I'll check first with Twila, and then with some of the tavern owners up in Pioche. As soon as I know anything, I'll call."

"You don't think there's been an accident or anything, do you?"

"Naw. If there'd been an accident, someone would have called me already. Don't be imagining things. It never turns out to be something you imagine."

Julie stood on the doorstep again. "My bed's made and my chores are done," she said to Liddy. "Can I go now?"

"Got your lunch?"

In answer Julie held up a brown paper lunch bag.

"Yes, you can."

"Thanks, Liddy. 'Bye. 'Bye, Brother Latham."

As soon as she was off the porch, she was replaced by another neatly dressed, blonde-headed child, one size larger. Like nesting Russian dolls, two more appeared to report. Then the four sisters went off down the street together, holding hands and swinging arms, and looking back at Spider and giggling.

Spider watched them to the corner. Then he held out his hand to Liddy. "I'll go now. Remember, don't go worrying."

"I won't," she said, shaking his hand and smiling bravely. She stood on the porch with her arms folded as Spider went back to his cruiser. She waved as he pulled away.

Spider sketched an answering wave and watched in his rearview mirror as she turned to go back in the house. There was something about the set of her shoulders that tugged at his heart. "Great Suffering Zot, what's that woman thinking?" he muttered to himself. "She'd better hope I don't find her right away, because right now I'm of a mind to shake her till her teeth rattle."

CHAPTER

IT SEEMED THAT ROSE'S teeth were safe. It took Spider a while to locate Twila's house, which was hanging off the side of a hill in Pioche. He parked on the street and climbed twenty narrow cement stairs to get to the walk that led to a small, square cottage with red, fake-brick asphalt siding and a mopped tar roof.

As he waited for someone to answer his knock, Spider looked around at the little town that lurched precariously down one side of a ravine and up the other. Here and there was a neat domicile with new paint and manicured yard. But mostly the houses were tired looking and forlorn. *Prosperous* was not an adjective one applied to Pioche.

Knocking again, Spider heard a petulant voice holler something from inside. He was being asked to hold something, but he couldn't quite make out what. Finally the door opened a crack, and Spider saw one high cheekbone and one brown eye, ringed with smudged mascara and half hidden by hair hanging down in front.

"Morning, Twila," Spider said. "I'm sorry to get you up so early."

The eye blinked. "Spider? What are you doing here, Spider? What time is it?"

Spider looked at his watch. "It's eight o'clock."

"In the morning?" The door opened wider, revealing the county's lone lady of the night clad in a pink gingham quilted bathrobe over a flannel nightgown. Twila sagged against the door, laying her cheek against the edge. "Spider, do you know what time I got to bed?" Her mouth opened wide, and her mascara-streaked eyes squeezed shut in a huge yawn.

"Ah, no. I'm sorry, Twila. I wouldn't come bothering you so early, but I need to know if Rose Markey spent the night here with you."

The yawn was stifled and the eyes snapped open.

"Oh, please! Do you think I've decided to become a Girl Scout leader? Why would I ask her to spend the night at my place?"

"Well, didn't you take her with you last night?"

"I told her I'd take her and introduce her to a couple of people, and I did. I even let her work for me for a half hour or so to try it out, see how she did."

"How did she do?"

"She doesn't think there's any difference between whiskey and bourbon, she kept calling a screwdriver a drivescrewer, and she can't make change. She's hopeless. And she giggles too much."

"I see. So, after she worked that half hour, what did she do?"

"Oh, I don't know. Sat around. Talked with the guys who were sitting at the bar. I was busy."

"And you didn't take her home?"

"No, she left with that guy. Spider, why are you here asking me all these questions?"

"Rose didn't come home last night."

"No, I mean, why are *you* here asking me all these questions?"

"Oh, the kids called me when their mom didn't show up. I'm the home teacher."

"Oh."

"I'm also the new deputy sheriff."

"You took Tharon Tate's place?"

"Yeah. What guy is that? The one you say she left with?"

"I don't know his name for sure. He's not local, but I see him every once in a while. He's an older guy. Old enough to be her father. He's got a real weather-beaten face—lots of wrinkles, you know."

"Is he big or small? Short or tall?"

"He's not too tall. I think you'd call him wiry. He gives that impression. Small, but still he's strong."

"Color of hair?"

"Gray. Kind of bald at the top. He's got dark eyes that kind of stare at you, and he has this habit of rubbing his hands together. Ugh! He gives me the shivers. The last I saw of Rose, she was walking out the door with him."

"Do you know what his name is?"

Twila shrugged. "I never heard it. He usually drinks alone. Doesn't seem to have any friends in the area. I just serve him and take the money. He always pays cash."

Spider stared at the toe of his boot, trying to think how to frame the next question.

"Is this going to take long?" Twila asked plaintively. "I'd really like to get back to bed."

"No. No. I was just wondering, did you ever, ah, see this guy outside of the bar?"

"Uh-uh. Oh, do you mean did I ever have him come over after hours?"

Spider nodded. His face was feeling warm.

"Well, I'll tell you, Spider, some people might look at the oddballs I've had over, from Dudley Weese, who thinks he can find gold with a map and a plumb bob, to Nate Allen, who is getting ready for the end of the world. Or Mr. Higarten, who wants to abolish—"

"Uh, Twila," Spider broke in. "If you don't mind, I'd rather not have a list of your clientele."

Twila tipped her head back and closed her eyes and laughed a noiseless, knowing laugh. "Oh, Spider," she said, looking at him from under her lashes. "You've got a lot to learn. What I was trying to say was, strange people don't bother me. But this one isn't strange. He's spooky."

"Listen, Twila. Thanks for getting up and talking to me. I'll go now, check a few other things out. If you happen to see Rose, will you have her give me a call? Thanks."

"Don't mention it."

Spider turned away and walked down the narrow walkway to the steps set steeply into the hillside. Just before descending, he looked back at the house and saw Twila, her angular frame still leaning against the door, watching him. "Go back to bed," he called.

Twila waved languidly and stepped away to push the door closed.

As he descended the narrow steps, Spider eyed the neighboring houses and hoped that anyone who saw him leaving Twila's house had also seen him arrive ten minutes earlier.

But he spared only that moment on the stairs for worrying about his reputation. As he walked to his car and got in, he was dogged by the remembrance of Twila saying, "He gives me the creeps." Absentmindedly, Spider drummed on the steering wheel with his fingers while he played over the conversation in his mind. "He's spooky," Twila had said about the man who left the bar with Rose. Spider was just about ready to bet the ranch that the spooky man was Kurt Wiggins.

"Oh, dear, dear, dear, dear, dear." he said aloud. "I wonder what's going on here." Looking at his watch, he saw it was 8:10. Misliking the feeling that lay in the pit of his stomach, he started the car and drove down the narrow, snaking road that led from Twila's house to downtown Pioche. It was a distance of four blocks with a drop in elevation of a hundred feet. He headed first for the county courthouse, but it was closed and dark. A sign on the door said hours were from 8:30 A.M. to 5:00 P.M. After unsuccessfully looking around in the car for something to write on, he drove to the new gas station and convenience store down by the intersection with Highway 93 and went inside to buy a small spiral notepad that he could stick in his pocket. Then he drove to the Trail's End Motel located a quarter mile north of the intersection.

As he pulled into the parking lot, Spider saw Christy Fellows emerge from the utility shed located at the end of the only fifteen motel rooms in the county. Christy was talking to someone in the shed, and as Spider got out of the car and ambled over to speak to her, Steven Fellows emerged pushing a laundry cart. Steven was Ben and Christy's only son, and the reason they had elected to put their life savings into the precarious existence of offering shelter to the few wandering souls who traveled the lonesome miles of Highway 93. Steven had Down's Syndrome and at age thirty-four led a happy and diligent existence vacuuming floors, changing sheets, and chatting about his postcard collection with those customers who were comfortable with his disability. That collection grew daily as travelers continued to remember the happy child with the almond eyes and the five o'clock shadow and to send him picture postcards from places all over the world.

"Morning, Christy," Spider said. "Morning, Steven."

"Good morning, Spider," Christy greeted, glancing at the deputy's car and back to him. "I heard you took Tharon Tate's place."

"Yeah. Yeah."

"You're out and about kinda early." She turned to her son. "You go on down to number one and get the beds stripped off, Stevie. I'll be there in a minute."

"Okay, Mom." Steven paused only to say good-bye to Spider before heading purposefully down the sidewalk, pushing his laundry cart before him.

"What can I do for you, Spider?" Christy asked.

"Well, I need to know about Kurt Wiggins."

"He's not here. He checked out last night."

Spider took his pen and notebook out of his pocket. "Yeah. I need to ask you about that."

Christy shook her head. "I can't tell you anything. I was in with Stevie when he left. Ben took care of checking him out.

He's in the office." She nodded toward the first door at the foot of the L-shaped motel. "Go on in and talk to him."

"All right, I will. Thanks." Spider touched the brim of his hat and turned to stride across the gravel parking lot to the door marked *Office*. Ben was there, and after a couple moments' conversation, Spider made some notes and took his leave. As he crossed the parking lot to the deputy's cruiser, Steven Fellows, trundling a vacuum cleaner down the sidewalk, called to him and waved, and Spider waved back.

He got in the car and looked at his watch. It was 8:20. *Dang, but I'm efficient,* he thought as he started the car and drove back up Main Street toward the courthouse.

There were no other cars in the courthouse parking lot, so Spider pulled into a space between fading white lines, turned off the key, and sat making a list of priorities as he waited for Randi Lee.

He hadn't long to wait. Randi was early, and her broad, pleasant face lit up when she saw him coming to meet her as she reached the door.

"Good morning, Spider," she greeted, selecting a key from a well-filled ring and opening the door. "You're here early."

"Yeah. I've got something I need help with, and I figured I'd better get at it. Is the sheriff in town?"

Randi slipped her keys into her slacks pocket and flipped on the lights. "Uh-uh. He's still up in Reno." She was a good-looking woman, tall and big-boned, with apple cheeks and honey-colored hair that curled in a well-ordered fringe around her face. Honesty was written in her candid blue eyes, and competence in her strong, supple hands.

Spider strode down the hall beside her, admiring the way she made the light precede them, flipping the switches on the wall as she went without hesitation in either her pace or her conversation. The dark fears that had driven Spider to the courthouse so early in the morning began to seem more fanciful than real in the presence of such a solid personality.

"So, what's Sheriff Brown doing in Reno still?" he asked.

She smiled at him. "The deputy attorney general for the state of Nevada is up there . . ."

"Since we're coming on to an election year," Spider supplied.

"Well, yes," Randi agreed. "And it turns out he and Sheriff Brown are third cousins."

"Is that so!"

"Yes. And Sheriff Brown was invited to stay for a few days at the deputy attorney general's cabin at Tahoe, and he accepted." Randi unlocked the door to the County Sheriff's complex of offices and led the way back to her private cubicle. "Come in and sit down," she said. "If you need to talk to Sheriff Brown, I can get hold of him. Or maybe I can help."

Spider took off his hat and sat in the chair Randi indicated. Placing the Stetson on the chair beside him, he took the new spiral notebook out of his pocket and opened it. "There's a woman who lives in Panaca who didn't come home last night," he began. "Her oldest girl called me this morning, concerned. I found out that this woman left the bar last night with a man."

"And?"

"I know that the man was leaving town. He lives up around Reno."

"Okay." Randi sat with those capable hands folded on the blotter in front of her and waited expectantly. When Spider didn't go on, she said, "You realize, don't you, that what you've just described happening goes on all the time in the county. What is this woman's name?"

"Rose Markey."

"All right. Is Rose married?"

Spider shook his head. "She's just divorced, and she's walking around with quite a sum of money available to her."

"And she went to a bar and left with a man and didn't go home. It's fairly obvious what happened. Especially if the man isn't from around here. It makes it easier for all concerned. A one-night stand. No strings. Happens all the time."

"Yeah. But . . ."

"But what?"

"Oh, I don't know. The guy she left with knows about the body of that woman I found last week. He read about it and came out to tell me that he saw someone out there parked by where the body was buried, last spring. He was too far away, he says, to see anyone. He says."

"And?"

"And . . . well, I've got this gut feeling that he knows more than he's telling. I think about her going off with him, and I get sick thinking about what could happen to her. He was supposed to be heading back up to Reno today."

"Uh-huh," Randi said, as if the tumblers had clicked. She drew a notepad to her and picked up a pencil. "What's this fellow's name?" she asked.

"His name's Kurt Wiggins. Ben Fellows at the motel said he checked out at nine o'clock last night. There was someone with him in his pickup when he paid his bill, but Ben couldn't swear who it was. Says it was a woman, but he didn't pay any attention."

"You say he was driving a pickup?"

"It's a blue Ford pickup with the Keystone logo on it."

"I don't suppose you got the license number?"

"Got it from Ben," he said, and read it to her.

Randi wrote the number and put an emphatic period after it. Then she looked up at Spider. "So, what do you want to do?"

"Well, I tell you, Randi, I'd feel mighty foolish to make a big thing about this and then have her call me this morning and say they had a flat tire or they'd been out dancing all night, or something."

"On the other hand . . ." she prompted.

"On the other hand, I've got a creepy guy heading off in the middle of the night with a feather-headed young woman who is altogether too trusting, and who also has a lot of money lying around loose. He's from the Reno area—"

"Where there are bodies turning up by the gross," Randi supplied, "if you'll pardon the pun."

"Yeah, and he's connected with a body that's turned up here, and which fits the Reno profile."

"So, do you want to call the sheriff?"

Spider thought a moment. "I don't know that that'll do any good. What I thought was, if we can get the word out to the highway patrol, and maybe the county sheriffs between here and Reno, they'll spot him on the way. They can stop him, and if Rose is with him, they can tell her the kids are worried and she needs to call home. If she's not with him, and she hasn't turned up at home yet, they can find out where he says she is and check it out."

"All right. I can do that. I'll get right on it."

"I figured you could," said Spider. "I've got a couple of other things I want you to check, too. First, I heard that there's some BLM land out towards Delmar that is going to be available to lease. People who have the lease are letting it go. Can you find out for me if that's true?"

"You thinking of applying for it?"

"No. It might be a piece of another puzzle I'm working on." Pulling a folded-up piece of paper out of his pocket, Spider laid it on the desk in front of Randi. "I found a car buried in the bank of Hughes's Wash, not too far away from my house."

"No kidding!" Randi picked up the paper and studied the information written on it.

"Yeah. That's the name and address of the registered owner. Now, I don't know if that's who was driving when it ended up in the wash. But I do know that the lady I found out by the Lucy Roberts was in this car when it wrecked." Spider noted the questioning look on Randi's face. "The body was missing two teeth and one shoe. I found them in the car," he said in answer.

"Boy, you have been busy!"

"Yeah. You could say that. What I need to know, Randi, is, was that car reported as stolen in the last year or two? I also need to know if the registered owner has been reported as a missing person. Can you check those things out for me?"

"Sure. It won't take but a moment."

She was as good as her word. Her fingers flew, clickety-click on the keyboard of her computer, paused, clickety-clicked again. Then pause, click, pause, click-click, pause, and then finally the verdict: "Negative on both counts. No report of that car stolen. No report of that name as a missing person."

"Huh!" Spider grunted. "Well, shoot. I thought I was on to something."

"I think you are! It's not clear right now, but I'll bet finding that car was a real stroke of luck."

"If I didn't have this Rose Markey thing, I'd run on up to Vegas this morning and check out this address."

"I understand. Why don't we wait a few hours, give her time to come home or call home. Is anyone there?"

"Yeah, her fifteen-year-old daughter is there with her three-year-old."

"Mmmmm. Okay. Here's what we'll do. I'll get in touch with people between here and Reno and see if we can locate the Keystone pickup and Kurt Wiggins. If we don't find out anything by noon, why don't you run on over to Vegas. You can always touch bases by phone. If they're halfway to Reno there's nothing you can do by hanging around here. Are the kids all right?"

"Yeah. I think the oldest daughter is raising them, anyway. I'll call the bishop, let him know what's going on." Spider picked up his hat and stood up. "I'll call you if she turns up. If not, I'll check in in a couple of hours to see if you've found out anything."

"Everything is going to be fine, Spider."

"Yeah. I know." As he walked down the hall to the double doors leading outside, Spider reflected that neither he nor Randi was a very good liar.

C H A P T E R

SPIDER TOOK A CHANCE that Oliver Higarten might be in early and drove from the courthouse down the hill to the *Sentinel* office. Angling in to park against the curb, Spider noticed that the shades were drawn over the windows, and he read the sign painted in black on the glass: "Office open 10:00 A.M. to 5:00 P.M., Monday through Friday."

Spider glanced at his watch. It was nine o'clock.

He read the sign again. He drummed his fingers on the steering wheel a moment and then looked up and down the sidewalk. There weren't many people about. Three doors up, two men in bib overalls and baseball caps stood in front of the hardware store discussing something that seemed, from the measurements they were describing in the air, to be about four feet wide and five feet tall and pretty serious business. Looking the other way, Spider saw a tiny, gray-haired lady toiling up the hill, leaning forward as she marched purposefully along.

Spider turned off the ignition and got out of the car, reaching the high curb in time to help Mrs. Siebert down so she could jaywalk over to the post office. Accepting her thanks and pausing to see that she came to no harm from the odd car that might be passing, Spider stepped up on the curb and walked over to the *Sentinel* office.

Feeling a little uncomfortable, as if he were making a spectacle of himself in public, Spider rapped on the door and stood listening. Knocking again, Spider called out, "Mr. Higarten? Are you in there?" The two overalled gentlemen paused, one with his hands four feet apart, to look at him.

No sound from the *Sentinel* office. Spider shrugged his shoulders and was turning to leave when he heard Mr. Higarten call, "Who is it?"

Spider turned back to the door. "It's Spider Latham. Deputy sheriff. I need to talk to you."

"Well, come on in."

Spider opened the screen and waited a moment, thinking that Mr. Higarten must be going to come and unlock the door. There were no footsteps. No rattle of a lock. Spider tentatively tried the door. It swung open easily.

"Be sure and close the door behind you," Mr. Higarten commanded. "I don't want anyone thinking I'm available. I'm a busy man."

Mr. Higarten was sitting in his wooden swivel chair, tilted back with his feet up on his desk and an open newspaper held up for reading. Spider grinned, thinking the editor was making a joke, but the fierce eyes behind the spectacles didn't twinkle, and there was not the least hint of a lift to the thin lips.

Spider cleared his throat. "I'm sorry to trouble you, but I

needed to talk to you about something, and I'm leaving town in a moment."

"Well, come on over. Sit down. Sit down." Mr. Higarten closed his paper and took his feet off the desk. "What do you want to talk to me about?"

Spider removed his hat and walked to the chair Mr. Higarten indicated. He sat down. As he did so, he noticed that the newspaper in the editor's hand was the *Church News*.

"I was wondering if you had a chance to chase down the name of that lady for me?"

"What lady?"

"The one you told me about. The one that came from back east and had the run-in with Bud Hefernan. The environmentalist."

"I told you I'd find out her name?"

"Yes, sir."

"When?"

"The day I came in to tell you about finding the body out at the Lucy Roberts."

"And asked me to put an article in the paper that was coming out next day. I remember. I had the front page all ready to go to press, and here you walk in with that! No wonder I forgot." Still holding the newspaper in his left hand and marking his place with his index finger, he dragged a Post-It notepad to himself with his right hand, scribbled a reminder, and posted the note on his telephone. "Who's going to pay for the calls?"

"The calls?"

"I'll be calling New York several times during prime time. Who's going to pay for the calls?"

Spider ran his fingers around the brim of his hat for a moment, studying the curve and thinking. "Well, I tell you,

Mr. Higarten, I figured the *Sentinel* would stand the charges in the interest of investigative journalism. If it turns out that she's missing and is tied to this, well, you'll have a scoop."

"A scoop? Where did you pick up that word? I'll tell you what I'll have. I'll have a deputy who owes me one."

"Within limits, yes."

Mr. Higarten leaned back in his chair and regarded Spider. "So, what?" he asked. "Is the sheriff's department so strapped for cash that they can't pay for some long-distance calls?"

"I don't know that it would be for me to say," Spider answered. "Sheriff Brown would be the one to talk to about the department's budget."

Mr. Higarten scribbled another note and posted it on the wall above his desk. "I'll talk to him," he said, "if he ever decides to come back and spend time with the people who elected him."

"Oh, he'll be back," Spider said mildly. "Next year is an election year."

"And so it is," agreed Mr. Higarten, smiling a thin-lipped smile. "And so it is."

Spider stirred in his chair. "About that lady," he said. "I'll be leaving for Vegas about eleven, if I can get away. Any chance you'll know anything before then?"

"Can't say. Maybe, maybe not."

"Well, I'll call from Vegas and check in with Laurie. If you find anything out, could you call her? She can relay the information to me."

"It can't wait till you get home?"

"I don't know. It may be tied to the information I have in Vegas. Maybe not. I don't want to have to make two trips down if I can take care of it in one."

"And what information do you have in Las Vegas?"

Spider made a deprecating gesture. "It's so scanty, I don't hardly want to admit I'm driving six hours because of it. I'll let you know if anything comes of it."

"Promise?"

"If I can."

"You don't give much away, do you?"

"I like to be able to keep my word." Spider looked at his watch. "I need to get on my way." He walked to the door and paused. "I'll check with Laurie this afternoon if I don't hear from you before I go."

Mr. Higarten was back behind his paper. He didn't reply, but just as Spider stepped outside he yelled, "Shut the door!"

Spider pulled the door gently to. Then, crossing the sidewalk, he stepped off the curb just as Mrs. Siebert came trundling back across the street from the post office, clutching her mail. She caught Spider's eye and smiled at him, waving the packet of letters she had in her hand. Spider couldn't understand what she said, and waited for her to get closer.

"I got a letter from my great-grandson!" she announced when she was safely across the street. "He's in the service in Germany and has written to me. Help me up on the curb. I've got to go show Stella that I have a letter from Germany."

Spider did as he was bid and stood for a moment watching her progress down the sidewalk, flashing the letter at everyone she met. Each passer-by smiled at the news, though she hadn't time to do any more than announce the arrival as she marched on home to share it with Stella.

Spider was grateful for the sweetness of that moment to take away the astringency of the minutes spent with Oliver Higarten. He got in the cruiser, taking a moment to cross

Bucketa Blood off his list, and to see what was the next task he had set for himself this particular morning. Then he started the car, backed out of his parking place, and threaded his way down the steeply winding streets of Pioche to the intersection with Highway 93. When he got there, he turned north, making for the Lazy H ranch. He had a couple of questions to put to Bud Hefernan.

TURNING OFF HIGHWAY 93, the gravel road to the Lazy H
Ranch lay straight as a string for three miles. Then it snaked for
three more through a small mountain range to a beautiful little
valley, spring-fed and green. As Spider emerged from the pass
through the mountains, he turned right and drove past a water
tower and stock tank, past a maze of chutes and corrals and
over a cattle guard. He pulled up in front of the adobe head-
quarters of the Lazy H Ranch.

Spider noticed that Bud Hefernan's pickup wasn't in the
yard as he got out of the county car and strolled up the walkway to the house. Chrysanthemums still bloomed in flower
beds flanking the flagstone path. Someone had been digging in
them. Mounting the steps to the covered porch, which ran
around three sides of the house, Spider could see that the front
door was open. He knocked. No answer.

Leaning forward to peer through the screen door, Spider

saw the rustic tidiness of the living room. Navajo rugs lay scattered on shiny hardwood floors. Handmade wood-and-cushion furniture was grouped for swapping stories underneath a chandelier made of a wagon wheel. Spider knocked again. "Myrna? Bud?" he called. Still no answer.

Spider was trying to decide whether to take the time to search out anyone who might be home, when he heard footsteps on the veranda. A moment later Myrna Hefernan rounded the corner. She was carrying a bucket in one gloved hand and a small garden spade in the other.

"Why, Spider," she said, "what a surprise to see you! Is anything wrong?"

"No. I was just on my way out of town, and I wanted to ask Bud something. Is he around?"

"No, he's out with Murray, putting in a reservoir. Can I tell him something for you?"

"Naw. That's all right." Spider paused in the act of turning away from the door, and Myrna waited expectantly. "I wonder . . ."

"What?"

"When you do the wash, do you check Bud's pockets?"

"Of course! He's always leaving things in his pockets that either foul up the washer or melt in the dryer. Why do you ask?"

"Well, the other day when Bud came out to help me, I saw him put something in his pocket. I thought it might have been something I dropped. I was going to ask him about it, but I got distracted by what we had to contend with. I don't know that it's important, but . . ."

"All I found in his pocket was a button. It came off his glove, and I sewed it back on. What was it you lost?"

"It was a . . . a . . . well, it wasn't important, I guess." Spider pulled off his hat and shifted his weight to his other foot. "Say, Myrna."

"Yes?"

"Does Bud have a turquoise and silver watchband?"

Myrna bent over to set her bucket down and leaned her short-handled spade beside it. The straw hat she wore shielded her face. "No."

"Uh, I was over at Ethan and Jessie's yesterday, and they said they fixed a watchband that Bud had."

"He did have one. He doesn't anymore."

Spider ran his fingers around the brim of his hat as if the answers to the questions in his mind were written in the texture of the felt. Intent on framing the next query, he kept his eyes on his hands. When he looked up, he met Myrna's eyes. They were brimming with unshed tears. "Bud had Ethan fix the watchband so he could sell it. He needed the money."

Spider's mouth felt cottony. His mind was stuck. Again he studied his hat. The silence lengthened. At last Myrna spoke again.

"We had a son. I mean, we have a son. He's an adopted son. We got him when he was four. He was to be the child we weren't able to have ourselves." She shrugged. "Life never turns out like you think it will. He lives in Prescott, where we used to live. He's schizophrenic. When he stays on his medication, he does pretty well."

"I didn't know, Myrna."

"We have a better relationship long distance than we do when we live close. He's only been over to see us once in the fifteen years we've lived here. Anyway, he went off his medicine about six months ago and beat his wife up pretty good. He heard voices that told him she was evil. We needed some extra money to help out over there, so Bud sold the watchband."

"Who did he sell it to?"

"There's a guy in Prescott that's wanted it ever since Albert Begay gave it to Bud. He bought it. Why are you so interested in Bud's watchband, Spider?"

"Um, I'd never seen Bud wear a watch. I didn't think it was like him to have something as fancy as a silver watchband." Spider felt foolish. He couldn't lie. Shouldn't have tried. He put his hat back on and awkwardly backed away, feeling the blood rising to his cheekbones. Touching the brim in farewell, he turned, but, catching the porch railing post with his boot toe, he tripped and went clattering down the stairs, arms windmilling to keep his balance.

"Are you all right?" called Myrna.

"Yeah." Spider ducked his head and made for his car, hoping desperately for a clean getaway. Yanking open the door, he piled in and almost got his wish, though the view as he burned rubber across the cattle guard was through a water-streaked windshield.

Angry at being in the position of asking prying questions, hating to appear foolish, Spider gritted his teeth and pushed the accelerator to the floor. As the cruiser roared over the gravel road, a plume of ecru dust hung in the air behind, the only blight on the clear tranquillity of the desert landscape.

Coming through the mountain pass, each power drift around an S-curve skated close to the edge of disaster and raised Spider's mood a degree. Free of the mountains, he raced down the straightaway to Highway 93, and his handling of the ninety-degree corner when he turned from gravel road to highway was such a thing of beauty that he actually smiled. Fifteen eighty-mile-an-hour minutes later, when he reached the turnoff onto his own gravel road, he was whistling "Put Your Shoulder to the Wheel."

Laurie was in the kitchen shaping bread dough into rolls when Spider came through the back door. "Hello," she called. "Whatcha doing?"

"I gotta go to Vegas."

"What for?"

"Check on that registration. Car isn't listed as stolen." Spider pinched off a piece of dough and put it in his mouth. "Mary Margaret Barnett isn't listed as missing," he continued thickly. "Maybe she's still there at that address and can shed some light on this whole thing."

"Have you tried Information? Maybe she has a listed number."

"That's an idea." Spider walked to the phone, and after he swallowed the last of the dough, he dialed Information.

There was no Mary Margaret Barnett listed in Las Vegas, North Las Vegas, or Henderson. Spider hung up the phone. "Dang. I thought I was going to get lucky."

"The luck will come some other way. So what's going on at the House of Fluff? Liddy Snow just called and said her mom still hadn't come home."

"I'd like to strangle that woman! Will you run in and check on those girls today? I'll call Bishop, too, in a minute. I need to get going. Could you iron my gray shirt?"

As Laurie finished forming the rolls, Spider got a loaf of bread out of the breadbox and cut off two large slabs. "No other calls? Nothing from Randi Lee?"

"Uh-uh." Laurie washed her hands and disappeared into the laundry room.

With a peanut-butter sandwich in one hand, Spider opened the Panaca Ward directory with the other. Munching on his first bite, he dialed the bishop's home number. "Oh, hello, Sister Stowe. Is Bishop home by any chance? No? Is he at the funeral home? Fine. I'll call him there." Too late, he realized he should have asked the number before she hung up. Taking another peanut-butter bite, Spider pulled out the phone book and looked up the number. Bishop answered on the seventh ring.

"Hello," he barked.

Taken aback, Spider paused. "Ah, is this the mortuary?"

Silence. Then a calm, well-modulated voice answered, "Yes. May I help you?"

"Ah, Bishop, this is Spider Latham. Deputy Latham. I need to talk to you about Rose Markey."

"You're the home teacher, Spider. You handle it."

"Ah, no. You see—"

The bark returned. "I don't have time for this now. My refrigeration unit went kaput last night and I've got to go pick up Mrs. Smith from Caliente."

"Is that Denny Smith's mom?"

"Yes." Impatient. Clipped.

"That's too bad. She's a fairly young woman. What'd she die of?"

"Spider, I don't have time for this! I've got a crisis here!"

"Well, where's old Shorty? I thought he was supposed to keep your refrigeration system going."

"He's gone. Left the county. Went to St. George to live with his sister."

"I'll tell you what, Bishop. I'll leave you to your crisis. Maybe I'll drop by in a while and talk over this other matter."

"Fine. Whatever. Good-bye." Click.

Spider finished his last bite of sandwich, staring through the window at nothing as he chewed. Then he called Randi Lee, who had nothing to report. BLM was going to get back to her about the lease out near Delmar.

Spider hung up the phone and stared out the window again. Then he ambled back to the bedroom to shine his boots. He had one foot up on a chair and was bent over wielding a brush when Laurie brought in the gray shirt.

She smoothed a wrinkle out of the bedspread. "So, when do you think you'll be home?"

"I don't know. I'll call late this afternoon, before I start back. Old Bucketa Blood is supposed to call you with some information. I want to have it before I leave Vegas." He glanced out the window at the pile of gravel Murray had dumped on Monday. "I was hoping old Mur would be here. I need to talk to him, too."

"He said he'd be by this afternoon to spread the gravel."

"His pickup was there when I passed his house, but his dump truck and trailer were gone. I thought he might be here."

"He might be home. I think he's got some of his equipment out where he's building a tank for Bud."

"I'll stop on the way." Spider tucked in his shirttail and picked up his deputy's badge from the dresser.

"What are you doing?"

"I'm putting my badge in my wallet. I feel silly wandering around with it on my shirt. Like a little kid playing cowboy."

"Is it all right for you to do that?"

"I read the handbook. It doesn't say anything about where I have to wear my badge."

She followed him down the hall. "I thought it was supposed to be over your heart. Symbolic, you know."

"Well, if it's symbolism we're after, I think it's in the right place." Spider patted his back pocket and kissed Laurie. " 'Bye, Darlin'. I'll call you this afternoon."

Laurie watched from the front door. Instead of going to the county car, Spider strode to the barn. In a moment he emerged with a toolbox in his hand. He put it in the trunk and got in, then backed around and waved just before he set out over the cattle guard. The wave she returned was meager, with fingers curled down.

Driving by Murray's place, Spider slowed down. He looked at his watch and drummed his fingers on the steering wheel. Finally he muttered out loud to himself, "You're a coward, Spider Latham. You want the paycheck, but you don't want to do the job. Now just get on in there and get the job done."

He turned into Murray's drive and parked by his pickup. Striding up to the house, he rapped on the door, but no one answered. He opened the door and called, "Mur? You here?"

Closing the door again, he went around the house and back to Murray's shop. Murray wasn't there. He wasn't in the barn or around the corrals where Slick and Dan, Murray's two cutting horses, were standing with heads up, watching Spider.

"Huh. Now what?" Spider wandered slowly back to the dooryard. Taking his notebook out of his pocket, he opened it and sat on the bumper of Murray's pickup. It was a skookum bumper, made of eight-inch angle iron and welded to the frame. It stuck out a foot from the truck and had a winch mounted in the middle, a handy place to perch while writing a note.

What to say? "Dear Murray, what was Missy's name? Did Missy have a real name?" Spider paused, considering: Is this a question to leave tacked on a door or under a windshield-wiper blade? Maybe not. Better wait and ask the question face-to-face. Friend to friend. Deputy to . . .

Recalling the session out at the Lazy H, Spider was glad that Murray wasn't home. He didn't know that he was ready yet to ask his old friend prying questions.

Spider stood and closed his notebook. He rubbed his leg where the edge of the bumper had cut off the circulation. "My mama told me never to borrow trouble," he said aloud. "I'm not going to borrow any here."

He got in the cruiser and headed for the highway. As he drove along, he could feel the imprint of Murray's bumper in his thigh, and he thought, *If I get lucky in Las Vegas, it won't matter what Missy's name was. I'll never have to ask Murray that question.*

When Spider got to the highway, instead of turning left toward Las Vegas, he turned right and drove to Stowe's Mortuary. As before, he parked in back and entered quietly through the double doors, toolbox in hand. Standing in the hallway, he pushed open one of the double doors to the right that opened onto the embalming room. No one was there. Next, trying the knob of the office door, he cracked it open and peeked inside.

Bishop Stowe was there. He was on his knees.

Bishop looked up and saw Spider peeking in at him. He stayed frozen in that position, hands clasped on the old wooden swivel chair, eyes turned up toward the door, and a blush spread up from his neck to his forehead.

"Ah, I didn't mean to intrude." Spider stepped back and began to close the door.

"No, Spider." Bishop scrambled to his feet and opened the door. "That's all right. Come in." He spread his hands. "I didn't know what else to do. I even tried Cedar City and Vegas. No one will come out. I didn't know what else to do."

"I don't know much about refrigeration. I probably can't do anything. But, if it's the compressor, I'm on my way into Vegas and I could pick up another one. That won't solve your problem right now. But I remember my Grandma Latham talking about when she was young and it took time for folks to gather for a funeral, they'd pack a body in ice. If you had to, you could do that until I got back with the compressor. I bet between what they've got at the Panaca Emporium and Vonda's Cafe, you could get plenty of ice."

"That's right! That's right! I never thought of something as simple as that."

"Where's the refrigeration unit?"

"It's out back. Here. I'll show you."

Bishop Stowe led the way through the doors and outside to a small brick addition. Inside were garden utensils, a lawn mower, and, over in the corner, a large and silent compressor with tubes leading in and out.

Spider set his toolbox down and studied the apparatus. "I don't know much about refrigeration," he offered again.

Bishop just spread his open palms and then clasped his hands back together, hovering, hoping.

Spider hunkered down, tracing with his eyes the wires leading to the compressor. He wiggled them at the connections. He sat back on his haunches and studied the unit as a whole. Then he opened his toolbox and took out his volt-ohm meter. Unwrapping the two wires, he placed the tip of one on one place and the other on another and watched the arm of the dial. He grunted and tried two different places. Nothing. He tried the first two places again, being very careful about establishing a connection. Nothing again.

"You're not getting any juice to the unit."

"What do you mean?"

"No electricity. Could be as simple as a tripped breaker."

"I checked the breaker box first thing. That's the first thing I checked."

"Where's your box?"

"It's inside. Right in the hall. I'll show you."

Again Bishop Stowe led the way. Just inside the double doors was the electric panel. Bishop pointed, then stood aside.

Spider opened the door and read the faint inscriptions written with an arthritic hand: office, prep room lights, prep room south and east wall outlets, prep room north and west wall outlets, compressor . . . "There it is."

"But it hasn't been tripped."

"No, it hasn't. But . . ."

"But what?"

Spider sniffed. "Something's wrong. Smells like . . ."

"Like what?"

"Bakelite. Hot bakelite. Smell it?" He pulled out the breaker and looked at it. "Here's the problem."

"What?" Bishop peered over his shoulder.

"Your breaker's gone bad. Heated up and went gunny sack. You need a new breaker. Whyn't you call the hardware store up in Pioche while I get my toolbox. Take this breaker and ask Hershel if he's got one like it. If he hasn't, I'll pick one up for you in Vegas." He looked at his watch. "I've got to get going."

"I'm on it!" Smiling, Bishop took the breaker from Spider's hand and bustled into his office. Spider closed the door to the electrical panel and retrieved his tools from the shed. Bishop met him at the door with hand outstretched.

"They've got one! My wife's on the way to get it right now. Thank you, Spider. You've saved the day."

"I don't know much about refrigeration. But I do know to check for power first."

"I'm grateful. I'm grateful."

"No problem. But I did need to talk to you about something."

"Oh, yes. Rose Markey, was it?"

"Yeah. She's disappeared."

Bishop stared. "What do you mean?"

"She didn't come home last night. Her daughter's worried, and, frankly, so am I."

Bishop kept his eyes on Spider's face. He swallowed. "What do you think? I mean, what could . . . ?"

"I don't know. I'm working on it. In the meantime, we need to keep an eye on those girls. Laurie is going to check on them today, but someone needs to be there with them this evening, spend the night, maybe. The older girl has things well in hand, but she's still a child, and she's getting pretty overwhelmed. Can you take care of that? Good. I'm off, now. I'll let you know if I hear anything." He held out his hand.

Bishop Stowe shook the proffered hand. "I didn't know it was anything like this. Let me know . . ."

Spider sketched a wave and held open one of the back doors. "I will. I gotta be going."

He stowed the tools in the trunk and got in the car, looking at his watch and frowning. "Well, that cost me a half hour," he muttered as he drove around to the highway. Then he turned the car toward Vegas and pushed the accelerator to the floor.

FINDING THE ADDRESS FROM the car registration turned out to be easier than Spider thought it would be. A city map, purchased at a service station, guided him to a run-down section of North Las Vegas. What he found was an apartment in a shabby fourplex that had a patchy lawn littered with tired-looking toys. Two boys, looking to be about four years old, sat in a bare patch in the lawn, digging with spoons. Spider parked his car and got out, checking his watch as he did so. It was two o'clock.

"Apartment four," he muttered to himself, stepping over a rusty Tonka truck on his way down the sidewalk. It was the last unit, and from the sound of a singer wailing about honkey-tonk angels inside, Spider judged that someone was home. He knocked at the door.

As he waited for an answer, he winked at the two boys who sat with idle spoons, watching him.

Knocking louder, Spider began to wonder what he would do if no one were home. He waggled a thumb at the door and asked the diggers, "Do you know who lives here?"

Both nodded.

"Is anybody home?"

Both nodded again. Spider knocked again, louder still.

"It's his mom," one boy said, pointing to his companion.

"Oh? Well, son, maybe you'd go in and tell your mom I'd like to talk to her."

"Uh-uh!" Son replied, wrinkling up his nose. "She told me she'd skin me alive if I came in before she was done."

"Do you know, I'm a policeman, and I'd like to ask her some questions."

"You don't look like a policeman," said Son.

"Yeah, but he's driving a police car," said the other.

Just then the door opened. Spider turned and found himself confronting a mane of tawny hair and a pair of forty-year-old, brown, bedroom eyes in a twenty-year-old face. A dressing gown of bronze satin hung artfully open over a bare shoulder. The young woman leaned her cheek against the doorjamb and pushed her tousled hair away from her face.

"Yes?" she breathed.

"Um . . . I . . . I'm . . ." Spider looked over his shoulder at the two boys sitting in the dirt, spoons forgotten, staring with interest at his interview. He cleared his throat and began trying to fish his wallet out of his pocket. "I'm, um, deputy sheriff of Lincoln County, ma'am, and I'm here looking for a lady."

"Will I do?" Brown eyes sparkled, and a coquettish dimple appeared in one cheek.

"Well, I don't know."

"Does that mean you don't think I'm a lady?" The lovely mouth assumed a playful pout, and the satin sank lower.

"Ah, no. No."

"Why do you have your wallet out?" She leaned closer, and Spider could smell the warm and musky fragrance of her body.

"I was going to show you my badge." He fumbled as he tried to get the wallet open.

At that she laughed, all the seductive mannerisms gone. The dressing gown was fastened properly and she stood with one hand on the doorjamb and looked past Spider to his car parked at the curb. "I knew you were a policeman," she said. "But not local." She looked back at Spider. "I couldn't resist putting you on. I don't have a lot of time right now, but if you want to come back in an hour . . ."

"I'm looking for someone named Mary Margaret Barnett. Her car registration gives this address. Is that you? Or a roommate?"

She shook her head. "I've lived here three months. I live alone, or at least Jimmy and I live here alone." She smiled past him at the boy on the lawn. "The manager lives in number one. She could tell you who lived here before I moved in."

Spider stepped back a pace and touched his hat brim. "Thank you for your help," he said. "I'll check with the manager."

The dimple appeared again. "I'm free in about an hour, if you want to come back."

Spider felt himself blushing for the second time that day and wondered if he were getting paid enough money for the hazards of his work. He managed to voice something inarticulately negative and fled down the walk to the manager's apartment.

His knock was answered promptly by a fresh-faced young woman with a sleeping baby on her shoulder. Spider was ready with his wallet and flashed his badge, introducing himself and asking for a bit of her time.

"Where is your car?" she asked.

Spider indicated the county cruiser, and she stepped out the door to look at it. "Where did you say you were from?"

"Lincoln County."

"It figures. *Sheriff* is spelled wrong on your car. Did you notice? Come in."

They stepped into a small living-dining-kitchen area. Moving a pile of shiny material off a kitchen chair with her free hand, she asked him to sit down. "This neighborhood has really gone downhill in the last four years. You can't be too careful."

"That's all right." Spider took off his hat and sat in the proffered chair. "I'm looking for a woman by the name of Mary Margaret Barnett."

The young woman pulled another chair away from in front of a sewing machine and sat down opposite Spider, glancing as she did so at the two boys playing outside. "I don't know where she is. She used to live here, but she disappeared, oh, about six months ago."

"What do you mean when you say, disappeared?"

"Just that. One day she was here, the next day she wasn't. Her apartment was intact, but her car was gone."

"Did you file a missing persons report?"

She laughed. "This is Vegas," she reminded him. "I have at least three tenants skip every year. It's almost routine—you wait until they're a month past due, and then you move their things out and put them in storage. At six months you sell their furniture to pay the storage and cleaning fees. We sold Ms. Barnett's at the beginning of this month."

"What about personal things? Checkbooks, letters, diaries?"

"Everything is sold together. Whoever bought the desk and chair got the letters and diaries too."

"Huh!" Spider said in disappointment. "Who handles the sale?"

"Ace Moving and Storage."

"Well, can you tell me about her?"

"About Mary Barnett?" The young woman glanced to check on the boys. "What do you want to know?"

"How old was she? Dark hair or light? Stuff like that."

The baby stirred. The young mother leaned her cheek against the downy head and rocked gently back and forth speaking softly. "She was a young middle-age. Forty or so, I'd say. Dark hair. Blue eyes. She wasn't pretty, but some might call her handsome in a cold kind of way."

"What did she do for a living?"

"I don't know."

"She wasn't a . . ." Spider indicated Number Four with his thumb.

"Prostitute? Could be. If she was, she did her business away from here. She said she was a bookkeeper, but she was always very coy about where she worked. I know one thing. If she was a hooker, she would have had a different clientele than Tiffany."

"Tiffany?"

"Number Four. Her clientele is blue collar—construction workers, like that. Ms. Barnett had pretensions to class."

"What do you mean?"

"She was always dropping names and flaunting labels. I

didn't have much to do with her—just collected the rent. But I always came away with a bad taste in my mouth. She would be, if she had any money, what my parents called 'nouveau riche.' Only she didn't have any money. She was as poor as we are, and that made her pretensions so pathetic."

"So, you wouldn't know anyone, friend or employer, who might give me a lead on where she is?"

"Uh-uh, unless . . ."

"Unless what?"

"Well, she had a business card on her table once when Geoff went in to fix a leaky tap. He came in and told me about it, because he recognized the name."

"Geoff is . . . ?

"My husband. We manage these apartments. Geoff does the maintenance."

"And the name on the business card?"

"It was some lawyer. My husband is in law school, and this guy is famous—or infamous. They call him the shark. Very dangerous to mess with."

"What was the name? Do you remember?"

She shook her head. "No. But Geoff gets home at four. If you want to call me then, I'll find out."

"If you'll write down your name and number, I'll do that."

"I'll give you one of my business cards." She checked the playing boys once more. Then she smoothly stood up and, one-handed, opened a purse sitting on the back of the sewing machine. Still one-handed she deftly opened a card case and extracted a business card. She handed it to Spider.

Spider looked at the inscription. Melodie Hale, Custom Sewing and Design. He stood. "Thanks, Melodie," he said. "I'll call just after four."

"There is one thing . . ."

Spider put the card in his shirt pocket and paused expectantly.

"Well, I almost think I should wait until Geoff gets home to talk to him about it."

Spider waited, hat in hand.

"Oh, what the heck. I'll be glad to get rid of it. Wait here."

Spider watched Melodie march purposefully down the hall to a closet at the end. Opening it, she dragged a box from a shelf and extracted a manila envelope. Leaving the box on the floor, she carried the envelope back. "Hold out your hand."

Spider switched his hat to his left hand and obediently held out his right. Melodie emptied the contents into his palm.

"She got behind in her rent towards the last, so she brought me these. She wanted me to hold on to them as surety until she could get me the rent she owed me. I didn't much want to, but she said it wouldn't be long."

"You didn't send these to Ace Moving?"

"No. Actually, I forgot about it. The new baby and all. And I was barely up and around after having Timmy when I had a wedding to do—brides, bridesmaids, mothers. The whole nine yards. When I finally remembered about this, the rest of the stuff was at Ace. I just let it go, figuring if she ever showed up, I'd give it back. But you can give it to her when you find her."

Spider examined the two objects. One was a plain gold ring. The other was silver and cigar-shaped, about three inches long and ornately decorated.

"It's a cigarette lighter," Melodie said. "She claimed it was sterling, but I don't think so."

Spider pulled back the hinged lid and spun the wheel with

his thumb. There was a spark but no flame. He rolled it twice more and was rewarded with a brief yellow flicker.

"Huh." He closed the lid again and examined the lighter.

"There isn't any monogram. There's something inside the ring, though."

Spider held the ring up to the light shining in through the window. "What does it say?"

"Forever."

"Ah. I see it. Forever. Huh."

"Can I get you to sign on the envelope that you took the things?"

"Sure." Spider put the lighter and ring in his jeans pocket. He set his Stetson on the sewing machine table next to where Melodie had placed the envelope and scratched his name and the date with the pen she provided.

Melodie read over his shoulder as he wrote. "Would you put your address in, too? That's fine. I just want to be covered when she comes back wanting her stuff."

"I doubt that she'll be back."

"Yeah. Me too."

Spider picked up his hat and offered his hand. "Thanks for all your help. I'll call back after four to get the name of that lawyer."

Melodie shook his hand with a firm clasp and then turned to open the door. Ushering him out, she stood in the doorway swaying back and forth, patting the sleeping babe.

As Spider got in his car, he heard her call to the two little boys to come in and have some juice. They shouted hooray and dropped their spoons. The last thing Spider saw in his rearview mirror was Melodie Hale with her baby on her shoulder, closing the apartment door behind her.

AS HE DROVE AWAY from the apartments, Spider considered his next move. What he needed was a phone book. A mile down the road he spied a phone booth outside a convenience store. He parked in the shade and bought a Pepsi and a bag of corn chips before he consulted the yellow pages and found that Ace Moving and Storage sat on the corner of Olive and Bridger. Spider wrote down the address in his spiral notebook and returned to the car to spread out his map. Munching on chips, he located the intersection. It was clear across town. Spider checked his watch. Quarter to three. He folded his map and finished his Pepsi. Then he tossed the cup and the crumpled-up chips bag out the window into a garbage barrel and left his shady spot to catch the cross-town arterial.

As he traveled, the housing developments became more upscale and the lawns and desert landscaping became neater. The booming prosperity of Las Vegas showed itself in teeming traffic and thriving businesses. How different from shriveled-up Lincoln County, he thought.

Past the center of the city, the five-lane arterial shrank to four lanes. Businesses became sparser and less prosperous looking and advertised low overhead on large billboards. Housing developments were interspersed with mobile-home parks, and all had great expanses in between, vacant except for tumbleweeds and windblown trash. The four lanes became two, and Spider looked around him with little hope for the errand ahead.

The outlook brightened when he found the moving company. The plant was attractive and well kept. Even the parking-lot stripes were newly painted. Spider parked between two crisp yellow lines and stepped out of the car, surveying. In front of him were four large roll-up doors and two regular doors, all painted the royal blue that trimmed the off-white of the square cinder-block building. Spider followed a sidewalk to the west corner, which was floor-to-ceiling windows. A glass door with bold royal blue and silver lettering said: "Ace Moving and Storage. Walk In."

Spider did.

He found a motherly, middle-aged receptionist with green-tinted bifocals parked behind a counter and under a huge banana tree. She smiled as he took off his hat and gazed up at the plant's full eight feet. As he looked around at the collection of ferns and palms that turned the office area into a mini-jungle, she said, "I like houseplants."

"So, the green thumb is yours, is it?"

She held up one of her thumbs and nodded.

"If you've got it, flaunt it."

She chuckled. "What can I do for you?"

"Well, if I had some things that were seized for non-payment of rent and sold at an auction by you folks, could I find out who bought my stuff?"

The eyes behind the bifocals changed. The smiling lines disappeared, and disapproval networked through the wrinkles on her grandmother face.

"It didn't happen to me," Spider assured her, setting his Stetson on the counter and fishing out his wallet.

"It happened to a friend, I suppose?"

"No, no. I'm a deputy sheriff."

"Yes, and I'm Raquel Welch."

"I thought I recognized you!" The joke fell flat. Spider finally got his wallet out and showed his badge.

The receptionist tilted her gray head back to examine it through her reading lenses. Without moving her head, she looked up into his eyes. "You don't look like a deputy. You don't dress like a deputy."

"I drive a deputy's car."

"Where?"

Spider indicated with his thumb, thankful that he had parked so the rear of the car was facing the window and not the offending, misspelled door panels. Grandma Raquel stepped to the window and parted a fern to look out. When she returned, the approval lines were back. Spider almost expected her to offer him milk and cookies.

She didn't offer anything. "I'm sorry, but I can't help you. Ace is the only one who can release the information you want."

"Ace?"

"The owner. This is Ace Moving and Storage."

"Yeah, I know. Well, then, I guess I need to talk to Ace."

Grandma held up her finger for silence and dialed a number.

"Ace, please." Pause. "Where?" Pause. "Thanks." She put down the receiver and said, "Ace is on the loading dock. Down the hall, first door on your left."

"Thank you, ma'am." Spider picked up his hat and sketched a wave with it as he headed down the hall.

The first door on the left opened onto a cavernous, unpainted, concrete room filled with trucks and forklifts and hand trucks, ramps and railings, crates and boxes. Several men in royal blue coveralls were busy as ants, ferrying loads to and from the trucks. Spider stood for a moment just inside the door, searching for some clue, either in dress or demeanor, as to who was the owner-ant, Ace. He was intent on reading the names on the coveralls: Boyd, Hal, Jack, when a door across the room opened and Ace walked out.

She was wearing a dark gray, pinstriped pantsuit that accentuated her leggy length. A snowy blouse, draped at the neck, muted the severity of the suit. It also set off black, shoulder-length hair cut in a carelessly elegant style, and olive skin, dark eyes, and perfect teeth. She was stunning.

Spider stood at the door with his hat in his hands and wished for the first time that he was wearing a uniform.

She saw him immediately. Impaled him in a long, lingering stare. Then she gave the clipboard she was holding to the man who followed her through the door and walked across the loading dock in a long, loose, confident stride.

"Are you Ace?" Spider asked as she approached him.

"Yes."

"How do, ma'am." He stuck out his hand, thinking, *How do? What kind of a greeting is that? Might as well announce you're from the sticks.* "Ah, I'm Spider Latham. Deputy sheriff from Lincoln County." *The sticks. I'm from the sticks.*

She was almost as tall as he was. Taking his hand in a firm clasp, she met his eyes with a frank look and a half smile. "Come into my office." The line would parse into a command, but Ace's smoky contralto made an invitation of it. No RSVP necessary.

Spider stepped aside as she passed by, and then followed her through the door at his back. She led him down the hall to a spacious office that was decorated in shades of gray, with black lacquer furniture and some brilliant foliage, as tall as the banana tree, cascading scarlet blossoms down a trellis in a corner. "I like your gardener," he said as she stood at the door to usher him in.

She closed the door. "My receptionist."

"Yeah. I met her."

"Sit down—I'm sorry. What did you say your name was?"

"Deputy Sheriff Spider Latham."

"From Lincoln County."

"Yeah. Lincoln County."

"What can I do for you, Deputy Latham? Please sit down."

Spider waited for her to sit behind her desk before he took a chair in front. A small smile turned up the corners of her mouth as she watched him place his hat on his lap. He took the spiral notebook from his pocket. "Your company held some furniture and personal effects in storage for the Ellis Apartments and sold them at auction the first of the month. I'd like to find out who bought those things."

"For what reason? Was any of it stolen goods?"

"No. The property belonged to someone that turned up dead in the desert in Lincoln County. We have a name, but we really don't know who she was. Don't know about family or anything like that."

"You said she turned up dead."

"We have reason to believe that there was foul play involved." *Foul play? We have reason to believe?* Spider shifted in his chair and crossed his legs and wondered how to sound less like a B movie.

"You mean she was murdered?"

"Maybe. Looks like."

Ace leaned back in her chair and regarded Spider. Her head was cocked to the side and she rested her cheek on one long, scarlet-nailed finger. "It is completely against our policy to give out the information you ask for."

Spider met her gaze but said nothing.

"So, what do you intend to do?"

"Do?" Spider stood. "Danged if I know. But it was worth a try."

"Sit down, Deputy Latham." Again, the husky voice turned the command into an invitation.

Spider sat.

"You intrigue me."

"Beg pardon?"

"You intrigue me. You're not the first officer of the law to come here looking for information. You are, however, the first gentleman. I will be most happy to do what I can to help you. Tell me again the name of the apartments and the date?"

Spider gave her the information and then waited as he was bid while she left the office. *A gentleman,* he thought to himself. *Well, I'll be.*

She wasn't gone long. Spider hadn't had time to do more than look at the furnishings and decide that his gray shirt was the right shade to go with the decor. When Ace returned she had nothing in her hand.

"I'm sorry. The person who bought that lot paid cash. There must not have been much, because it went for $50. Barely paid the storage. When someone pays cash we don't record the name of the buyer."

Spider stood. "Well, that's that." He looked at his watch. It was 4:05. "I wonder . . ."

"Yes?"

"Could I use your phone to make a call? The manager of the apartment had some information for me, and it would help out if I didn't have to go chasing down another phone booth."

"Be my guest."

"It's a call to North Las Vegas."

"That's all right." Ace pushed the button for line one and turned the phone around so it was accessible.

Spider fished the business card from his pocket and dialed the number. Melodie answered it on the third ring.

"I thought it must be you," she said when Spider identified himself. "Geoff told me the name of that lawyer. It's Jonas R. Vantage." Spider wrote the name down on the back of the card and wondered where he had heard it before. He thanked Melodie and rang off, then looked up to see Ace eyeing the name he had written.

"Jonas R. Vantage," he said. "Do you know the fellow?"

"The R. stands for Rattlesnake. Yes, I know him. He's an attorney. I've had business dealings with him, both here and in Reno."

"Reno?"

"He has offices there as well as here. So do I."

"Tell me about him."

"What's to tell? He's a snake."

"What dealings have you had with him?"

217

"They usually had to do with divorce. Maybe we had things in storage and the party of the first part was trying to get them away from the party of the second part."

"So, what happened?"

"It depended on who had Jonas Rattlesnake as his lawyer. Whoever had him won."

"As simple as that?"

"As simple as that."

"Fair means or foul?"

"Ostensibly, everything he did was legal. But I had one person say that he used intimidation on her."

"How's that?"

"She never could prove that the snake sent them, but two big, scary-looking thugs came one night and promised to cut up her face if she didn't sign the papers releasing the storage. She came in the next day and signed. She had a pretty face. It was her primary asset."

"Where was this? Here, or in Reno?"

"That was here."

"Huh. Jonas R. Vantage. I've heard that name before. Can't place where I heard it."

"Is he tangled up with the woman you're looking for?"

"I don't know. I guess I'd better find out."

"How are you going to do that?"

"Go on over to his office. Talk to him."

Ace shook her head. "You'll never get in to see him. Doesn't matter if you have a badge or a subpoena. If he doesn't want to see you, you won't get past the waiting room. Just a moment."

She picked up the phone and dialed a code. "Rocky? I need an appointment to see Jonas Vantage. Today. No, I know what time it is already." Pause. "I know what kind of a man he is."

Ace's voice showed a hint of steel. "Rocky, I need that appointment. Save the warnings and get it for me, please. Yes. Thank you. 'Bye."

Ace set the receiver down. "She mothers me."

"Is this the lady out under the banana tree?"

"No, it's my secretary. Next office down." She opened a desk drawer. Taking out a calling card, she uncapped a fountain pen and wrote a line on the back. The phone rang. "Hello? Good girl! Oh, he did? Well, that's fine. Let him think that."

She rang off and pushed the card over to Spider.

"Your appointment is at seven," she said. "You'll have to deal with the fact that he thinks he's taking me out to dinner afterward."

Spider picked up the card. It was off-white, of heavy, textured stock, with *Ace Lazzara* engraved in flowing script across the middle. Very discreetly, in the corner, was printed an address and telephone number. Spider turned the card over. On the back she had written, "This man is my friend. Treat him well."

Spider looked up and met her dark eyes. Her gaze held his, and he was the first to look away. He stared at the card. Running his thumb over the engraving, he felt the contours of the letters and the grain of the cardstock. Choosing his words carefully, he said, "You've said how you feel about this man. I get the idea that he feels differently about you."

"Are you afraid that you are going to put me under some obligation to him?"

Spider looked up. He didn't reply.

She shook her head. "He wants two things from me. The first is an entree into a circle in Vegas that I'm connected to by blood. The second . . ." She shrugged. "He won't get either."

Silence.

The dusky voice had a softness about it. "Don't worry, Deputy Latham. And by the way, tell me again. What is your name? I can't keep calling you Deputy."

"Ah. Folks call me Spider."

"I thought you said Spider. How did you get that name?"

"I was born in the spring. By the time I started crawling, the floor was cold, so I'd crawl on my hands and feet instead of my hands and knees. My daddy said I looked like a daddy longlegs, and he started calling me Spider. The name just stuck."

She smiled, showing a row of beautiful teeth. "That's like my story. My name is Maria Gabriella Angelina. But my father, who has an interest in several casinos, kept calling me his ace in the hole. I've been Ace all my life."

"It fits you."

"Well, thank you." She looked at her watch. "Your appointment isn't until seven. Let me take you to dinner. I know a little place just near Jonas's office. It's quiet, the food is great, and they have a wine cellar that's as good as any in New York."

"Ah . . . thank you. The invitation is . . . ah, I appreciate it. Thanks. But, I can't."

"Can't? Or won't? There's a difference."

Spider looked down at the card he still held in his hand. He stuck it in his left shirt pocket and picked up his hat. Only then did he meet her eyes. "I think they both come to the same thing. I have the time. I'm hungry. But I'm also married."

"I thought you probably were, Spider. But in this day and age people often go to dinner with other people's husbands and wives in the way of business."

"Well, I come from Lincoln County, and we haven't quite come to this day and age yet. Besides, I don't believe business had anything to do with it."

"It didn't. Aren't you the least bit tempted?"

Spider smiled. "Well, of course I am. And flattered." He stood. "And I appreciate your help with old Rattlesnake Vantage. If I'm ever in a position to return the favor, I'll be glad to."

"But you won't go to dinner with me?"

"No, ma'am." He transferred his hat to his left hand and held out his right, reaching across the desk. "Thanks again."

She took his hand without rising. "Good-bye, Spider. Good luck."

He smiled down at her. Then he released her hand and walked out the door.

★ ★ ★

Spider blinked as he stepped out of the green-shaded reception area into the bright desert afternoon. He put on his hat and surveyed the surrounding neighborhood as he walked to his car. "Half my time is spent looking for phone booths," he muttered.

He found one at a convenience store back toward the center of town. Standing in line at the checkout stand to get change for a dollar, he smelled fried chicken that reminded him how long it had been since his peanut-butter sandwich. The deli clerk was lifting sizzling, crusty pieces out of the pressure fryer and laying them neatly onto a tray. As she slid it into the deli case, she saw Spider watching. "Better have some. It's good chicken."

"Smells good." The dollar that Spider was changing was one third of the money that he had on him. He looked at the drumsticks lying neatly in a row and wished he hadn't spent his money on corn chips. Then he thought of the card in his pocket and the phone number written in script in the corner.

What if he were to call Ace Lazzara and tell her he had changed his mind? She had only offered him dinner. Nothing wrong in that, in this day and age.

The person in front of him left. Spider stepped forward and asked for change. The clerk gave him a half-dollar and two quarters.

Outside at the phone booth, Spider took the card out of his pocket. He read the number. He set the quarters on the shelf.

"I'll call Laurie first," he said out loud and punched 0 and then his own number. He waited as the operator asked Laurie if she would accept the charges. Then he said, "Hello, Darlin'."

"Oh, Spider, I'm so glad you called!"

"What's the matter?"

"Nothing's the matter. I have messages for you. Randi Lee called about the BLM land that's coming up for lease out by Delmar. Jonathan Chamberlain had the lease. Bud Hefernan has already filed for it for the Hughes family. Also, Bucketa Blood called and wanted me to tell you he found out the name of the Elk Woman. The journalist from back east."

"What was it?"

"Isabel Blunt."

"Huh."

"And Spider . . ."

"Yeah?"

"I remembered where I had heard that name!"

"Isabel Blunt? You never said you remembered it."

"No, the other one. Mary Margaret Barnett."

"You did! Where did you hear it?"

"It was at Bobby's university graduation. Remember, when they were giving out diplomas and they called the name and nobody came up to get it, and they called again."

Spider noticed he was still holding the calling card in his hand and absentmindedly stuffed it in his pocket. "I don't remember."

"That's because it was a B at the beginning, and you were only interested in Bobby, who was an L and coming later. But she was in Bobby's graduating class! Her picture would be in the yearbook—or maybe they have a copy of the picture on her student body card on file at the registrar's office."

"Well, I'll be hanged."

There was a silence while Spider digested this information, and finally Laurie asked, "Are you still there?"

"Yeah. I'm just thinking. The university is clear across town from here, and there's no way I could reach it before the registrar's office closes up shop. Great Suffering Zot."

"Well, you could look in the library. Her picture is probably in the yearbook, and they would have one of those in the university library, wouldn't they?"

"Good idea. I'll give it a try."

"Okay. One more thing. Murray came by and graded that gravel. He wanted to know where you were, and I told him you went to Vegas on business. But Spider . . ."

"Yeah?"

"On my way to check on the Fluff children this afternoon I passed Murray's pickup parked alongside the road there at the bridge across the wash."

"Huh. Was he there? Did you see him?"

"No. I slowed down and looked around, but I didn't see anyone. Do you suppose he was down in the wash?"

"Maybe. Bud must have told him I was down there digging. He was just probably interested in what was going on. Any sign of Rose? Randi Lee didn't say anything about her?"

"No."

"Shoot. I don't suppose a man by the name of Kurt Wiggins has called?"

"No. But I was gone for a while. Do you want me to make some calls and call you back there?"

"No. Look, Laurie, I'll probably be home late tonight, so don't wait up."

"That late, huh?"

"Yeah, that late."

★   ★   ★

It was indeed that late. It was ten o'clock at night before Spider climbed into his cruiser and headed for the freeway. The librarian at the university library had been helpful, and within five minutes Spider was staring at the face of Mary Margaret Barnett. She was, as Melodie had said, handsome in a cold kind of a way.

His mission at the office of Jonas Rattlesnake Vantage was not accomplished with such dispatch. The polished and brittle receptionist had taken the information about the substitution of Spider for Ace along with the calling card and disappeared into the inner sanctum. Returning, she announced that Mr. Vantage would give Spider ten minutes in a half hour. Spider thanked her, then eyed the vacant waiting room. The couches, done in muted mauve and teal, looked deep and soft. He chose a straight-backed chair in a corner. He sat, put his hat on the lamp table beside him, and leaned his head back against the angle in the wall. When he closed his eyes he saw again the middle-aged eyes looking out at him from among the banks of fresh young faces in the yearbook. It would be no bad thing if Mr. Vantage decided not to see him at all. Spider didn't want to pursue this any further. He was tired of the whole thing. Tired, tired, tired.

Spider woke himself up snoring. He had to blink his eyes and scramble mentally to remember where he was. The waiting room was dusky, lit by a single mauve ceramic lamp across the room. The window that had let in the late afternoon sun was now a black rectangle hung on the wall. The reception desk was vacant and tidy. Spider walked over to it, stood still, and listened. The only sound he heard was the faint hum of blue-finned screen savers swimming across the face of the computer monitor. Then another intermittent, rhythmic whistling noise reached his ears.

It seemed to be coming from down a hall. Spider stepped behind the receptionist's desk and poked his head through the doorway. The hallway was wide and dimly lit from sconces on the wall. There were four generous-sized doors spaced along the hall, each set off with opulent, dark molding. One of the doors stood open, allowing a shaft of light to fall through and slice across the dusky blush of the carpet.

Spider listened. There it was again, a faint and wheezy whistling.

He walked down the hall toward the open doorway, his footsteps muffled by the deep pile of the carpet. Pausing just at the edge of shadow and light, he leaned slightly to allow one eye a peek into the room.

What he saw caused him to step into the light and lean a shoulder against the doorframe, surveying the scene.

The room was large and decorated for power. The credenza, bookcase, and armoire were substantial and satiny dark. Pictures were massive, done in bold colors and framed in the same sleek brown wood as the furniture and moldings. The desk was a huge wooden expanse, designed to intimidate who-ever was sitting in either of the two straight-backed chairs in front of it. But there was nothing intimidating about the paunchy, balding, middle-aged man who sat in the high-backed swivel chair behind the desk.

He wasn't actually sitting. He was lolling. His arms hung down and his head was tilted over and back into an uncomfortable-looking position. His eyes were closed and his mouth was slack, and after each long-drawn breath, a wheez-ing whistle escaped from between the flaccid lips. On the desk in front of him were a Big Mac container and a paper cup with a lid and straw. Spider paused only a moment to reflect on the old saw about being caught napping before he tapped on the open door with the knuckles of his right hand. Then he watched in appreciation as lids opened, mouth closed, limbs came to order, scattered wits were marshaled, and beady, cal-culating eyes were bent his way.

Ace called it right, he thought. *Snake.*

"Ah, good evening, sir. I'm Deputy Sheriff Spider Latham of Lincoln County. Your receptionist said you'd see me a while back. I wondered if you were free yet. I won't take much of your time."

The reptilian eyes flicked to the clock on the wall and back to Spider. "Sit down." He picked up the fast-food garbage and dropped it into a wastebasket beside his desk. "I can give you ten minutes."

Spider stayed a half hour.

At first the lawyer denied any knowledge of Mary Margaret Barnett. When Spider stood abruptly and, fists clenched, told him to cut the crap, Jonas Vantage picked up the phone and pressed a speed-dial button.

Spider took two steps, grabbed the phone cord, and yanked it out of the wall. "Now, I've had a long day," he said. "My patience is wearing thin. I have good reason to believe that this woman was a client of yours, and I'd appreciate a little effort expended before you try to brush me off. Where are your files?"

The smaller man did not shrink as Spider stood over him. He made a steeple of his hands. "They are in the vault, but my secretary has gone home."

"Well, you just slither on in there and see what you can find yourself. I'll come with you."

Spider stood away and allowed Jonas Vantage to rise and precede him out into the hall and down two doors to a windowless room across from the receptionist area. Banks of mahogany file cabinets flanked all four walls. A heavy library table with four green-shaded reading lamps and a telephone took up space in the center of the room.

Jonas Vantage stopped just inside the door and opened the drawer of a cabinet. Spider strolled to the table and moved the telephone across the room. Then he pulled out a chair and sat down as the lawyer pulled an accordion file from the drawer and carried it to the table.

Jonas Vantage turned on the nearest lamp. "I'll need a few minutes to acquaint myself with what's in here."

"Take your time."

The lawyer took his time. Unhurriedly, he read through the documents in the file box, placing each one in a neat pile, face down, as he finished with it. Then he leaned back in the chair, put his fingertips together, and gave Spider a complete and precise rendering of his dealings with the woman in question.

When he was finished, Spider thanked him. He stood and went unaccompanied across the dim hallway to the waiting room to retrieve his hat. As he passed the receptionist's desk, he saw a light on the switchboard light up, and through the open doorway he heard Jonas R. Vantage hissing, "Get over here right now!"

Spider carried his hat as he left the office suite and rode the elevator down to the lobby. Once outside, he paused to put it on and to look around at the downtown area. The neon lights of the Jack-O-Diamonds Casino flashed on and off two blocks away. They sold breakfast twenty-four hours a day at the restaurant there. He could get a short stack of pancakes with sausage and eggs for two dollars. Spider looked at his watch. Nine o'clock. Torn between the desire to be home and the hunger in his belly, he stood for a moment, undecided. The malevolent command that Jonas Vantage issued—to whom? bodyguards?—lurked around the edges of Spider's consciousness and made him uneasy. It might not be wise to hang around too long. But, he reasoned, the cruiser was parked out of sight on a side street four blocks away, and he doubted anyone would look for him in a casino. "My kingdom for a pancake," he muttered, and set off walking toward the Jack-O-Diamonds Casino.

An hour later, squinting at the lights of Las Vegas in his rearview mirror, Spider wondered if this was any way to make a living. Then he set his mind to making sense of the things he had found, and wondered when and how he would be able to deal with the heartache.

CHAPTER

COMING THROUGH WINDMILL Canyon at midnight, Spider nailed a five-point buck in his headlights. The deer stood motionless, held frozen just long enough for Spider to note the magnificent rack of antlers. He hit the brakes, but in that instant the deer wheeled and bounded off into the darkness.

"So where were you," Spider muttered, "last October when I was tramping through these hills looking for something to fill my freezer? I had to settle for a runty two-point buck."

As Spider resumed speed, winding his way through the serpentine canyon, his mind drifted back to deer season a month previous. He and Murray had taken two days to pack into the hills, gaining access to territory where the hoards of wealthy-but-rushed weekend hunters from Las Vegas didn't go.

During the week they were out, he and Murray had gone through their repertoire of stories. The annual deer hunt was more than a way to get meat for the family. It was a ritual, a celebration of a common beginning and a common upbringing. Though their lives had taken different roads, in the telling of old tales they reaffirmed the bonds of time, place, blood, and religion.

Murray was the one who had told the story about Brother Heaton. It was the evening of the day they both got their deer. The carcasses were dressed and quartered and hung from the limbs of a piñon tree. Both men were tired, and as the campfire cast a comfortable glow against the brisk October night, Murray had leaned back against a log, patted his pocket, and withdrawn a battered package of Marlboros. "You remember old Moses Heaton?" he asked Spider as he felt inside the package with his index finger. "Every testimony meeting, you'd figure on at least twenty minutes shot by him telling how he went on his mission without purse or scrip. You remember all us deacons sitting there on the front row would make bets as to which of his five stories he was going to tell." Murray had paused to light his cigarette, and then ticked them off on his fingers. "The miracle of the five-dollar gold piece, being tarred and feathered, shelter in the lightning storm, his one-and-only convert, or . . ." Murray paused in thought, index finger poised on his pinkie. Finally he looked expectantly at Spider. "I can't remember the fifth one," he said.

"Receiving a witness of Christ," Spider had supplied.

"That's it. I remember we'd all put a penny in the pot, and you were usually the one who won the nickel."

"Yeah, five cents would buy a lot then. A candy bar or a Milk-Nickel."

They had sat in silence for a moment, both gazing into the campfire and remembering those hot summer Sundays with the tall windows of the old rock chapel open top and bottom in the hope that an afternoon breeze would come through, and the congregation quietly sitting through the long silences, fanning themselves with cardboard fans provided by Stowe's Mortuary as they waited for the next person moved upon by the Spirit to stand and address his brothers and sisters.

"Brother Heaton's ninety-five years old now," Spider had said.

"He still get up every time?"

"Yeah."

"Still take twenty minutes?"

"No. He's on oxygen, one of those little roll-around tanks that follows him around, and he takes it off to come up to the pulpit. Can't be off it more than about five minutes, so when he gets to sounding faint, Bishop hustles him back down to his pew."

"Poor old feller. Does he still cover the same ground?"

"Naw. Oh, every now and then he hits one of the other stories, but mostly he talks about his witness of Christ."

"I don't suppose the young folks pay him any more mind than we did."

"Naw. I suppose not."

Again the silence stretched out between them. Murray had finished his cigarette and flicked the smoldering remnant into the fire. "Have you ever wondered," he asked pensively, "who you would be if you had made different choices early on?"

★   ★   ★

The blinking hazard lights of a vehicle in the distance brought Spider back to the present, and he realized that while he was thinking about Murray and the deer hunt, he had driven through Caliente and was just a mile from the turnoff to his place. Hoping that this wasn't something that was going to take a block of the deputy's already depleted night, Spider slowed to a stop, parking behind an older pickup truck with Utah plates that was sitting on the shoulder of the road with the hood up.

Leaving his key in the ignition, and taking his flashlight from under the seat, Spider left his headlights on and got out. As he walked around the pickup, he could see that there were two men standing there, hidden from the waist up by the shadow of the car hood.

One of them spoke, "Are you Deputy Latham?"

Spider recognized the southern Utah twang, though not the voice.

"Yeah. What's the trouble?"

"Dunno. That's what we're trying to figure out."

"Need a flashlight?"

"Yeah. Why don't you shine it down there."

Spider caught a glimpse of a white Stetson and a weathered face in the peripheral light as he turned on his torch. The other man had faded into the shadows. "Down where?" he asked.

"Down there, alongside the intake manifold."

"What do you think is wrong?" Spider directed his beam at the place indicated.

"I thought there might be a vacuum hose that come loose or something."

Spider smelled the warm and yeasty odor of beer on the fellow's breath as he leaned closer. "I don't see anything. What was the motor doing?"

Leaning over the grille of the pickup, shining his light on a greasy engine block and listening to the nasal whine of the driver's voice, Spider suddenly had the feeling that all was not well. The hair at the back of his neck began to prickle, and, sensing movement behind him, he abruptly straightened and looked around. Feeling self-conscious about responding to his unease, he had left the light pointed inside the pickup hood, and he saw only in shadows the tall, lean form standing with hand upraised. There was no mistaking the menace in that stance, and instinctively Spider brought the hand with the torch up in front of himself in a defensive gesture. He felt the jolt as it connected with his assailant's hand, which was wrapped around a tire iron. The tall fellow swore, and there was a ringing clatter as the metal bar went bouncing on the pavement and the flashlight went out.

Spider's wits finally caught up to his involuntary reactions, and he realized that he was out-manned and ill-armed. His only weapon was the now-torchless torch.

He went with what he had. Charging at the tall form he could see outlined in the cruiser's headlights, he swung the flashlight with all the force he could muster. He was stopped in mid-stride by a pile driver of a blow that caught him on the shoulder and spun him around. He stumbled against the pickup fender, caught his balance, and turned back to his attacker.

"Get 'im, Clint!" he heard the other man call.

Clint tried to oblige. He bored in, aiming first a right and then a left at Spider's midsection. Spider grunted at the force of the blows, but stood squarely, waiting for a chance to wield the flashlight. He took another right to the belly, and then Clint's head was down and in range as the blow carried through. Spider brought the flashlight down behind his ear, and then watched, half surprised, as he crumpled.

Without waiting to see where Clint's companion was,

Spider sprinted toward his cruiser. He had the door open and was in and turning on the key before the other man was out from in front of the pickup. Spider was aware of his running approach, but figured that, discretion being the better part of valor, flight would make more sense than fumbling with a locked glove compartment and trying to get his gun. Cursing his inexperience as a deputy, he jerked the lever on the steering column down and stepped on the accelerator. The moment the wipers started spreading cleaning fluid, Spider realized what he had done, but he had already lost precious, needed seconds. Clint's friend was reaching for the door with one hand, and he had the tire-iron in the other. Just as Spider thought to press down the driver's door lock before shifting gears, he realized that the crafty son-of-a gun had opened the back door instead, and before he could find drive with the floor shift, the tire iron came down in a shower of stars and everything went black.

★   ★   ★

The next sensation Spider had was of cold. He was lying face up on a frigid and rocky surface with his hands tied together in front of him. He opened his eyes, but there was no lessening of the blackness, and he blinked once to make sure his eyelids were working. Telling himself that this was a dream and that in a moment he would waken in his bed with Laurie beside him, he tried to stay calm. Turning his head to see if he could see anything to his right, he felt such a stab of pain that it almost made him sick. So he lay still with his eyes squeezed shut, breathing in shallow pants until the nausea subsided.

Definitely not a dream, he thought.

He opened his eyes again, blinking in an effort to see, to get some bearing, to find out where he was. There was a sense of unreality about the whole thing. He couldn't for the life of him figure out why he should be so cold, why his head should be throbbing, or why he could not see. Common sense told him that complete and engulfing blackness like this came only with being shut away from sun, away from moon, away from even the scanty light of stars. But the dry, rocky ground that he lay on, and the cold breeze blowing over his face, told him he was shut in no house.

He was blind.

Tears welled up in Spider's open and staring eyes. Cursing himself for being a ninny, he squeezed his eyes shut. The tears spilled over and ran down the furrows around his eyes and into his ears. As Spider lifted his tied-together hands to wipe away the wetness, the pain in his midsection brought everything back.

He remembered the nasal voice asking, "Are you Deputy Latham?" He saw in memory his lanky attacker, coming from the shadows with a bludgeon, and he felt still—here and now—the effects of that final blow that had left him in darkness. In a futile gesture, Spider lifted his bound hands and held them in front of his face, staring hard with eyes wide open.

Nothing.

Dropping his hands, he lay still, biting his lower lip.

When he felt he had control of himself, in order to ease the discomfort from a rock that was digging into his hip, Spider cautiously moved his left leg to the side, being careful not to move his head and court that searing pain again. The heel of his cowboy boot hit something hard and unmoveable, and the sound rang unnaturally loud through the blackness. It took a moment for the significance of that sound to cut through the layers of pain and despair, but presently Spider tentatively kicked the object again with his boot heel and listened to the metallic thunk that echoed around him. Instantly alert, he ran his boot heel along the metal object, bending his knee to slide his foot as far as possible. Then he lay quietly and considered.

If I were to guess, he thought, careful not to jump too hastily to a conclusion that would give him hope, *I'd say that was a rail.*

He lay still a moment longer, letting his mind play out the possibilities, and then he shouted "Hello!" into the blackness and listened to the sound bouncing back into his face.

He had heard that sound before.

With hope the unbearable can be borne. A tiny spike of hope had shown itself, and with it came an impatience with cringing in the dirt. If he could not move his head to the right, perhaps he could move it to the left. Slowly he began the attempt, noting a soreness and a definite increase in the throbbing headache, but not the stabbing, sickening pain he had encountered earlier.

Heartened, he decided to sit up.

Bad idea.

Because his hands were tied together, he had held them out in front and used his stomach muscles to jerk himself to a sitting position. Every place that Clint had landed a blow screamed in protest, and as Spider sat up, the tensing of neck muscles caused a pain to slice through the right side of his head. Defensively, he held his hands over his ear, awkwardly cradling the hemisphere, holding it tightly lest it fall off. He broke out in a clammy sweat as the waves of nausea returned, along with a buzzing in his ears.

Knowing that if he fainted he'd be flat on the ground again, Spider carefully drew up his knees and bent over so that his head was hanging between them. Gradually the nausea left and the buzzing subsided.

There. He was sitting up.

Spider decided to rest a while and savor this small victory.

The cool breeze evaporating the sweat made him shiver, and he realized he was better off to keep moving, even if it was slowly. So he reached to the right with his hand, groping through the pebbles until he found the cold, hard surface that he was looking for. It was definitely a rail.

Another victory. By identifying this track and the echoing sounds, Spider had established that he was in a mine. He didn't know which one, or where. He knew that bumping around an abandoned shaft in the dark was a risky business. But hope was recently fledged and could not be kept from soaring.

The next business at hand was—the hands. That was easily, if awkwardly, taken care of. Spider's pocketknife was in a scabbard at the back of his belt, and he strained to get his left arm to stretch enough to allow his right hand to reach back around.

Maybe it wasn't easily taken care of.

The snap that closed the leather case was just beyond his fingertips, and even if he could open it, he didn't know that he could get hold of the knife.

He was sweating again. Grunting, he strained once more, trying so hard to gain those extra fractions of an inch that inadvertently he moved his head to the right and felt the base of his skull explode into red-hot splinters. Immediately penitent, Spider froze, bracing himself for the sickening waves of nausea. Miraculously, they didn't come.

Spider waited only long enough for the fiery prickles to subside, and then he unbuckled his belt and pulled it out of the belt loops. He heard with satisfaction the sound of his knife scabbard hitting the ground. Gingerly, he inched himself around on his backside to where he could easily pick up the case with both hands. After a minimum of time spent groping in the dirt, he found it. Opening the knife, he clamped it in his teeth while he sawed back and forth with his hands. He felt the tickle on his nose as individual strands were cut through and sprang back. Finally, one of the cords gave completely away. Another minute and his hands were free.

Spider waited for a trembling weakness to pass, thinking how susceptible he was to the least little emotional feeling. Then he took the knife from his teeth and closed it, putting it in its scabbard and leaving it in his lap while he fumbled in the darkness with his belt. The knife could go in his pocket—he wouldn't worry about trying to put it back on the belt right now. With the knife in his hand, he scooted on his haunches away from the rail, inching across the uneven surface until his back touched a rock. Feeling behind him with first his right hand and then his left, he determined that this must be a wall. Oh so carefully, he rolled to his knees. Then slowly, and with the aid of the wall in front of him, he gained his feet.

He was sweating again.

Spider leaned in and pressed his cheek against the rocky face, grateful for the coolness even though the uneven, jagged points dug into his flesh. *I'll just stand here a minute,* he thought, *and then I'll figure out what I've got to do next.*

But, propped against the wall like a rag doll on a shelf, Spider realized that the throbbing, radiating pain at the back of his head kept spreading into an ever-widening circle. He felt it sopping up every thought, every feeling that wasn't manually and forcefully thrust forward. He knew he had to keep concentrating on a plan of action or he could die. His would be the next bones lying hidden in the desert waiting for some wandering, curious adolescent to find them by chance.

"All right," he said aloud, trying to focus his efforts. "So what now?"

He thought for a moment. "Put the knife in your pocket," he told himself out loud. That would leave both hands free and keep him from dropping it in the dark.

Glad to have purpose again, Spider began to push the leather-sheathed tool into his pocket, only to puzzle at the object that was already there. What was it? It was shaped like a small cigar, but hard and metallic. Spider slipped his hand in his pocket and felt the smooth surface. Then he remembered. It was the silver cigarette lighter.

Such was his mental torpor that it was a moment before the importance of his find occurred to Spider. When it hit him, he had to grasp the wall again because his knees began to buckle, and he feared that he would go down. As he clung there waiting for the beating of his heart to return to normal, he whispered over and over, "Please, God . . . Please, God . . . Please, God . . ."

When he felt that he could turn loose of the wall, Spider took the lighter from his pocket. With hands that felt like they were new on the job, he finally managed to get the lid off. Turning it in his hand until his thumb was on the little wheel, he flicked it.

There was no yellow flame, but Spider couldn't resist a small shout of triumph. A blue spark had jumped from his fist, a tiny pinpoint of light that was erased in a millisecond. There was no doubt that it had been there. His eyes had seen it.

He was not blind.

Heartened, Spider tried the lighter again. And again. Each time the blessed blue spark danced in the darkness, Spider felt a quiet surge of returning strength. When the wick finally caught and a light flickered in his hand, Spider found that he was standing without support.

He held the lighter aloft, peering into the shadows for some clue as to where he was. He was rewarded with the sight of a set of shelves, familiar because he had seen them just days before. They were the shelves his father had built and placed in the Empress Mine.

Excitement drove him forward, and he stumbled over the uneven footing in his haste to push open the door and get out. But the door didn't swing open at his touch. Thinking it might have become wedged, he kicked at the bottom. There was no give at all in the two-by-twelves that made up the gate. With rising panic, Spider slammed his shoulder against the door. For his efforts, his head threatened to split open again. He sagged against the wooden breastwork and waited for the pain to subside.

"Great Suffering Zot," he whispered. "How'm I ever going to get out of here? I'd need a chain saw to cut through this. All I've got is a pocket knife and a little old silver . . ."

Spider's voice trailed off as an idea began to take form in his mind. Standing in the darkness of the mine, he saw in living color all the resources, all the steps needed to free himself from this prison. Chuckling, Spider said to himself, "My daddy has left me quite a legacy this week."

Using his lighter only when he had to have it to see, Spider first gathered up all the newspapers that his mother had placed on these shelves forty years before and set them in a pile by the wooden wall. Then, heedless of the pain it caused, he jerked on the shelves until they fell crashing to the ground. Grunting because of the weight, he turned them edgeways, and, bracing his back against the wall, he stood on one leg of the unit and pushed his foot against the other, rocking it back and forth until he had destroyed the structural integrity of the set. Finally, he sat on it, straddling it as he would a bronco and gritting his teeth as it buckled under him and he hit the ground. For a moment his head split and his ears rang, but Spider knew that if he let pain get in the way, he would never get out. Determinedly, he picked himself up and began tearing the boards apart.

It was hard work. Spider was sweating and panting long before he was through, but he drove himself to finish the task before he allowed himself to rest. Even then, he paused only a few minutes, sensing that if he waited too long he wouldn't have the courage to go on.

Working mostly in the dark, he broke the one-by-twelves up into kindling by the process of laying one end of a board on the rail and jumping on it. Each time he landed, the jolt to his frame ended in a searing pain at the back of his head. When his ears started ringing and a light flashed at the back of his eyes each time he jumped, Spider decided he had enough.

All this took a fair amount of time and so much energy that, in the end, Spider's hands were trembling. When he was finished, the crumpled newspaper and kindling, along with the leftover, unbroken boards, were piled against the wooden barrier. Resting only long enough to steady his hands so he could work the lighter, Spider conjured up the tiny torch and lit the edges of the newspaper all around the bottom of the pile. Then he stood back to watch.

It was amazing how light the cavern became with the glow of six or seven tiny flames. *Compared to pitch black,* Spider thought, *anything seems bright.*

The tiny flames were larger now, licking over the kindling

and flaring up against the dry wood of the barricade. Spider began to smell pungency in the air. Already he could feel a warmth on his face. The snapping and crackling of the kindling pine echoed all around as the fire caught and held.

The mine was filling with smoke, and Spider took advantage of the firelight to move farther along the shaft. He felt the breeze blowing by and hoped that enough could get through the chinks in the wall to carry the smoke away. He didn't want to have to go too far in to escape it. There was always the danger of rotten timbers and the roof caving in, not to mention unexpected vertical shafts or pools of water. It was all pretty dicey if you couldn't see where you were going.

The mine shaft angled sharply down into the mountain after the first twenty-five feet or so, and Spider soon found himself in a shadowy tunnel, able to look on the wall above and see the rosy flickering of the fire, but unable to see ten feet ahead. The smoke, in spite of the breeze blowing through the mine, was sent billowing back on waves of heat. When it hit the cooler air, it dropped down around Spider, making him breathe in shallow drafts. He pushed cautiously deeper into the darkness.

He had not gone far when he barked his shins on something jagged and hard. Igniting the lighter, he saw that it was a broken timber that was sticking out of a pile of rocks. There had been a cave-in. Holding the lighter high, he peered through the smoke and discovered that the timber just above him was sagging.

Spider's eyes were burning. The smoke was beginning to gag him. The cavern roof behind him was lit with an eerie, flickering orange glow, and the crackling sounds of combustion bounced from one wall to another, creating a constant din that was overlaid with a whooshing roar. Spider retraced three or four steps and hunkered down. Breathing was instantly easier, but just at that moment, from the direction of the entrance, he heard a sound like a rifle shot, and then the crashing rumble of the roof falling in.

Squatting in the rubble from one cave-in, and listening to another, Spider was terribly aware of his peril. Instinctively, he went from a squat to a kneeling position, and, heedless of the rocks digging into his knees, he spoke to God aloud in words that he couldn't hear above the infernal sounds in the cave.

He quit praying when the blanket of smoke settled low enough to make breathing a problem again. Thinking that the noise seemed to be a little less intense, and hoping that he wouldn't be driven back farther into the mine, Spider carefully lay down on his back so that he could watch the firelight on the ceiling. Grateful for cleaner air at floor level, he folded his hands over his chest and listened again in memory to the order Jonas R. Vantage had hissed into the telephone. It was inconceivable that Spider could have bartered his life for a short stack. But Clint and company had been definitely been waiting for him. Who else would have done this? And why?

★   ★   ★

Two hours later, the fire was a barely discernible glow on the hillside, and Spider was hoofing it south on Highway 93, figuring that at five in the morning he didn't have much chance to catch a ride.

His exit from the mine had been easier than anticipated. Only a few rocks had fallen from the roof. The sound had been magnified by the close quarters and his heightened awareness. He had picked his way among the rubble on the cavern floor.

Then he had made two giant leaps to clear the glowing coals at the entrance, and all at once he had found himself standing in cool, clean desert air. The moon had not yet gone down, and he could see quite plainly the old railroad grade and the dirt road that led down to the highway.

He had been halfway down, playing over in his mind the experience he had just had, and thinking how grateful he was to have come out of it as well as he did, when he remembered the heavy praying he had done toward the end, remembered asking the Lord to delay any imminent cave-ins until he was gone. Maybe a word of thanks would be in order.

Spider hadn't stopped right then. Though his mind hadn't formed the words, "I'll do it later," his legs had kept on marching down the hill. The thought even flickered through, just the tiniest impression of a thought, really, that the prayer hadn't been necessary. There had been no real danger of a cave-in. The danger had been all in his head.

As tiny as the thought had been, it made him ashamed. He stopped. Looking around, and feeling silly at doing so, he made sure he was alone. Then he knelt in the soft dirt at the side of the road. A small animal scurried away and rustled into a clump of sagebrush. A bat went squeaking above him. Far in the distance, Spider saw the headlights of a car. If he started down to the highway right now, he might be able to catch a ride at least as far as Pioche. Stifling the urge to jump up and run, he closed his eyes and cleared his mind, and began to speak softly, fashioning a thank-you from the feelings in his heart. He had just said amen and gained his feet again when he heard a rifle shot.

As he dived down behind a clump of sagebrush, a thousand thoughts ran through Spider's mind. Damning himself for a fool for presenting such an inviting target, silhouetted against the moon, and thinking that he had this all figured out wrong, he cautiously raised his head and searched the hillside in the direction of the report.

What he saw was a cloud of sparks swirling around the entrance to the mine. He heard, too, the clatter of rolling rocks, and realized that what he thought was a rifle shot was really the sound of a heat-stress fracture in the stone at the entrance to the mine. The roof had caved in. Spider stared at the spot where embers still glowed in the night and said to himself, "Huh. Boy, am I ever glad I said thanks."

As the car drove by below him, Spider stood up. Then, disregarding the dull ache at the back of his head, he began ambling down the dirt track whistling "Count Your Blessings."

As it turned out, he had barely gained the highway when he heard a car approaching. Turning around so that he was walking backwards, he stuck his thumb in the air and tried to look benign. The car slowed, and Spider stepped to the side waiting for it to stop. It was no one familiar. The license plate was from Elko County, and it was an older Mercedes limo. A diesel, he decided from the telltale gnarling under the hood. The car came abreast of him, and he could see that it was driven by a woman. She was young and slender, and the dash lights played off blonde curls.

The electric passenger-side window glided down, and a little-girl voice spoke from inside. *Boy, this is my day to mingle with the tarts,* Spider thought.

"Is that you, Bishop?"

It was Rose Markey, on her way home from Elko. She was glad to take him wherever he needed to go, chatting gaily about her trip and displaying not the least curiosity about why he should be fifteen miles away from his car at five-thirty in the morning, or why he reeked of smoke and looked like his complexion had blackened overnight.

When Spider mentioned that the girls had been worried about their mother, she exclaimed, "Oh, didn't I tell them? I was so excited I must have forgotten. Well, they will forgive me when they see what I have done."

"There's the car," Spider said when he spied his cruiser. Mentally he gave thanks that it was still there. Now, if the keys were still in the ignition . . .

He sat clenching his teeth as Rose jockeyed the boat of a car back and forward, back and forward, turning around in the middle of the deserted road. When she finally pulled up parallel with the county car, Spider asked for her to wait for a moment and left his door open while he stepped out to check the ignition. The keys were there. He was in business.

Turning back to Rose, he was just about to close the door when he picked up on what she had said. "What have you done, Rose, that is going to make the girls so happy?" he asked.

"I've invested the money."

"Your insurance settlement?"

"Yes. I bought this car. What do you think?"

"You bought this car? As an investment?"

"Yes. I bought it from Mr. Wiggins's brother. It's a classic." The breathy little voice continued with an explanation that Spider knew must have been learned by rote. It could never have sprung from the dust motes of her mind. "In a few years it'll be worth six times what I paid for it. In the meantime, I have transportation. That's not only an intelligent investment, it's an efficient use of my resources." When Spider didn't reply, she asked again, "What do you think?"

"I'm speechless, Rose. Plain speechless. I'd like to find out more about it. Can we talk about it tomorrow?"

"Make it tomorrow evening! I've been up all night, and I'm going home to bed," she giggled.

"Okay. Tomorrow evening." Spider closed the door, and Rose drove off, leaving behind the oily smell of diesel exhaust. Spider stood and watched Rose's twenty-thousand-dollar tail-lights disappearing into the distance and said, "Huh!" Then he got in the deputy's car and drove home.

27

SPIDER MANAGED TO SHOWER and shave without waking Laurie. Then he went into the kitchen and hunted through cupboards and drawers for Laurie's blank recipe cards. When he couldn't find any, he took down her recipe box and searched through it. There were no blank ones there, so he pulled the recipe for Orange Kiss Me Cake and turned it over. Taking his *Law in Layman's Language,* he sat down at the table and began to copy something onto the back of the recipe card. He finished just as he heard Laurie's alarm ring at 6:30.

Quickly, he put away the recipe box and his Triple L and went back to the bedroom, pausing to lean a shoulder against the doorjamb. "Good morning," he greeted as she turned off the buzzer.

Yawning, she turned to focus sleepy eyes on his haggard face. "Been up all night?" she asked.

"Pretty near. I'm going out to the shop right now. There's something I've got to do. Call me in for breakfast. Okay?"

"Is everything all right?"

"That depends on what you mean by everything. Call me when it's ready." And he was gone.

He came promptly when Laurie hallooed out the back door, washing his hands at the kitchen sink and attacking his pancakes with obvious appetite.

"So, how did it go yesterday?" she asked. "And how did you get that cut on your face?"

Spider gingerly touched the abrasion on his jaw. "That's nothing," he said. "It looks worse than it is." He added, with a twinkle in his eye, "I got propositioned by a hooker yesterday."

"No! Did you really? Is that how you got that?"

Spider shook his head, and between mouthfuls he told about his visit to apartment four.

"And she's a mother," Laurie said. "How sad."

"I imagine she's a woman alone with no skills, and that's what she does to support her family. That's reality."

Laurie smiled a bleak little smile. "Well, we know a bit about reality, don't we?"

Spider pushed back his chair and stood up. "Yep. And we're learning more all the time!" He walked to the back door and took his hat off the peg. He looked at the hat, rather than Laurie, as he said, "I asked Murray to bring his four-by-four over and help me drag that car out of the wash. He'll be over soon. I told him to come on in the barn."

"Tell him thanks for spreading the gravel," Laurie called. She spoke to empty space, for Spider had already pulled the back door closed and was striding across the yard to the barn.

She stared after him for a moment, then shrugged and turned back to her dishwater.

In the barn, Spider was struggling to unlatch one of the tiny safety pins holding the flowered sheet around his lodger, all the while wondering if he had gone out of his mind. "It isn't going to work," he muttered.

He heard the sound of a pickup truck rolling across the cattle guard and gave up fumbling with the safety pin. Taking out his pocketknife, he sliced through the muslin at the hem and tore the sheet clear across, flinging it open to reveal the grisly figure resting uneasily with the head turned sideways. Dried, half-eaten eyes looked expectantly toward the doorway.

A car door opened and slammed shut. Spider found that his hands were sweating. He wiped them on his pantlegs and looked around. There was a cement mixer standing in the shadows of the corner by the barn door. As quietly as he could, Spider made his way there. The sound of his own breathing was loud in his ears, but over it he heard a slow, stealthy approach outside.

Is this the approach of a friend? Spider wondered. And then he answered his question with another: *Is this the welcome of a friend?*

Dang it, it's not going to work, he thought next. Then, as Murray paused just inside the barn door, Spider realized just how wrong things were going.

Murray had a rifle in his hand.

Spider heard the sharp intake of breath as Murray caught sight of the lodger. He saw Murray's lips move, but no sound came out.

As Murray began to walk unsteadily toward the gruesome

mummy, Spider stepped from his corner. "Murray?" he said softly.

Murray whirled, levering a shell into the rifle in one swift motion and pointing the gun at Spider.

Spider tried not to think about how good a shot Murray was, and how close the range was. He forced himself to ignore the muzzle of the gun yawning in front of him as big as a cannon, and instead focused on the eyes of an old friend.

"I know all about it, Mur," he said quietly. "I know that she served divorce papers on you and told you that she'd have your ranch away from you. And I know that when she left, you were mad and followed her and ran her off the road up there by the wash."

Spider waited, but Murray made no sign of having heard. The rifle stayed, unwavering, pointed still at his heart.

"Why'd you carry her off, hide her like that?" Spider asked gently. "Even if you did run her car off the road, no jury in this county would convict you of murder."

Silence. But Murray's hands had begun to tremble.

Spider's hands were sweating again. *Oh, great!* he thought. *He's going to end up shooting me accidentally.* Trying to keep his voice gentle and persuasive, he spoke: "Give me the gun, Mur. I know you don't want to shoot me. Stop and think, Murray. I'm your oldest friend."

Holding out his hand, he walked slowly forward, speaking softly all the while. "You and I did lots of hunting together, and I never knew you to break the hunter's code. You wouldn't shoot me, your best friend, Murray. I just know you wouldn't."

Spider put his hand on the muzzle and pushed it to the side. Murray gave a convulsive sob and crumpled. At the same time the rifle went off and went clattering to the concrete floor. Spider grabbed Murray and supported him.

"Stand up, fella! Come on. You're a better man than this! Stand up!"

Murray stood. Spider let go of his elbow and looked away, giving him time to compose himself. When he looked back, Murray was staring at the pitiful remains lying on the old plywood gate slung across two sawhorses.

"Spider! Spider!" Laurie's frantic voice rang out from the house, and he heard her running toward the barn.

"Everything's all right, Laurie," he called. "Don't come in! Go on back to the house!"

The footsteps stopped.

"Go on back to the house!"

At the sound of her unwilling retreat, Murray turned his head and looked at Spider with anguished eyes. "You asked why I hid her body. You said no jury would convict me. Well, I convicted myself," he rasped. "I had murder in my heart, Spider. I was angry enough to kill her. I only meant to stop her, to try to reason with her. But when I found her dead, all I could think was that I had murdered her."

"So you took her up by the Lucy Roberts."

Murray nodded.

"And then what? No, wait! Mur, I have to read you your rights." Spider pulled the recipe card from his pocket and read from it precisely what he had written, and then stuffed the card back in his pocket. "Now," he said, "do you want to go on and tell me what happened, or do you want to wait until you can have a lawyer with you?"

Murray shook his head. "I knew you were out of town at Bobby's graduation and no one else would be along here to see the wreck, so I left it while I got rid of her body. I came back and got the loader so I could bury the car, but by the time I got back, the wash was flooded, and it carried the car down to where the water had eaten into the bank. The whole thing caved off on top of it. As soon as the water went down, I put some bushes in front of the bank. I was always going to take the loader and do a better job, but I couldn't face it. It was like, if I went and hid the car better, I would be admitting that I had really killed her."

"You know, Mur, I have to take you in."

"Yeah, I know, Spider." Murray turned and walked slowly out of the barn and into the sunlight.

As Spider followed, his attention was drawn to a cloud of dust off to the east. "Someone's driving like the devil was after him," he commented. "Now, who'd do a fool thing like that on a gravel . . . is that a hearse?"

Murray was taking little notice. He stood with sagging shoulders and arms hanging limply at his side.

As Spider watched, the opulent gray Stowe Mortuary hearse came roaring up, nosed forward as it braked, and then bounced diagonally across the cattle guard before skidding to a stop in the middle of the yard. The door opened and Bishop Stowe stepped out, clad in pajamas and a bathrobe. He stood indecisively for a moment, then shut the car door and spread his hands.

"I don't know why I'm here," he said. He cleared his throat. "But I just had the most incredible . . . it was like . . ."

"Never mind, Bishop," Spider said. "I know why you're here. Give us just a minute, will you." He grabbed Murray by both shoulders. "Listen, Mur," he said. "This is the beginning of the beginning. That man over there came out here because

Someone is looking out for you. Do you have the courage to tell Bishop what you just told me?"

Murray's eyes held a puzzled expression.

Spider shook his shoulders gently. "The Lord loves you, Murray!" he declared. "Do you believe it? Here's Bishop Stowe in his pajamas, come to tell you so. He's come to help you through this. He's come . . . to tell you about grace."

The eyes began to focus. A gleam of hope appeared.

"It's not going to be easy, Mur," Spider cautioned. "It's going to be painful—like giving birth to a new man. But it will be worth whatever it costs. Do you want to try?"

Murray nodded, and Spider signaled to Bishop Stowe to come over. Shaking his bishop's hand warmly, Spider said, "I'll leave you two together," and retreated to the barn out of earshot.

He busied himself covering up Missy's body, getting it ready to go back up into the rafters. As he worked, Spider glanced briefly every now and then at the two men standing in the yard. Murray stood with his battered Stetson in one hand, a white handkerchief in the other, letting his pent-up secret flow out in anguished phrases. Bishop Stowe, hands in the pockets of his bathrobe, looked now at his feet, now at the hard-bitten face of the man in front of him, and nodded as each sordid part was laid out in the morning sunlight. When Murray was finally done, the bishop spoke briefly. It was Murray's turn to nod as Bishop counted off each point on his fingers. Then Bishop Stowe put his arm around Murray, and they walked back to the barn.

"He's ready to go now," Bishop said, patting Murray's shoulder and then offering his hand to the penitent. "I'll be in touch," he assured him.

As his eye fell on the rabbit-wire cage, the bishop cleared his throat. He gestured toward the body and said, "I was wrong, Spider. I should have given her a place to stay. Can I take her now?"

"Sure, Bishop." Spider shook the hand that his bishop proffered. "I guess I've been wrong about a thing or two myself, lately." He turned to Murray. "Let's get going," he said. "Waiting doesn't make it any easier."

As they walked to the deputy's car, Murray cleared his throat. "Bishop said I needed to get everything confessed. There's something I got to tell you, Spider."

"I'm listening, Mur."

"I got to tell you about last night," he said. "I was out drinking with a couple of old rodeo buddies and trying to blame you for my problems. I knew you were on to me, and I guess I was hurt. I don't know why, but I told them you were ragging on me. They said they were going to put you out of commission for a while. A favor to an old friend. I told them to go ahead."

Spider opened the cruiser door for Murray, who sat heavily in the passenger seat. He looked up before Spider could close the door. "I need to tell you how sorry I am," he said.

"You've told me. I believe it." Spider closed the door and walked around to the driver's side. When he got in, Murray was sitting with his elbows on his knees and his head in his hands.

"I didn't run her off the road," he said.

"Beg pardon?"

Murray looked up and met Spider's eyes. "You said you knew I ran her off the road. I didn't."

"Well, Murray, there was a dent mighty like your pickup bumper in the rear fender."

"That happened before she was out of the yard. I clipped her and she stopped, and I got out to try to reason with her, and she took off again. I was chasing her when she lost control there by the wash. I didn't run her off the road, but it comes to the same thing."

"I don't know that it does, Mur."

Murray shook his head and buried his face in his hands again. "I was married to her for thirteen years," he said in a muffled voice.

Spider waited to turn the key. "Yeah, Mur?"

"She took my self-esteem; she took my manhood. She was going to take my granddaddy's homestead."

"Yeah, Mur, I know." Spider patted his friend on the knee; then he started the car and drove out over the cattle guard and turned toward the county seat. As he looked in the rearview mirror, he saw the silver hearse backing up to his barn door.

LATER THAT EVENING AT supper, Laurie asked, "So, why didn't Missy just tell us that she was going to school?"

"I don't know. Maybe she thought that we'd try to talk Murray out of paying for it."

"She'd have been right!"

"Yep."

"And how about the name? I'll swear her name was Marlow when she moved here."

"It was. She had been married before. When she told you she had taken back her maiden name, you assumed it was Marlow. But it wasn't. It was Barnett."

"And why didn't someone report her missing?"

"Well, she was through with school. She had quit her job. The apartment manager figured she had skipped town. She didn't have any friends who cared enough, apparently. No close family."

"How about her lawyer?"

Spider shrugged. "She wanted to serve the papers herself, and he figured that she had changed her mind. I guess that often happens."

"And did you really suspect Bud?"

"No. But think about it. The car ended up on Hughes land. The only reason it would have been on this road would have to do with us or Murray or Bud."

"Or that fellow out at Delmar."

"That's right. Did you know Bud has a son who's schizophrenic?"

"Yes."

"You did? Well, I didn't. Anyway, here this fellow shows up out there, and I wouldn't bet a nickel on him being sane. Next thing I know, Bud's traveling out toward Delmar. It was too many coincidences."

"And that's all they turned out to be: coincidences. We can be grateful for that!"

"Amen."

"So what now?"

"Well, Murray's future is in the hands of the courts. He's talked to the bishop, and I think he's found hope and maybe a bit of peace. I told him we'd take care of his horses and his place for as long as we need to. I told him, too, that we'd see that Missy had a proper burial."

"And what did he say to that?"

Spider sat silently for a long time, and then he said quietly, "He wept."

The telephone rang, jangling through the stillness of the kitchen, and Laurie went to answer it. She said hello and then listened, little crow's feet appearing at her eyes as she held the receiver a ways from her ear.

"It's Bud Hefernan," she said to Spider, when the caller paused. "He wants to know if the county knows it's paying you to track down lost buttons. He says you should be earning your keep by taking care of the ee-co-system."

Spider laughed, and he stood to take the phone away from Laurie. "Thanks for calling, Bud," he said. "I'll meet you first thing in the morning at the turnoff to the Lucy Roberts. We'll take care of the ecosystem. And bring a shovel. I'll call Bishop to meet us at the graveyard, and we'll lay our lodger to rest."

ELIZABETH SHOOK ADAIR WAS born in 1941 in Hot Springs (now Truth or Consequences), New Mexico. Her father worked for the Bureau of Reclamation, and they traveled all over the western United States and Alaska.

Liz attended BYU and then Arizona State College, where she graduated with a B.S. degree in education. She married Derrill Adair, and they had four children of their own and adopted three more. Liz became a reading specialist and taught school for several years, but decided she needed to stay home to be a full-time wife and mother. The family lived in an old farmhouse with a cavernous barn. They milked cows, had chickens and pigs, put up hay, and raised a huge garden. Later, Liz established a specialty wholesale bakery next to the farmhouse in a little building that Derrill built into a commercial kitchen.

These days, Liz has lots besides Spider Latham to keep her

busy. She works full time, has two Church callings, and feeds and cuts the hair of numerous family members wafting in and out of the old farmhouse. She is also the director of the Barr Road Family Band and a beginning baritone horn player.

AFTER
GOLIATH

A SPIDER LATHAM MYSTERY

by

LIZ ADAIR

THE SUN WAS WELL UP, AND Spider could smell bacon fry-ing as he made his way down the hallway to the kitchen door. He leaned his shoulder against the doorjamb and surveyed the scene before him. Laurie and his mother were seated at the table, and Laurie was squeezing a drop of blood out of his mother's finger onto a paper strip that she then inserted in a small machine sitting on the table.

"Morning, Mama."

Mrs. Latham flashed a smile at him as Laurie cleaned off her finger with an alcohol swab. "Good morning."

"I'll have breakfast ready in a minute," Laurie said. "I have to get this routine tightened up."

"No hurry. I just want to check first, before I have break-fast, that this kitchen is on The List."

Laurie shot him a fulminating look. "Careful, or you may be wearing your breakfast."

Spider threw up his hands. "Okay, okay. Just thought I'd ask. Can I help? Want me to make the pancakes?"

"That would be fine." Laurie got out a small notebook.

Spider looked over her shoulder at the readout on the machine. "What does it say?"

"One hundred thirty."

"Is that good?"

"It's in the acceptable range, I think." Laurie scanned the page in the log book. "It's certainly lower than it's been. Deb hasn't been able to monitor your mother's diet when she's away at work." She put down the book and began unwrapping a syringe, but paused to listen, cocking her head and then leaning over to look out the kitchen window. "Who would be coming to see us at this time of morning? Do you know anyone who has a red convertible?"

Spider walked to the window to get a better look. The car was coming across the drive too fast, and he could see the wide eyes of the white-faced woman inside as she clutched the steering wheel. She must have finally put on the brakes, because the car nosed down as it skidded on the gravel, bumped over the walkway, and rolled onto the lawn.

"Great Suffering Zot," Spider muttered. "What've we got going on here?"

"Who is it?" Laurie held the naked syringe point-up in midair as she stood behind Spider at the window.

Mrs. Latham stood too, peeking around her son.

"I've got to get out there," Spider said. In his haste he pushed his mother aside and strode to the back door. Flinging it open, he was down the steps, breaking into a trot as he rounded the corner of the house and headed toward the car.

Annie Ridge was still sitting in the car, but when she saw

Spider, she got out. The color had drained from her face, and her mouth moved in voiceless words. Finally she croaked, "Brother Latham," and dropped from sight behind the door.

By then Spider was at the car. He knelt down by the inert form crumpled on the grass. Her eyes were half open, eyeballs rolled back and only the whites showing below the line of lashes. Seized with awful dread that he had another body on his hands, the second in six months, Spider lifted her wrist and felt for a pulse. It was there, and Spider gave silent thanks as he sat back on his heels and looked over the woman lying in front of him. Her long, fair hair was spread out under her. She had on Levi's, a black Rocky Ridge T-shirt, and fluffy white bunny house slippers tinged with red around the bottom.

He was just about to investigate the bottom of the slippers when he heard a small voice murmur, "Don't cry, Lorna. I'm sure Mommie's not dead."

Spider looked through the crack between the driver's seat and the doorway of the car and met a pair of clear gray eyes set in a round, freckled face. A sturdy-looking girl of around ten had her arm around an ethereal blonde angel whose limpid blue eyes were brimming with tears.

"No, your mama's not dead," Spider said to the gray-eyed girl. "I'm Brother Latham, but I'm also deputy sheriff. Can you tell me . . ." But Annie Ridge began to stir, and Spider leaned over her as the eyes opened and focused. He saw them register disorientation and confusion, then recognition, then fear.

"Don't worry, Sister Ridge. You're all right. You drove to my house, remember?"

Annie Ridge nodded and tried to sit up. As Spider assisted her, he noticed for the first time Laurie hovering nearby.

"Do you want me to get the girls out and take them inside?" Laurie asked.

"Not yet. Let's find out first if anyone's been meddling with the car before we go opening doors." He spoke quietly to Annie Ridge. "Are you feeling better?"

She inclined her head a fraction. Her eyes were open, but she was staring at the ground.

"I want you to tell me what happened, but I wonder if maybe the girls shouldn't go in with Sister Latham while you do that. Is there any reason I shouldn't send the girls in the house?"

There was a negative shake of the head. Just a fraction of a motion, but Spider understood.

"Then I want you to stand up, if you can, Sister Ridge, and let's let the girls get out this door, if you please."

With Spider's help, Annie stood and moved tighter into the corner between the door and the car while he folded the driver's seat forward and invited the girls out. Bonnie, the sturdy, stalwart one, came first, her short, straight hair swinging forward over her cheeks as she bent to climb out. She turned and offered her hand to her slip of a sister, Lorna, who emerged sideways, sliding through with uncertain steps, one hand clutching her sister, the other pushing a tumble of shiny curls away from her face.

"Sister Latham will take you inside," Spider said to Bonnie. "Have you had breakfast?"

Bonnie shook her head, her gaze traveling to Laurie, who stood back a ways on the grass, and beyond her to the older woman who started forward, holding out her arms.

"What have we here?" Mother Latham exclaimed. "Two angels come to visit me. What pretty girls you are! Come and see me." Obediently, the girls went to Mrs. Latham, who put an arm around each and shepherded them toward the back door.

Laurie's and Spider's eyes met, and then Laurie turned and followed, leaving Spider to wonder, momentarily, if Alzheimer's robbed one of all except the very core of what one was.

Spider didn't have time to ponder, though, for there was this slender mother-waif still standing in her red corner, one hand on the door, one on the cloth top of the car for support, her hair blowing in the early-morning breeze and her blue eyes fixed on Spider.

"All right, now. Let's find out what brought you out here," Spider said, extending his hand to Annie and guiding her away from her sanctuary, around the door, and up onto the lawn. Catching the corner of the door with his boot, he pushed it shut and then led Annie to the front steps and had her sit down. Sitting beside her, he again noticed the russet stain around the sole at the front of the fuzzy slippers.

"My husband is dead," Annie said in a flat, raspy, almost-whisper even before Spider was seated.

Wondering if he had heard correctly, Spider looked at her intently and asked her to repeat. She did, in the same flat tone.

"Are you sure? Where is he? When did this happen?" Spider stopped and mentally told himself to slow down. This wasn't helping. More gently he said, "I'm sorry. Can you begin at the beginning?"

Annie took in a great, shuddering breath and then exhaled. Tears began spilling out of her eyes and rolling down her cheeks, sliding down her jawline to her neck. She turned up the bottom of her black T-shirt and wiped them away while Spider fished in his back pocket, hoping that his handkerchief was clean. It was. He extended it to her, and she took it with softly murmured thanks.

She cleared her throat. "I had gone to Vegas," she began. "I took the girls and we spent all day. We looked at materials for flooring and bathroom fixtures. They're supposed to begin construction next week, even though . . . even though we don't have the phone line in yet. Since there's no cell phone service out there, the contractor has put us off because we don't have a land line in yet. Rocky's brother, you know . . ."

"I know about that. Go on. What happened?"

"After that we went to a movie and then stopped for ice-cream cones. We didn't get home until about eleven. Rocky's car was in the driveway, and the house was dark. I knew he wasn't there because when he's home, he never goes to bed before one or two in the morning. Though he's not home much since we moved here."

"You didn't think it was strange that his car was there but he wasn't?"

"No, because Arlene often sends José with her limo when she wants to see him."

"And Arlene is . . . ?"

"Arlene Richland. It's her husband who owns the casino where Rocky performs. She has taken a real interest in his career. Sometimes when she has an idea, she'll send for him to come, and they'll spend hours discussing it."

"So you didn't worry that he wasn't there?"

"No. Sometimes he stays over and sits in with one of the bands in the casino. It's not unusual for him to stay out all night. José brings him back the next morning." Annie wiped along her jaw and down her neck, then wiped her eyes. She blew her nose.

"So, you came home late, you and the girls. You came in and went to bed?"

"Yes. I woke up early this morning. I always do, since we moved out here. I think it's the quiet that wakes me up."

"Okay. Then what happened?"

"I was in the kitchen getting a drink of orange juice. The cupboard where the glasses are is right by a window that looks out to where Rocky parked his car, but on the passenger side. I looked out, and I could see this—this paint all over the side of Rocky's car, like someone had flung paint at it and it ran down in streams. And then I saw—sticking out from behind, I saw Rocky's boots. He was lying behind his car. He was dead."

"You're sure he was dead?"

"He was stone cold and white as a sheet. What I thought was paint was blood on the car. He's lying in a pool of blood." She wiped her jaw and neck and eyes again, and blew her nose, but she didn't meet Spider's eyes.

Spider looked at her slippers, and she saw his eyes turn to her feet. "Yes." Again the raspy whisper. "That's his blood."

Spider sat for a moment, considering. "Did the children see him?"

She shook her head. "I couldn't call. We have no phone, you know. His brother . . ."

Spider nodded sympathetically.

"I drove around to the front before I woke up the girls so I could take them out the front door. I put them in the car and came on. I didn't tell them anything, only that I had to come see you about something important. I'm so glad you told me the other night where you live. I wouldn't have known what to do otherwise."

"Okay," said Spider. "Here's what we need to do. I need to

get the coroner out there. That's old Dr. Goldberg. After we check things out, we'll get Bishop Stowe to come and get the body and take it to his mortuary. I know it's hard, but I'm going to ask you to go back out with me." He paused and waited for her to process that information before going on. "As soon as I can, I'll send you back here. Who are your visiting teachers?"

"My visiting teachers?"

"I'm going to ask one of them to come and get you, bring you back here. I won't have her come up to the house, because no one else needs to see your husband like that. But I'll have her wait at the gate, and when you're ready to go, she can bring you on back."

"Oh. Okay."

Spider stood. "Who should I call?"

"Oh. Sister Wallace."

"Now, I'm going to go make a couple of phone calls." Spider took off his watch and handed it to Annie, who looked at him in puzzlement. "I'm going to try to keep it to no more than five minutes. You can time me. If you will wait right here, I'll check on the girls and make sure they're doing all right, too."

Annie nodded mutely, holding the watch with both hands. Spider turned and strode toward the back door, glancing back just as he turned the corner. She was still sitting on the top step with her hands on her knees, staring at the watch.

Laurie was alone in the kitchen when Spider entered, but the remains of four breakfasts were still on the table. She looked a question, and he said tersely, "Rocky Ridge is dead."

"Oh, no! Oh, no! Did those poor children see?"

"No, thank heaven. Listen, Laurie, I need to leave the girls here while I take their mama back out to their house. Then I'm going to send her back here. I need you to watch over all of them. They need to stay here until I get back."

"I think we can manage that."

"Good. Now I've got to make a couple of calls."

Spider quickly called Dr. Goldberg and Bishop Stowe. He asked the bishop to make arrangements for the visiting teacher to pick up Annie at the gate and then to pick up Dr. Goldberg and bring him out to the Ridges' house. "His palsy is so bad they won't let him drive anymore," Spider explained.

"I'll meet you out there as soon as I can," Bishop Stowe assured him before he rang off.

As Spider hung up the phone, he heard his mother's voice. He followed the sound to the living room and peeked in. Lorna was seated cozily in the chair beside her. Bonnie had a hairbrush and was brushing Mrs. Latham's silvery hair.

"When I was a girl," Mrs. Latham was saying, "a lady would have a jar on her vanity table. It was called a hair receiver. She would save the hair out of her hairbrush and put it in the jar. When she had enough hair saved, she would have it made into a rat."

"A rat!" Bonnie made a face.

"Yes, indeed. A rat is something that is made out of hair that you put under your own hair to make it seem fuller. We would wear our hair piled up on top of our heads . . ."

Judging that the children were doing well, Spider went into his bedroom and got his camera, the same one he had taken on his mission as a young man. Slinging it over his shoulder, he stopped off next at the linen closet in the hall and grabbed a sheet. As he passed through the kitchen, Laurie looked at the sheet in his hand and shook her head. "I never got the last one back," she complained.

"Send a bill to the county." Spider took his Stetson off the peg on the service porch and jammed it on his head. "I've got another body on my hands," he muttered as he pushed through the back door, letting the screen door slam behind him.

Annie was still sitting where he had left her. She looked up when he approached and held the watch out to him. "Seven minutes."

"Sorry." Spider tucked the neatly folded sheet under his arm as he fastened the watch, then held out his hand to help Annie up. "I checked on the girls. They're doing fine."

Spider guided Annie over to the deputy's cruiser and put her in the passenger side. As he was getting in, he saw Laurie watching from the kitchen window. He threw the sheet and camera in the backseat, gave her a wave, and then headed out over the cattle guard toward the highway.

The early morning sun was behind them, and they pushed a long shadow in front as they rode in silence. Finally Annie spoke. "I know who killed him."

"Who said that someone killed him? You don't know that."

"I know. His brother killed him. I know."

"Mo? How do you know?"

"He hated Rocky." Annie's voice, which had been flat and colorless, now became determined. "He was jealous of Rocky. He would do anything to get rid of him. Why, only last week he tried to kill him when Rocky went to see him. He's a dangerous man, and I want you to lock him up. Lock him up and throw away the key."

"Ah, I think we shouldn't make any hasty decisions. Let's

look around and see if it was an accident or not. If it's not, then is the time to try to see who was involved. Right now we don't know anything."

"I've seen my husband lying in a pool of blood. I know." Annie looked straight ahead and pronounced in implacable syllables, "Mo Ridgely is an evil man and he killed his brother."

Spider couldn't think of anything to say, so he just grunted, "Huh," and drove the rest of the way in silence.

FOR MORE OF THIS EXCITING MYSTERY, LOOK FOR *AFTER GOLIATH*, A NEW SPIDER LATHAM BOOK BY LIZ ADAIR.